TEL : *Stories*

TEL : Stories

Jay Lake
Editor

 Wheatland Press

http://www.wheatlandpress.com

TEL : Stories

Published by Joseph E. Lake, Jr. and Wheatland Press
http://www.wheatlandpress.com
P.O. Box 1818
Wilsonville, OR 97070

Library of Congress Cataloging-in-Publication data is available upon request.

ISBN 0-9755903-3-2

Printed in the United States of America.

Book design and cover collage by Stephen R. Stanley.

Cover photography by Jay Lake and Stephen R. Stanley.

Table of Contents

This book owes much to many, and I cannot credit you all. My thanks to Deborah for making this happen, to Bronwyn for lending it purpose, to TL for making it possible, and most especially to FG for making it fun. And of course, the authors, without whose contribution you would be holding a blank-paged journal in your hand even now.

Introduction
Jay Lake

*E*very book has a voice. Wiser authors and editors might be able to control their discovery of that voice, but it has snuck up on me unawares. When Deborah Layne launched both Wheatland Press and the *Polyphony* anthology series in a raving swoop, dragging me into the maelstrom with her, we learned how a slush pile can give an anthology a voice that was never quite envisioned in the guidelines. When we were putting together *Greetings From Lake Wu*, much the same thing happened: a voice emerged unplanned, unheralded from the great pile of paper with which we had to work. Again, when David Moles invited me to work on *All-Star Zeppelin Adventure Stories*, the book found a voice that was more vibrant and stronger than he or I had dreamt.

I wound up thinking a lot about slush piles and voices and how some stories cried out for paths we could not or did not take. A certain story in this book surfaced in a slush pile, and it was wondrous. It just wasn't right for the project at hand. (No, I won't tell you which one — story or project.) But it haunted me for quite some time after. Meanwhile, I read Greer Gilman's "Jack Daw's Pack" in Ellen Datlow and Terri Windling's *Fourteenth Year's Best Fantasy and Horror*. That story haunted me too.

Both pieces haunted me because they represented extremes of style, radical positions taken in the great field and arc of story telling, approaches to fiction that for the most part are untenable.

But not completely untenable.

Hence this book. *TEL : Stories* is a labor of love, paid for out of my own thin pockets, worked on in time robbed from paying projects. The inestimable Stephen Stanley displayed great patience with my errant schedule and woolly-headed thinking to pull together an admirable book design. Deborah Layne mentored and encouraged me, and mostly left me alone, in my little foray into the jungles of publishing. (I can edit quite well, thank you, but let's not talk about typos in the contracts or problems with funding...)

And here we have it, this space for experiments and extremes of style and vision. Twenty-eight brave authors, willing to risk their reputations and efforts on my hopeful project. A book for you to enjoy or hurl across the room as you see fit.

My hope is that you do enjoy it, as I have. If nothing else, applaud with me the skill and courage of these writers, and voyage with them toward the edges of literature. —JL

Jack Daw's Pack
Greer Gilman

The Crow

He is met at a crossroads on a windy night, the moon in tatters and the mist unclothing stars, the way from Ask to Owlerdale: a man in black, whiteheaded, with a three-string fiddle in his pack. Or in a corner of an ale house, querulous among the cups, untallied; somehow never there for the reckoning, though you, or Hodge, or any traveller has drunk the night with him. A marish man: he speaks with a reedy lowland wauling, through his beak, as they say. He calls Cloud crowland. How you squall, he says, you moorland ravens; how you peck and pilfer. He speaks like a hoodie crow himself, all hoarse with rain, with bawling ballads in the street. Jack Daw, they call him. A witty angry man, a bitter melancholy man. He will barter; he will gull. In his pack are bacca pipes, new ones, white as bones, and snuff and coney-skins and cards. He plays for nothing, or for gold; packs, shuffles. In a game, triumphant, he plucks out the Crowd of Bone, or Brock with her leathern cap and anvil, hammering at a fiery heart, a fallen star. (It brock, but I mended it.) Death's doxy, he calls her, thief and tinker, for she walks the moon's road with her bag, between the hedges white with souls; she takes. Here's a lap, he says, in his shawm's voice, sharp with yelling out for ale. Here's a blaze needs no bellows. Here's a bush catches birds. He mocks at fortune. The traveller in the inn forgets what cards he held, face down, discarded in the rings of ale; he forgets what gold he lost. He'd none in his pockets, yet he played it away, laid it round and shining on the sanded board, a bright array. On each is stamped a sun.

And elsewhere on that very night, late travelling the road between Cold Law and Soulsgrave Hag, no road at all but white stones glimmering, the sold sheep heavy in his purse, another Tib or Tom or Bartlemy will meet Jack Daw. He will stand at the crossroads, bawling in his windy voice, a broadside in his hand. There'll be a woodcut at the head: a hanged man on the gallantry, crows rising from the corn. Or this: a pretty drummer boy, sword drawn against the wood, and flaunting in her plumy cap. Two lovers' graves, entwined. A shipwreck, and no grave at all. You must take what he gives. Yet he will barter for his wares, and leave the heavy purse still crammed with coppers, for his fee is light. He takes only silver, the clipped coin of the moon: an hour of the night, a dream of owls. Afterwards, the traveller remembers that the three-string fiddle had a carven head, the face his own. With a cold touch at his heart, he knows that Jack Daw's fiddle wakes the dead; he sees their bones, unclad and rising, clothing with the tune. They dance. He sees his girl, left sleeping as he thought; Joan's Jack, gone for a soldier; his youngest child. Himself. They call him to the dance. He sees the sinews of the music string them, the old tunes, "Cross the Water to Babylon," "The Crowd of Bone." Longways, for as many as will, as must, they dance: clad in music, in the flowers and the flesh.

What the Crowd of Bone Sang

She is silent, Ashes, and she dances, odd one out. In the guisers' play, she bears a bag of ashes of the old year's crown to sain the hearths of the living, the hallows of the earth. The children hide from her, behind the door and in the shadow of the kist; not laughing, as they fear the Sun. Click! Clack! He knocks the old man dead, that headed him before. And tumbled by the knot of swords, he rises, flaunting in their gaze. The girl who put on Ashes with her coat of skins, who stalks them, bites her cheek and grimaces so not to laugh; she feels her power. She looks sidelong at the Sun.

They say that Ashes' mother got her gazing in her glass. *Undo*, the raven said, and so she did, undid, and saw her likeness in the stony mirror, naked as a branch of thorn. The old witch took it for herself; she cracked the glass, she broke the tree. They bled. Devouring, she bore her daughter, as the old moon bears the new, itself again; yet left hand to its right. And they do say the old one, Annis, locks her daughter in the dark of moon, winterlong and waning, and that Ashes' birth, rebirth, is spring. They say the sun is Ashes' lightborn brat. She is the shadow of the candle, the old moon's daughter and her mirror; she is tarnished with our breath and death. She's winter's runaway.

They are old who tell this.

But the girl who put on Ashes with her tattered coat walks silent, flown with night and firelight and masking. She is giddy with the wheel of stars. She sees the brands whirled upward, sees the flash of teeth, of eyes. The guisers shout and jostle. They are sharp as foxes in her nostrils: smoke and ale and eager sweat. She moves among them, nameless; she wears her silence like a cloak of night. Ah, but she can feel the power in her marrow, like a vein of stars. Her feet are nightfall. She could tuck a sleeping hare within her jacket, take a hawk's eggs from its breast. Her hand could beckon like the moon and bid a crone come dancing from the chimneynook to sweep about her and about; could call the sun to hawk at shadows, or a young man to her lap, and what he will.

And in the morning, she will lay by Ashes with her rags, and wash her face, and comb the witchknots from her hair; but Ashes in the tale goes on.

In spring, she rises from her mother Annis' dark; they call the snowdrops Ashes' Steps. The rainbow is her scarf. She dances, whirling in the April storm; she fills her hands with hailstones, green as souls. And there are some have met her, walking backward on the Lyke Road, that they call the white hare's trod, away from death; she leaps within the cold spring, falling, filling up the traveller's hands. She is drunken and she eats.

At May, the riddlecake, as round as the wheeling sun, is broken into shards, one marked with ashes; he that draws her share is Sun. But he was sown long since, and he's forgotten harrowing. He rises and he lies. Light work. He breaks the hallows knot of thorn; he eats the old year's bones for bread. Sun calls the stalk from the seeded earth, draws forth the green blade and the beard to swell his train. He gives the meadows green gowns. And flowers falling to his scythe lie tossed and tumbled, ah, they wither at his fiery kiss. They fall in swathes, in sweet confusion, to his company of rakes, his rade of scythesmen all in green. The hay's his dance. Vaunting, he calls the witchstone, Annis, to the dance, for mastery of the year, and wagers all his reckless gold. But he has spent his glory and must die. The barley is himself.

Ashes reaps him. By harvesting, she's sunburnt, big with light. She wears a wreath of poppyheads; her palms are gashed, they're red with garnering. They open like a cry. Her sickle fells the standing corn, the hare's last hallows, and he's gathered in her sheaf. She's three then, each and all the moon, his end: her sickle shearing and her millstone trundling round, her old black cauldron gaping for his bones.

The Harper's Lad

His hair was yellow as the broom, as ragged as the sun. A ranting lad, a spark for kindling of the year. His name was Ash. It was Unhallows, in the grey between May Eve and morning. On the hills, the fires died. He'd leapt the nine hills in a turning wheel, from dusk to dusk, and rode rantipole with witches. Ah, they'd raged, howking at the earth with long blue nails. When they shook their tangled hair, the soulstones clattered, red as blood, and eyestones, milky white and black; and birdskulls, braided through the orbits, in their nightlong hair. He was drunk with dancing. He'd another girl to meet; had lingered, waking with his blue-eyed witch. *The owl flew out, the raven in,* sang mocking in his head, like Ashes in the old play. As he slouched along the moor, he heard a hoarse voice, in windy snatches, singing. Some belantered rantsman, he thought.

"*Oh, my name it is Jack Hall, chimney sweep, chimney sweep…*" A crow's voice, chanting, hoarded iron in a hinge.

There were some had sung all night, thought Ash; he'd gone to other games. It was lightward, neither sun nor moon, but the grey cock's hour. He was late. He hastened toward the beck.

"*And I've candles lily white, oh, I stole them in the night, for to light me to the place where I must lie.*"

They met by the trey stone, back of Law. A fiddler from a dance, it seemed, in a broad hat and battered jacket, with his face like the back of a spade. His hair was white as barley. "Out," he cries. "D'ye call this a road?"

"Flap ower it then, awd corbie. D'ye call that a voice?"

"Called thee."

A glance at the three-string fiddle. "Canst play us a dance on thy crowdy, catgut? Light our heels, then."

"What, is thy candle out?"

"I've a lantern to light it at."

"Of horn?"

But Ash was thinking of the blue-eyed witch, as rough as juniper, as fierce. She'd scratched him. Ash thought of the fire, how it whirled and crackled when they burned the bush; the sparks flew up like birds. The fire was embers: for a coal of juniper will burn a winter's night. Would burn a nine month at the heather's roots. Closing his eyes, he saw late-risen stars whirl round, the Flaycraw all one side afire, and rising, naked to his bones. The hanged lad in the sky. He played for the dancers in the starry hey. He played the sun to rise. But that was Hallows; they were winter stars, another turning of the wheel, and other witches. Vixens in a cage of straw. Hey up, he must be giddy drunk. Were all yon ale and randy turned his wits. But he'd a spark in him yet. And Ash thought of the dark-eyed lass who waited, like a sloethorn and a clear gold sky. A traveller. Whin. He'd best be going on. He tossed a coin to the fiddler. "Here's to thy bitch."

"And for thy pains."

They found the broadside in his jacket, after. Some said the woodcut was a high green gallows, and the harper's boy hanged dead. And others, it were nothing like: the white hare running and the hag behind. The black hare's bonny, but the white is death, they say: the moon's prey and her shadow.

Ash thrust the broadside in his pocket and went on down the road. His tousled head was bare, as yellow as the weeds called chimneysweepers, that are gold and come to dust.

Scythes and Cup

Poor Tom a' Cloud, and so he died?

His husk, an old wife says, and drinks. *Scarce bearded when he's threshed and sown.* Another, brown as autumn, broad-lapped, takes the cup; she kneads the cake. *Wha's dead? He's for thy belly, when he's risen, girl. He's drunken and he sleeps; his dreams are hallows, all a maze of light, of leaves. When's time, he'll wake wood.* And says the third, as thrawn as frost, the youngest of the three: *At dusk, at Hallows Eve, he rises, starry wi' a ceint o' light: t' Sheaf, Awd Flaycraw, clapping shadows frae th' fields of night. Yon hanged lad i' th' sky.*

And Ashes?

Ah, she mourns and she searches. And rounding wi' his child, she spins. D'ye see yon arain webs ont moor? Tom's shrouds, they call 'em. Bastards' clouts. And she may rive at Mally's thorn for shelter; owl's flown, there's none within. No hallows. So she walks barefoot and bloodfoot, and she lives on haws and rain. And moon's her coverlid, her ragged sheet.

Sheath and Knife

The girl lies waiting in the high laithe, knife in hand. Hail rattles on the slates. She cannot hear — what? Hunters. Closer still, she holds the knife, the same which cut the cord. Her breasts seep milk, unsuckled. Ah, they ache. Her blood wells, she is rust and burning; blood will draw *them*. Talons. Wings. Her mind is black and bright with fever. She would slip them, fight them, but her body clags her. It is sodden; it is burning. Sticks and carrion. The wind wauls, the rooftrees creak; below is muck and sleet and stone. She's drawn the ruined ladder up. Holed up. She stares at dark until the earth cants, until the knife's edge calls her back. Sharp across her palm: a heartline. White, then red. Her blood and milk spilled on the musty straw. That will call them, that will draw them from the dark, the tree, the bairn. But the earth starves for what she will not give it. Their voices tell her she is famine, she is hailseed, withering, the cold share in the dust.

She was Ashes. Ah, she'd flyted with them, wives and lasses, as they'd stripped her of her guising, scrubbed her, tugged the witchknots from her hair. *Cross all and keep nowt*, they'd told her, turning out the sooty pockets, folding up the tattered coat; and late and morning, privily, desperately, she'd drenched and drenched, but could not rid her belly of the seed. She's Ashes still. Still guising, in a tinker's jacket, oh, a brave lad, with her bloody hole. Caught in Ashes. Holed up. Crouching, clenching, in her darklong pain, she'd heard the shadows of the women mocking, turning out the pockets of the coat. Knife. Haws. Pebbles. Eggshells. There, the whirligig she'd cried for, that she'd broken, long years since. They hold up a skint and bloody hare. *Here's one been poaching*. Shivering, she shuts her eyes, but still she sees the brat like bruised fruit trodden in the grass, the cry between her legs. Windfall for the old ones. Ashes to ashes. His furled hand, like bracken. His blind mouth at her tit. If they'd found him there, they'd slain him, for the earth to drink. *Keep nowt*. She'd hung no rags to the hallows tree, when she'd left him. She'd not beg awd ones. And she'd nowt to give. Her hair was cut long since and burned. Her tongue was dry. But she'd wrapped him in a stolen jacket, nowt of Ashes. Twined a stranger's tawdry ring about his neck. Why? For the daws to pyke at? She's seen the crows make carrion of halfborn lambs, their stripped skulls staring from their mothers' forks. On the slates, the dry rain dances, shards of Annis, shards of souls. Heel of hands against her aching eyes, until it's red, all red as foxes, and their green stench in the rain.

Coffer and Keys

At Hallows Eve, Ashes' mother hunts, unthralled from her stone. She is the wintersoul, the goddess of the high wild places, fells and springs and standing stones, the mistress of the deer. Her child's her prey.

Her mother Annis hates her, that her child (her child) is not herself. She wears her daughter at her throat in chains of ice, her blood as rings; she tears the new Sun, red with birthblood, from her daughter's side.

In winter, Ashes dies, is graved within her mother's dark.

And her bairn's shut up in Annis' kist, says an old wife, jangling her bunch of keys. *Down where she sits i' dark, and tells her hoard of souls. And he's Sun for her crown. So all t' world's cold as Law and blind as herself.* She leans and whispers. *D'ye hear her at window with her nails?* The dark-eyed children huddle by the hearth and stare at her, the old wife crouching with her cards of wool. Her shadows cross her shadows, like a creel unweaving. *Ah, but he's for Mally's lap, she haps him all in snow. It's winter and her loom is bare. Wood's her cupboard, and her walls are thorn; her bower's all unswept. Thou can't get in but she lets thee. And she's Tom Cloud's nurse. But Brock — ah, well now, Brock's death's gossip and she's keys to all locks. Will I tell ye how Brock stole him?*

Why? says the boldest.

For a bagpipe that plays of itself, says the eldest, as she rocks the babby. *Hush, ba. For a bellows til her blaze.*

Not for Annis.

But there are some say Ashes journeys on the river of her milk, that she's the lost star from the knot of stars they call Black Annie's Necklace, or Nine Weaving, or the Clew, that rises with the fall of leaves, a web like gossamer and rain. The Nine are sisters, and they weave the green world and the other with a mingled skein of light and dark, weave soul and shroud and sail; but Ashes winds the Sun within her, that the old Moon shears.

And some say no, that Ashes is a waif on earth, and scattered with the leaves. She rocks the cradle in the midnight kitchen, where no coal nor candle is, in houses where a child has died. And some have heard her lulling in the dying embers; seen her shadow in the moonspill, in the leaf's hand at the pane.

Poppyheads

The woman in the stubble field moves slowly, searching. Her palms are creased with blood. Her tangled hair is grey. There is something that she's lost: a knife among the weeds, a stone from off her ring. Her child, she says. If you suckle at her dry breast, drink her darkness, she must speak your fortune, love and death. She once told other fates, with other lips. And still she squats among the furrows, lifting up her ragged skirts for anyone or none. She holds herself open, like an old sack in a barn. No seed within, all threshed to chaff and silence. She was Ashes. She is no one. By the sticks of the scarecrow, she crouches, scrabbling at the clodded earth and crying, "Mam. Mam, let me in!"

Sieve and Shears

There must be one called Ashes at the wren's wake, when they bring the sun. At Hallows, she is chosen. All the girls and women go with candles, lating on the hills.

And if a man by chance (unchance) should see one, she will say she's catching hares, she's after birds' nests, though it rattle down with sleet and wind. They both know that she lies. Her covey are not seeking with their candles, but are sought. And one by one, the tapers dwindle, or are daunted by the wind; the last left burning is the chosen. Or they scry her in an O of water from the Ashes spring, at midnight, when the Nine are highest. They will see her tangled in their sleave of light, as naked as a branch of sloethorn, naked as the moon. And though the moon in water's shaken by their riddling hands, its shards come round and round. Then swiftly as the newfound Ashes runs, longlegged as a hare, she'll find the old coat waiting at her bed's head, stiff with soot and sweat and blood. She walks in it at Lightfast, on the longest night, the sun's birth and the dark of moon. She smutches children's faces with her blacknailed hands. And their mothers say, *Be good, or she will steal thee. Here's a penny for her bag.* Her mother's tree is hung (thou knows) with skins of children, ah, they rattle like the winter leaves, they clap their hands.

The Scarecrow
The starved lad in the cornfield shivers, crying hoarsely as the crows he flights. He claps them from the piercing green, away like cinders into Annis' ground. Clodded feet, cracked clapper, and his hair like what's o'clock, white dazzle. *Piss-a-bed,* the sheep-lads cry him. What he fears is that the Ashes child will dance among the furrows, rising to his cry. What he fears is that the crows will eat him. They will pick his pretty eyes. And he dreads his master's belt. Yet he sings at his charing. At nights, he makes the maids laugh, strutting valiant with the kern-stick, up and down. *Hunting hares?* calls Gill. *Aye, under thine apron,* he pipes, as the Sun does, guising. And they laugh and give him barley-sugar, curds and ale. *Thou's a bold chuck,* cries Nanny. *Will I show thee a bush for thy bird?* And he, flown and shining, with the foam of lambswool on his lip, *I's not catched one. But I will, come Lightfast. I'll bring stones, I'll knock it stark.* How they crow! And Mall with the jug cries, *My cage is too great for thy cock robin, 'twill fly out at door.*

Now he shakes with cold and clacks his rattle, and the cold mist eats his cry. The Ashes child will rise, unsowing from the corn: a whorl of blood, a waif. Craws Annis will crouch in the hedgerow, waiting; she will pounce and tear him with her iron nails, and hang his tatters from the thorn. Jack Daw will make a fiddle of his bones. He knuckles at his stinging eyes. He wants to cry. He sings. Back and forth, he strides the headland, as the guisers do, and quavers. *My mother was burned for a witch, My father was hanged from a tree...* When he sees the hare start from the furrow, he yells, and hurls a stone.

The Hare, The Moon
The moon's love's the hare, his death is dark of moon. He is her last prey, light's body, as the midnight soul, night's Ashes, is her first: All Hallows Eve, May Eve, her A and O. In spring, the waning of her year, she hunts in green: not vivid, but a cold grey green,

as pale as lichened stone; afoot, for her hunt is scattered. And she hunts by night. Where her feet have passed is white with dew. Swift and mad, the hare runs, towards hallows, to the thicket's lap, unhallowing in white. He sees the white moon tangled in her thorn. Her lap is sanctuary. He would lie there panting, with his old rough jacket torn, his blood on the branches, red as haws. But at dawn, the hey is down. The white girl rises from the tree; she dances on the hill, unknowing ruth. Yet he runs to her rising, eastward to the sky. Behind him runs his deerlegged death, his pale death. There are some now blind have seen her, all in grey as stone, greygreen in moving. No, another says, as red as a roe deer or the moon in slow eclipse. At dawn, she will be stone.

They are sisters, stone and thorn tree, dark and light of one moon. Annis, Malykorne. And they are rivals for the hare, his love, his death: each bears him in her lap, as child, as lover and as lyke. They wake his body and he leaps within them, quick and starkening; they bear him light. Turning, they are each the other, childing and devouring: the cauldron and the sickle and the cold bright bow. Each holds, beholds, the other in her glass. And for a space between the night and morning, they are one, the old moon in the new moon's arms, the paling of her breast. The scragged hare slips them as they clasp. He's for Brock's bag, caught kicking.

Masks

Wouldst know thy fortune? her lover says. And laughing, as his bright hair ruffles at her breath, *Ah. What's o'clock?*

Not yet, she says, low-voiced. (The stone in his ear, like the blood of its piercing. The bruised root stirring on his thigh.) *Not dawning yet. Nor moon nor sun.*

Will not it rise? he says, rounding.

And go to seed. She smiles, remembering. *Not yet. I've plucked it green.*

The Rattlebag

The boy kneels, drunken, in the barn. They hold her down for him, the moon's bitch, twisting, cursing in the filthy straw. A vixen in a trap. He holds the felly of the cartwheel, sick and shaken, in the reeling stench. Cold muck and angry flesh. Their seed in snail tracks on her body, snotted in her sootblack hair. Their blood — his own blood — in her nails. She is Ashes and holy. He fumbles, tries to turn his face. He's not thirteen. "Get it into her, mawkin!" calls the bagman, wilting. Ashes and fear. "Thinks it's to piss with." "Hey, crow-lad! Turn it up a peg." "Spit in t'hole." And the man with the daggled ribbons, his fiddle safe in straw, cries, "Flayed it's thy mam?"

The Hare, The Moon (Turned Down)

The black hare's bonny, as they sing: she lies under aprons, she's love under hedges. And she's harried to the huntsman's death, the swift undoing of his gun. But the white hare's death, they say: a maid forsaken or a child unmourned, returning from her narrow grave. A love betrayed. Her false lad will meet her on the moor at dusk, a pale thing fleeting; he will think he gives chase. But she flees him and she follows, haunting like the ghost of love. She draws him to his death. And after he will run, a shadow on the hills, a hare: the moon's prey and her shadow. Love's the black hare, but the white is death. And one's the other one, now white, now black, and he and she, uncanny as the changing moon. They say the hare lays eggs; it bears the sun within a moon. A riddle. Break it and there's nought within.

Riddles

He holds her ring up, glancing through it with his quick blue eye; and laughs, and pockets it. A riddle. What's all the world and nothing?

O, says she, *thine heart. 'Tis for any hand. Thyself would fill it.*

And he, *Nay, it is th' owl in thine ivy bush. It sulks by day.*

Aye, says she, *and hares by night.*

Thy wit, all vanity and teeth.

Thy grave.

At midnight, then? I'll bring a spade and we'll dig for it. His white teeth glimmer, ah, he knows how prettily; and daring her, himself (for the thorn's unchancy, and this May night most of all), he says, *At the ragtree?*

At moonrise.

Waking Wood

Between the blackthorn and the white is called the moon's weft, as the warp is autumn, Hallows, when her chosen sleeps. He dreams of lying in her lap, within the circle of her flowering thorn; his dreams wake wood. Between the scythe and frost he's earthfast, and his visions light as leaves. He keeps the hallows of the earth. And winterlong he hangs in heaven, naked, in a chain of stars. He rises to her rimes. When Ashes hangs the blackthorn with her hail of flowers, white as sleet, as white as souls, then in that moon the barley's seeded, and the new green pricks the earth. He's scattered and reborn. As in the earth, so in the furrows of the clouds, his Sheaf is scattered, whited from the sky until he rises dawnward, dancing in his coat of sparks. He overcrows the sun; he calls the heavens to the earth to dance. And in their keep, the Nine weave for their sister's bridal, and their threads are quick, their shuttles green and airy, black and white and red as blood. They clothe her in her spring and fall. In the dark before May morn, the Flaycraw dances, harping for the Nine to rise, the thorn to flower and the fires to burn, the wakers on the hills to dance. *The hey is down,* they cry. *Craw's hanged!* They leap the fires, lightfoot; crown their revelry with green. Not sloe. The blackthorn's death and life-in-death; the white is love. The bride alone is silent, rounding with the sun.

Riddles, Turned

She looks at him though all her rings. There's mischief in her face, a glittering on teeth and under lids. *An you will, I may.*

Quickening

At quickening, the white girl rises, lighter of herself; she undoes her mother's knots. Alone of all who travel Brock's road backward, out of Annis' country, out of death, she walks it in her bones, and waking. Neither waif nor wraith nor nimbling hare, but Ashes and alone. The coin she's paid for crossing is of gold, and of her make: her winter's son. Yet she is born unknowing, out of cloud. Brock, who is Death's midwife, sains her, touches eyes, mouth, heart with rain. She haps the naked soul in earth.

All the dark months of her prisoning, in frost, in stone, her shadow's walked the earth, worn Ashes outward, souling in her tattered coat. She's kept the year alive. But on the eve of Ashes' rising, the winter changeling is undone. From hedge to hall, the women and the girls give chase, laughing, pelting at the guisers' Ashes, crying, *Thief!* Bright with mockery and thaw, they take her, torn and splattered, in the street. *What's she filched? Craw's stockings. Cat's pattens. Hey, thy awd man's pipe! And mine. And mine.* Gibing, they strip her, scrub her, tweak the tangles from her hair, the rougher for her knowing. All she's got by it — small silver or the gramarye of stars — is forfeit. All her secrets common as the rain. And they scry her, and they whisper — *Is it this year? From her Ashes? Is't Sun for Mally's lap?* They take her coat, her crown, her silence. Naked and nameless then, she's cauled and comforted, with round cakes and a caudle of the new milk. She is named. Then with candles they wake Ashes, and with carols, waiting for the silent children and the first wet bunch of snowdrops at the door.

They say that Ashes wears the black fell of an unborn lamb; her feet are bare. She watches over birthing ewes and flights the crows that quarrel, greedy for the young lambs' eyes. Her green is wordless, though it dances in the wind; it speaks. Her cradle tongue is leaves. And where she walks grow flowers. They are white, and rooted in the darkness; they are frail and flower in the snow. It is death to bring them under a roof; but on the morn of Ashes' waking, only then, her buds are seely and they must be brought within, to sain the corners of the hearth. The country people call them Drops of Ashes' Milk. She is the coming out of darkness: light from the tallow, snowdrops from the earth, Bride from the winter hillside; and from Hell, the child returned.

She is silent, Ashes; but she sings her tale. The guisers strung the fiddle with her hair, the crowd of bone. It sings its one plaint, and the unwed, unchilded, dance:

> My mother bare me in her lap,
> Turn round, the reel doth spin;
> As white the cloth she wove for me,
> As red my blood within.
> As black the heart she bore to me,
> As white the snow did fall;
> As brief the thread she cut for me:
> A swaddling-band, a pall.

The Ragthorn

It was lightward and no lover. Whin sat by the ragtree, casting bones. There were rings on her every finger, silver, like a frost. They caught and cast, unheeding, caught and cast. A thief, a journey by water. Sticks and crosses. All false.

The thorn was on a neb of moorland, at the meeting of two becks: a ragthorn, knotted with desires, spells for binding soul with soul and child in belly. Charms for twisting heartstrings, hemp. They were bright once and had faded, pale as winter skies. Bare twigs as yet. The sloe had flowered leafless, late; the spring was cold. In the moon-blanched heath a magpie hopped and flapped and eyed the hutchbones greedily. He scolded in his squally voice. "Good morrow, your lordship, and how is her ladyship?" called Whin. She knew him by his strut and cock: his Lady's idle huntsman, getting gauds in his beak. The bird took wing. The bare bones fell. "Here's a quarrel," she said, and swept them up, and cast again. When Ash came, she would rend him, with his yellow hair. Or bind him to her, leave him. Let him dangle, damn his tongue. She'd dance a twelvemonth on his grave. Ah, but she would be his grave, his green was rooted in her earth. And she thought of his white teeth in the greeny darkness and his long and clever hands. His hair like a lapful of flowers.

Whin was long-eyed, dark and somber, with a broad disdainful mournful mouth and haughty chin. But there was mischief in her face, as there was silver glinting in her hair: nine threads, a spiderwork of frost. Her clothes were patchwork of a hundred shades of black: burnt moorland, moleskin, crows and thunder; but her scarf was gold, torn silk and floating like a rag of sunrise. Looking up, she started — even now — and then she sighed and whistled softly, through her teeth. "Yer early abroad," she said. "Or late. T'fires are out."

Down the moor came a woman, slowly, feeling with a stick, and a child before her on a leash, its harness sewn with bells. Its hair was hawkweed. When it stumbled, it rang; she jerked it upright. Whin watched in silence as the two came onward: the beggar groping with her blackshod stick, the white child glittering and jangling. They were barefoot. She was all in whitish tatters, like the hook moon, scarved about her crowblack head, and starveling, with a pipe and tabor at her side. When she felt the rags on the branches brush her face, she called, "Wha's there?"

"A traveller," said Whin. "Will you break fast wi' us?"

"Oh aye," said the beggar, with her long hands in the ribbons, harping, harping. "Gi's it here." The blind woman slung down her heavy creel and sat, her stick across her knees, and held out her palm. Whin put bread on it. "Hallows with ye," she said. The long hand twitched like a singed spider; it snatched.

"Since ye'd be casting it at daws afore t'night," said the beggar.

"Wha said I's enough for twa?" said Whin.

The beggar crammed. She wolfed with her white eyes elsewhere, as if it were something else she wanted, that she tore. Her brat hid, grimed and wary, in her skirts, and mumped a crust. "And why else wouldst thou be laiking out ont moor, like a bush wi' no bird in it?" said the beggar. "Happen he's at meat elsewhere." She listened for Whin's stiffening. And grinning fiercely through her mouthful, "D'ye think I meant craw's pudding? Lap ale?" The bluenailed hand went out again, for sausage and dried apple, which she chewed and swallowed, chewed and spat into her fledgling's mouth. "Ye'd best be packing."

Whin drank. Too late to whistle up her dog, off elsewhere. The beggar took a long swig of Whin's aleskin. As she raised her arm to wipe her mouth, her sleeve fell back; the arm was scarry, roped and crossed with long dry welts. "Will you drink of mine?" she said, mocking; and undid her jacket for the clambering child, for anyone. Her breast was white as sloethorn.

Whin was cutting sausage with her streak of knife, and whistling softly through her teeth, as if her heart were thistledown, this way and that. *"...if I was black, as I am white as the snaw that falls on yon fell dyke..."*

The child suckled warily; it burrowed. The beggar pirled its hair; she nipped and fondled, scornfully. "It fats on me. D'ye see how I am waning?" She was slender as the moon, and white; and yet no girl, thought Whin: the moon's last crescent, not her first. Her hair was crowblack in a coif of twisted rags, the green of mistletoe, and hoary lichen blues. At her waist hung a pipe of a heron's legbone and a tabor of a white hare's skin. She had been beautiful; had crazed and marred. Her eyes were clouded, white as stones. There was a blue burn on her cheek, like gunpowder, and her wolfish teeth were gapped. Yet her breast was bell heather; her hands moved like moorbirds on her small wrists. They were voices, eyes. Looking elsewhere, she called to Whin, "You there. See all and say nowt. Can ye fiddle? Prig petticoats? I c'd do wi' a mort."

Whin said, "I's suited."

"And what's thou here about?"

"Gettin birds' nests," said Whin, all innocence.

"What for, to hatch gowks?"

"Crack eggs to make crowds of."

"And what for?"

"Why, to play at craw's wake."

The beggar wried her mouth. "Thou's a fool."

"And what's thou after?" said Whin. "Has thy smock blown away?"

"Hares," said the beggar.

"Black or white?"

"All grey to me." The beggar set the child down, naked in its cutty shirt. "Gang off, I's empty as a beggar's budget."

"Wha's brat is thou?" said Whin to the babby.

"No one's. Cloud's," said the beggar.

"Ah," said Whin.

The beggar did up her jacket. The child sat by her petticoats with a rattle: a wren tumbled round within a clumsy cage. "Will we do now?"

"How's that?" said Whin.

"Ah," said the beggar. "I give and take. My ware is not for town." She looked sidelong. Like a snake among heather roots, her hand was in her petticoats. She found something small and breathed on it, spat and rubbed and breathed. "Here," she said to Whin, holding out a round small mirror. "Is't glass?"

"It's that." It was clouded, cold; she held it gingerly. There was earth on it, and in the carving. It was bone. She looked in it and saw another face, not hers: a witch, a woman all in green, grey green. A harewitch. A green girl, gaunt and big with child. The beggar was listening with her crooked face. "No," said Whin. "My face is me own."

"A pretty toy," the beggar said. "An ape had worn it in his cap."

Whin turned it; she ran her thumb round the edge. Earth bleared it. There was gravedust on her hands; she dared not wipe them. She kept her voice light. There are witches on the walk, between times. If you meet them, you must parry. "Here's thieving. Does they wake when yer come and go?"

"They keep no dogs," said the beggar. "And they sleep. This?" Between her hands was a scarf like an April sky, warped with silver. It was cloud and iris, changing. It was earthstained, like the sky in water in a road, a rut. She drew it through and through her hands. A soul.

"Here's a fairing," said Whin, and shivered.

"Aye, then," said the beggar. "There's a many lads and lasses gangs to't hiring at that fair, cross river, and they bring twa pennies til their fee." Her voice grew deeper. "'Here's fasten penny,' they says. And mistress til them, 'Can tha reap? And can tha shear?'" Her fingers found the wafted scarf; they snatched it from the air. "And then they's shorn."

Whin watched it fluttering. The scarf had changed, like brown leaves caught in ice. "That's not on every bush. Was never a hue and cry when you—?"

"Cut strings? Wha said I did?" Her fingers brushed, ah, lightly, at Whin's neck, where the gold scarf flaunted, like a rag of dawn.

Whin flinched, but flung her chin up. "I's a fancy to't drum."

"I's keeping that," said the beggar. "For't guising."

"Did yer gang wi' them? Guisers?"

"I were Ashes."

"Ah," said Whin.

The child in the heather clapped its hands, it crowed. At its jangling, the small birds rose and called. Whin looked sidelong at it, smiling through her rings. "And you getten yer apron full. Here's catching of hares."

The beggar twitched its string. "I'd liefer gang lighter."

"Cold courting at Lightfast. Find a barn?"

"Back of Law, it were, and none to hear us. It were midnight and past, and still, but for t'vixens crying out on t'fell. On clicketing, they were, and shrieked as if their blood ran green. But for t'guisers ramping. See, they'd waked at every door, they'd drank wren's death. And went to piss its health at wall. 'Up flies cock robin,' says one, 'and down wren'; and another, 'Bones to't bitches.' 'And what'll we give to't blind?' says third, and scrawns at fiddle. 'Here's straw,' they said. 'And threshed enough,' said I. But they'd a mind to dance, they'd swords. D'ye think brat's like its father sake? Is't Sun? Or has it Owler's face, all ashes? Hurchin's neb? Think it one of Jack Daw's get?"

"Nine on one?" said Whin, furious.

The stone-eyed beggar shrugged.

"Dogs."

"Boy and all," said the beggar. "They set him on." Thrub thrub went the fingers on the little drum and stopped the windless pipe. They pattered. "Happen not his brat. Nor old man's nowther. Cockfallen, he were." She leaned toward Whin's silence, secret, smiling with her wry gapped mouth. Her eyes were changeless. "But I marked 'em, aye, I marked 'em all." She drew a braid of hair from underneath her cap, undid the knot with swift sure fingers. Moving on the wind, the tress was silver, black and silver. It was wind, as full of blackness as the northwind is of snow. "There," she said. In her fingers was an earring, gold, with a dangling stone, a bloodred stone. "D'ye know its make?"

Whin sat. Her hands were knotted, rimed with rings. *False,* said her heart's blood. *False.* The black hair stirred and stirred, so much of it, like shadow. The beggar leaned toward her silence, with her scarred white throat. "Is't torn, his ear?" She flipped the earring, nimbly as a juggler, tumbling it and sliding it on and off each finger, up and down. "What will you give for't?"

The child's white hair was dazzling in her eyes, like snow, like whirling snow. Whin turned her face. "It's common enough." But the needles of the light had pierced her; she was caught and wound in hinting threads.

The beggar palmed it, pulled it from the air. "And which of nine?" she said, her white face small amid her hair. "There was one never slept that night, nor waked after. Drowned," she said. "Wast thine? They found him in Ash Beck. They knowed him by his yellow hair, rayed out i't ice. Craws picked him, clean as stars. Or will. Or what tha will. Wouldst barley for a death?"

Her fingers pattered on the drum. "That's one. And which is thine? There's one he s'll take ship and burn. He s'll blaze i't rigging, d'ye see him fall? And ever after falling, so tha'lt see him when tha close thine eyes. That's one.

"And one s'll dance ont gallows, rant on air. Is't thine? His eyes to feed ravens, his rags to flay crows. D'ye see them rising? Brats clod stones. And sitha, there's a hedgebird wi' a bellyful of him. And not his eyes. She stands by t'gallows. D'ye see her railing? That's one.

"And one s'll be turned a hare and hunted, dogs will crack his bones. There's a pipe of his thighbone and a drum of his fell. And tha s'll play it for his ghost to dance. And there's a candle of his tallow, for to light thee to bed. With such a one, or none, or what tha will. That's one. And which is thine?" She leaned closer. "D'ye take it? Is it done?"

Whin said nothing, caught in rime.

"Is't done?" said the beggar, chanting.

"And if it's done?"

Whin's fingers found the knot of the child's leash; undid it stealthily.

"Is't done?"

"Undone and all to do," cried Whin, springing up.

The whitehaired child had slipped his lead; he whirled and jangled as he ran. His hair was flakes of light. He whirled unheeding on the moor. And childlike fell away from him, like clouds before the moon, the moon a hare, the hare a child. He lowped and whirled and ranted. Whin caught him; he was light, and turning in her blood to sun. She bore it. By its light, she saw the beggar's shadow, like a raven on the rimy earth, that hopped and jerked a shining in its neb, a glass. A *thief!* the raven cried. Whin stood, as if the cry had caught her, in the whirring of the light like wings, a storm of wings; held fast. The child was burning in her hands, becoming and becoming fire. And she herself was changing. She was stone; within her, seed on seed of crystal rimed, refracted. She was nightfall, with a keel of moon, and branching into stars. She was wood and rooted; from her branches sprang the light, the misselchild. In that shining she was eyes of leaves, and saw her old love's blood, like holly, on the snow.

The child in the embers crowed, A *thief!*

And at his cry, Whin turned and ran, but still she held him fast. Behind her, the white-eyed woman shrank and whirred; the raven in her quillied out and rose, black-nebbed and bearded, with a woman's breasts. The waters of the beck leapt white. Amid the raven's storm of hair, its face, a congeries of faces, gaped for blood. Whitebrowed and ironbeaked; but its body was a woman's, cold and perfect to the fork: that too was beaked and gaping. It was shadow, casting none. Its very breath unhallowed.

Sun. The raven cried to its rising, "She's stolen my milk!" as Whin leapt the blackrocked foaming river. Cried and withered, like a flake of ash, and all its eyes went out.

The moor was sticks and ashes; frost and fire.

Whin held a heap of embers in her hands. They sang with dying, fell and faded into ashes. They were cold. She dared not spill them. With a shrug of her sleeve, she wiped her eyes, glittering with soot and tears.

The sun had risen. Whin turned from it and turned. White. A mist, a hag wreathed round and round her, cloud cold as Law. Beyond her, by the tree, she saw a white moor and a standing stone, unshaped. An iron crown was on it, driven deep with iron tangs, and rusting. There were nailholes where the eyes should be. The tree was silver, bowed beneath a shining weight of ice, in rattling shackles of glass. They cracked and glittered, falling. As she turned away, Whin saw a girl unbending from the tree, a knee as rough as bark; or nothing, wind among the rags.

And as she looked, the frost was flowering, the tree was white with bloom.

The Thief

At the moorsend guisers came, in rags, in ashes, garlanded with green. They wore their coats clapped hindside fore; and a man in petticoats swept round them with a broom.

A thief! A thief! they called, and clodded earth at the ravenstone. *Craw's hanged,* they cried. They paid no heed of Whin. A boy set garlands, rakish, on its crown. A girl in green tatters stooped for the beggar's blackshod stick, flung down; she strode it and she cantered, flourishing her whip. Moonbent and moledark, Hurchin tried his bagpipe, with a melancholy wheeze and yowl and buzzing, like a cat among wasps. Ragtag and bagpipe, they ranted and crowed.

There was one among them, in and out, unseen: a smutchfaced little figure, dark and watchful, with a heavy jangling pack. A traveller by kindred: breeched and beardless, swart and badgerly of shoulders. By its small harsh voice, a woman, so Whin guessed. And dressed as Ashes in the guisers' play. She wore grey breeches and a leathern cap, a coat of black sheepskins, singed and stained about the cuffs with ashes and with blood. Her hair was shorn across the brows and braided narrowly with iron charms. The hag had grizzled it; a hand undid the years.

"Hallows wi' thee," said Brock, nodding.

"And with ye," said Whin. What river had she leapt?

"Crawes Brig," the traveller said, and crossed to meet Whin at the beckside, stone to stone. Sifting through the flinders in Whin's hands, she found a something, round and tarnished; thumbed it to a gleam. A coin. She spun it round. The one side was obliterate — an outworn face, a bird? — on the other was a rayed thing, like a little star or sun. "That'll pay for't dance," said Brock, and smiled, small and sharp as the new moon. She took a bag of craneskin from her sleeve, and held it open for the ashes. There were coins in it and bones; she drew it tight. "Undone," she said. "And all to do."

Whin bared her throat, undid her scarf and jacket to the heart; she bowed her head beneath the cord. She saw at heart a shadow of the deepless water and the pale boat riding, shrouded with her soul. Brock hung the soulbag at her throat; she marked Whin's face with ash.

Whin gazed at her. "It's your coat Ashes wears."

"Aye," said Brock. "It's lent for travelling. Way's cold in but thy bones."

Whin said, "It's bonny on this earth, this morn; I'd linger."

And Brock said, "D'ye think it's dead alone as dance?"

Whin said, "I saw yon lady's scarf, her soul; she will not dance."

"Will she not?" A wind in the quickthorn shook the silver on the trees. Whin saw a grove of girls, of sisters, woven in their dancing, scarved in light. A hey as white as hag. Nine Weaving. "She dances now," said Brock. "She's rising into dawn, and rooted; she is walking from her mother's dark, toward winter, ripening until t'moon reaps her and she lies i' dark. Plum and stone. And she'll gang heavy til she's light."

"What's she?" But Whin had seen her in the glass, and barefoot in the shards of glass.

"Left hand til her mother's right, white's black. Not waning but t'childing moon. Unwitch, unmaiden and unwise. Her mother's sister and her make. Thysel."

"Her mother?" Whin did not name Annis.

"Aye, t'awd witch got her in her glass. And keeps her." Brock looked sidelong at the stone, the hill. Whin saw it, through and through, as black as sky. It was a woman sleeping, with the hooked moon at her heart, and stars and gatherings of stars within her side. She was the fell they stood upon, her hair unwreathing in a coil of cloud.

"How—?"

"She quickens wi' herself," said Brock. "She's moon, and mews her daughter in her dark. But I's keys to all locks, and I come and go. When's time, I s'll call on witch and steal her daughter to't dance. Will yer gang wi' me?"

Whin said, "I were Ashes."

"Ah," said Brock.

The scarf was in Whin's ashy hands; she ran it through and through a ring. "It were guising at Lightfast, and he'd bright long hair. Outlandish. I were fifteen, so I went down moor with him. I never see'd his face."

"So yer gotten a bairn?"

"Me mam and her gran — they'd've ta'en him and slain him. For an Ashes child. And sown his blood wi' t'corn. And they'd bind me til them, sleep and waking, while I's light of him. And whored me after. I left him under ragthorn." The scarf was knotted. "And I prayed no craws'd come, nor foxes. But I never stayed. I never turned til home. I's walking since."

Brock's eyes were shadowed in her hair. "And what d'ye think? Here's a woman weeping and she laps her child i't shroud; she lulls her fondling on her knee. Her nails are brocken, for she's graved it with her hands. Her milk is sore. And here's an old crone wailing, that she cannot comfort them. It's winter, and her loom is bare. And here's a fondbegotten brat, and nowther clout nor cladding til his arse. Tom Cloud. And thorn's his lap. And here's a vixen and her seven cubs; she dances like a flake of fire, crying, *Blood!* There's a many tales. And which is his?"

Whin said, "I'd want him well and growed."

"And thysel?"

"Away," said Whin. "I'd not be ended in a tale."

Brock tilted her face; the small cold iron clinked and jangled. "And here's a lad roved out wi' guisers—"

"No," said Whin, struck cold.

"And which?" said Brock. "And when? It's done, and long since done, and all to do."

Whin rubbed her hands against her breeches, crumpling the stormy scarf; the ash was pale against her clothes. Her blood was branching ice. *And which is thine?* the beggar said, herself met barefoot on the road. What child was sacrifice? And who had laid her down? "He's not — He's—"

"What moon makes of him."

Whin looked where the white tree shone. "And yet she dances."

"In her turn, and with him, in her turn. She bears him in her lap."

"I'd set her free."

"It's guisers turn all tales, and wake her to't dance. There's never endings. Will tha play for us?"

"A while," said Whin.

The rout came onward, fluttering with strips of rags. They shook a knot of bloody ribbons in her face. She knew them all by part. That broad-faced shepherd with the crown of horn. The old man with the bundled swords, the stripling with his pipe and drum. Those ranting lads. The Fool. The Awd Moon, with his petticoats and broom. Herself, with the box of coins, the bag of ashes. And the lad with bright unravelled hair. He bore a pole, with a cage of thorns, ungarlanded; the crow within it swung, down-dangled by a leg, its wings clapped open, and its beak agape and stark. Whin took her scarf and tore it, waif by waif, and hung the cage with rags of sun.

Aside and smiling, then she saw the white-haired fiddler raise his bow. Brock held the silver to him, beckoning Jack Daw; she called the tune.

And there began the wheedling of a little pipe, a small drum's thud.

The Guisers

They come like hoarfrost and are gone. In their packs are dreams, lies, memories: the old moon's spectacles; a bunch of rusty keys; a baby's rattle like a wooden wren; spindles and whorls; blunt shears; a half burnt doll; a tangle of bright silks, bent nails; a tallow candle and a knife; a crowd of bone. It sings its old plaint in an outland tongue. They strung it with her hair. Or there are gold rings, chaffered at the door, for nothing, for a gnarl of ginger and a rime; cast shoes of leather. The lady left them, walking into song. 'Twas they who put the grey hawk's feather in her bed. And there's a shirt, a little slashed, once fine, but stained with hanging. They had it from his back. His eyes went to the crows; his bones dance.

If they come as guisers, you must let them in: the slouched one with her bag of ashes; the patched one with his broom of thorn. They bring the sun. **T:S**

The Santaman Cycle
Ken Scholes

Muscles tire. Words fail. Faith fades. Fear falls. In the Sixteenth Year of the Sixteen Princes the world came to an end when the dragon's back gave out. Poetry died first, followed by faith. One by one the world-strands burst and bled until ash snowed down as huddled masses whimpered in the cold.

The Santaman came reeking of love into this place and we did not know him.

This is his story.

This is our story, too.

The Breaking of the Dragon's Back

Muscles tire. It's all we really knew. The dragon's back held up the world. The poetry and faith of the Singing Literocrats held up the dragon by the will of the Sixteen Princes. One Literocrat fell to the sword, another to plague, a third to famine. Halved in this way, the choir faltered in its song and the dragon caved in on its spindly legs. The Sixteen Princes had no time to act, to change the course of this sudden, sweeping end. They drank wine and spoke of lemon trees instead.

We sat in the cold until the Santaman came.

The Coming of the Santaman

Myth became life. No one really believed in the Santaman until he came with his tattered red robe and his dripping red sword. No one really believed in his undying love until he burst into our direst need to carve us a new home from the bones of the world.

We looked up at the whistle of his wolf-stallion. "Why do you weep and whimper?" the Santaman asked from the back of his mount.

"We whimper for the end of our world," one of us said. "We weep for the fall of the Singing Literocrats and the Breaking of the Dragon's Back."

The Santaman grinned and shook his sword. Blood rained down from it, mixing with the ashes. "Weep also for the Sixteen Princes who have failed you."

"Why, Lord?" someone asked.

The Santaman spun his mount. "For I have avenged you in the Name Above All and they are no more."

We did not waver in our weeping. There was no lull in our lament.

The Ending Rest of the Sixteen Princes
The Santaman drew a head from his pouch, held it high by its golden hair. Its eyes and mouth worked open and the Fourth Literocrat sang us the song of the Ending Rest of the Sixteen Princes:

Muscles tire. Words fail. Faith fades. Fear falls. Love avenges. Hope births.

The Santaman heard the faltering song and felt the faltering faith of the Half Dozen Choir. The Santaman saw the breaking of the dragon's back and knew from his Seeing Pool the inaction of the Sixteen Princes. He rode out in rage reeking of love. He roared his vengeance at the darkening sky. Click-clack went the claws of his wolf-stallion on the Purple Palace's marble floors. Snick-snack went the blade of his singing sword as sixteen heads came tumbling down amid spilled wine, spilled blood and lemon blossoms.

He burned their summer palace into the ground with stone-fire and rode East to seek the last of the literocrats.

The Last of the Literocrats
Dust rose from the West as the Santaman approached. The wolf-stallion growled and tore sod and the last of the Literocrats lay down their lyres by the Murmuring Stream as the dragon's eye faltered above them.

"Take up your tools and lift your song," the Santaman cried.

"We are halved," the Fourth Literocrat said. "Our song is lost. The world ends. The dragon's back, already broken."

The sword licked out, then pointed North. The Murmuring Stream ran pink. "Sing a new home," the Santaman cried again. "Beyond the ether at the Edge of the World."

Two voices rose and fell in song. A third burbled in the stream. Scooping the golden-haired head from the water, the Santaman came seeking us to tell us of our new carved home.

The Ether at the Edge of the World
"North of the faraway beyond the ether at the Edge of the World," the head sang and died. The Santaman cast it aside.

"The way is too hard," we told the Santaman. "And we are afraid."

He sheathed his sword and climbed down among us. He cast open his arms, his red robes hung like bleeding meat. "Do not be afraid. I walk with you."

North, he walked his wolf-stallion and we followed after. In twilight, we walked and as the ruined cities fell behind us, others joined our ragged band.

Lost also behind us, the last of the literocrats sang sunrise and sunset, sang muscles and sinew, sang bones and teeth.

Death crabs scuttled and scavenged. Snick-snack went the sword.

Black Drawlers shrieked and savaged. Snick-snack went the sword.

Some of us fell. Some of us faltered. All of us hoped.

The faraway wrapped us and the ash snows fell away.

Sunlight bathed us and we swam out into the ether at the Edge of the World.

Swam towards our new carved home.

Our New Carved Home

Motes swim. Light diffuses. Home rises.

We see it through a smoky glass. We watch it twitch and meep with each note of the framing song.

The Santaman laughs and beats his sword against his thigh: "Ho, ho, ho."

We few remaining weep and set our feet on emerald grass. We smell the reek of love upon the wind. We wipe our eyes. We wipe our eyes and look again.

Ahead a dragon.

Upon his back a world. **T:S**

Danaë at Sea

Carrie Vaughn

*T*hems that tells what's right and wrong to the rest of us decided I'd done wrong, more or less. How else is a girl like me s'posed to make a living? I shouted at them as they drug me out of Old Bailey. Then it was to Newgate, then to the docks, then away. Seven years transport was my sentence. They might as well have killed me. Seven years, they said, but it was really death. Who'd ever heard of someone coming back from transport?

I knowed they done it to a thousand others. But when the others went away it was easy enough to think 'em dead. I'd never see 'em again. Guess I would now. It was like dying, that last glimpse of the docks before they shoved me down into the hold with the rest of the convicts and closed the lid on us. That smell of London air, the wet shit and coal smoke smell, I breathed deep, so deep, because it was London and I was dying.

They shut out the light, leaving me in a damp, dark room with a hundred other women — whores, thieves, and swindlers all of us. How else were girls like us meant to make our way in the world, when our men beat us and the Queen herself couldn't think of anything better for us than to ship us to God-forsaken Australia?

I'd heard a story like this. An old story, one that I saw on a broadsheet or that some gent told me when he was all drunk and spent. A girl's father thought she was a whore, all on account that she wasn't married and she had a baby. He couldn't kill her — not right, killing your own daughter, even the worst of 'em knows that, usually — but he didn't want her 'round to shame him, not at all. So he put her to sea in a sealed box. Nailed the lid down tight over her and her baby both. How the babe must have cried, was all I could think. How they both must have cried. But since this was a story and just the start of it, no less, they lived. They washed up on a distant shore and a kind fisherman saved them, married her, adopted the baby boy as his own. I hoped he was handsome, or at the very least good to her, since she clearly hadn't much choice 'bout marrying him or no. Man saves your life, what else are you meant to do? The boy grew to be a hero. Killed monsters, saved a princess, went back to the start and killed his grandfather, the one that put him and his mum in the coffin. It's a story and revenge always comes 'round at the end.

I never knew my father.

•••

The first two weeks, most of us was sick as dogs. The few that weren't — lucky girls born with sea-legs, who didn't mind the swaying and rolling, the way the floor and your stomach never stayed still — took care of us that were. Poured water down our throats, no matter how much we puked it back up again. Soaked bread and made us eat. Molly, she's the one looked after me, and how I loved her for it. She said if any of us were to get through this alive, we'd have to help each other. Weren't no such thing as crime or hate down here, she said. Just keeping each other alive. I believed her, and I'd have done anything she asked after that.

Couldn't count how many of the girls got here by whoring. Couldn't count how many kept whoring after they got here. Wasn't this all meant to cure us of it, then? But it was an easy way to get an extra piece of bread or salt pork, or even a mug of ale. Couldn't put a hundred women on a boat with a hundred men and expect them to keep apart.

Molly never told me what she'd done to get here. We all told our stories to each other, and happy to, to pass the time, but not her. She must have done something awful. Murdered someone or the like. She might have been a murderer, even though she seemed right peaceful. My guess was she wasn't a whore, because she kept me from it on the boat. I almost did, then she asked me if it was what I wanted, if it made me happy. It didn't, though I'd never thought of it like that before. It was what my mother'd done, it was what I'd done. A job, like working in a factory. No pleasure to be had. So she says to me, don't. Simple as that. Don't. When one of the sailors turned his eye to me and made noises like he could help me — an extra hour up top in the fresh air, a boiled egg — I told him off. He didn't like that, saying he figured that once a girl was a whore she was always a whore and for sale. I screamed and hit him. I might have gotten lashes for that, but my screaming drew notice and he left me, shamed.

Didn't matter, when my belly grew. I counted back and yes, there was that guard at Newgate. Couldn't say no, then. Counting the time on the ship, I'd be so far along with a baby.

At least I knew who the father was.

There was the girl in her coffin, adrift at sea, crying and crying. I cried and cried, but there was nothing to be done for it but muddle on. A baby should be born on land, where things were dry and still, not rotten and moldy like our bread and our hammocks. I counted forward. I might get there in time.

I'd only ever gone to church when they promised a meal at the end of the service. They did that, some of the fine folk, bribed us to religion with food we were desperate for. They didn't realize we were so hungry the words drifted 'round us like a fog, we barely heard the difference between gospel and hymnal. But I sang their songs and thought the glass in the windows was pretty. Sparkled like rainbows. I'd not prayed much then, but I prayed now. Lord God, wash me up on land safely. I'm turning a new leaf, just like they said I should. I heard talk from the girls that the land we were heading for was filled with men who'd gotten rich with sheep and gold mines, all of them desperate for wives since women were scarce. The girls talked like this with stars in their eyes, and it kept 'em hopeful. They could live through the night and wake in the morning, if only they kept sight of those stars.

No man'll marry a whore with a bastard in her arms.

We were all getting so thin, even me with a baby in my belly. Molly was giving me half her bread — for the baby, she said — and I screamed at her, cried at her, worried her. She was getting so thin, and I couldn't do without her. But she wouldn't argue, she wouldn't take back her ration, and if I didn't eat it, it would have gone to waste or been taken by rats. I couldn't let that happen. Not with the baby.

Strange how I should want the thing to live so badly, when most like it'll have a life like mine — hard, hungry, with a long, drawn-out death at the end of it. But maybe it'll do better. It'll have schooling, learn figures, apprentice with some fine master, live in a pretty house with a garden. If it's a boy. If it's a girl — she could be a maid. A maid to some fine lady.

There were no such fine ladies in Australia, of course. A land of convicts. She'll turn out just like me, only they won't have no place to ship her off to when they decide she's done wrong.

•••

A fever came over the ship. Some of us died. The men wrapped the bodies in old sailcloth and took them up top, pitched 'em over the side. Buried at sea and they weren't even sailors, how d'you like that?

My turn to take care of Molly when she caught it. I told her she couldn't die. How'd I ever get along without her? She only smiled, said she didn't mean to die, but if she did she thought I'd do fine. She was cracked. I hated this place and so many times I'd gone to sleep hoping I'd never wake up, wishing I'd died back in England. Heaven or hell, either would be better than this. Drifting, a girl in a coffin, with nothing to do but sit in her box and pray.

Now I knew why Molly took such good care of me at the start: she knew I'd have to return the favor. Obligation. A couple of the girls came aboard hating everyone and cursing everything. They died alone, no one to sit with them, no one to cry for them. That hell was worse than the one I lived in. The littlest kindnesses kept us together and kept this hell from being worse.

When Molly was asleep, I told her of a little dream I'd been making up, a bit of a plan which I'd never think of trying in an old, cold place like London. I told her, we could make our own work, that if Australia really was a place filled with men and the dust of deserts thousands of miles wide, there's bound to be laundry needing done. I could do washing — or I could learn quickly, and Molly could help, I knew she could because she was smart. When our terms were up we could pay our own way, be our own masters. I'd never have had the courage to tell this to Molly when she was awake, being afraid she'd laugh at me and my silliness. So I told her when she slept, when I was afraid she'd die no matter how hard I prayed. I told her, whispering in the dark, my voice muffled by the sound of waves slapping the sides of the boat.

● ● ●

When they lifted the lid to the hold, I could barely climb the ladder, as big as I was. Not as big as I should have been, and I was afraid this was all for nothing and I wouldn't have a baby to show for it. But the babe was kicking. Weeks now, I'd felt kicking, tiny but strong.

Molly helped, coming up behind me with her hand on my back.

A week before the ship docked, she told me an idea she had, that we could pay our own way, be our own masters, by taking in the laundry of the hordes of men crawling over the continent, who were bound to need desert dust washed from their shirts. She said it with a smile, and I blushed, but we shook on it, and it gave me more hope than I deserved.

When I came up top, the sun was the brightest sun I'd ever seen. It hurt my eyes and made me dumb with its strangeness. The sky was big, clear of coal smoke, and the land went on and on.

I had washed up on shore with my baby, ready to slay monsters. **TiS**

Hex-Ray Hoodoo Rapture

Th. Metzger

Call Him Mr. H-Man

Hard meat, sexy sinew, gristle & sleek shimmy skin. His hairless head reflects the infrared and U.V. baleful as a bugzapper at midnight. Naked, handsome chest under leopardskin zoot-drape. His pants bulge with 40 ounces of pure panther cooties.

Hypmogoogoopizin' Eye

However, it is the eye, the great gorgeous eye, that is the primary instrument of his depravity. The erectile vision bulb, the unholy orb, the crown jewel, the swollen ground zero of manly ocular mojo funk. Look on a dollar bill — see the all-seeing eye looking back. Look into the abyss & the abysmal über-peeper looks back. Investigate the Pinkerton's logo: "We Never Sleep." The eye sees without ceasing.

XXX-Rays

Bulging, yearning, hard & sleek as a tainted beef extrusion, it is the eye which emits the endless triple-X radiation, the noxious orgone rays which no female biped can resist or even hope to resist, which is the ultimate locus & ultimate source of all the H-man's vilest transgressions against the state & crimes against nature herself. It is the great turgid glistering Hypmogoogoopizin' Eye that I, without hesitation, declare and condemn as utterly anathema.

I Accuse

The charges are as follows, that the defendant did: 1) appear on national TV smirking & smiling to gain world-wide fame 2) seduce with wanton disregard for reproductive rectitude a young virgin untouched by human hands 3) provoke and incite a riot which left countless dead and untold damage to property 4) take part in a shameful low-speed pursuit and televised motorcade flouting decency & due process of law 5) in contradiction to constitutional mandate take part in a travesty of D.N.A. research to mock and malign the forces of eugenic progress 6) appear at his tribunal unbowed and unrepentant & 7) by means of sorcery and sortilege foil the instrument of justice, the electric high chair fitted especially for him with Easo-matic footrest & rocker-recliner head-support system.

Sweet Vengeance

I will see him fry. I will see him strapped squirming in the hot squat. I will, I will, I will see him raised up in the PowerDeath Throne of Glory, flame broiled to seal in flavorful juices, transmuted Heavenward to meet his final fate. I will sit by his side as he rocks all night in the queasy chair, violet volts sizzling in his foetid flesh. I will not cease from mental fight until Jerusalem Slim returns & says to me "Well done, good and faithful servant of the Law."

And Again: Sweet Vengeance

I will not rest until this blighted knight, this errant errand-boy of Eros, is brought in chains, mouth gag, and asbestos eye patch (to seal in the foul rays), until he is taken once more before the High Bad Boy Bench and condemned to life in the electric chair. This wound in me will not heal until I see the grinning mouth, the too-tight-trousers, the sleek hairless cranium under lock and key damned for all eternity to fry in the blue bolts of justice juice. I will not rest until my shame, my secret festering psychic wound, is healed by the pure balm of vengeance.

Deposition #1

"For me the Hypmogoogoopizin' Man will always be a hero. No matter what they say, he was somebody for us to look up to. He got on TV that time with the honey-coated hoochy-coo girl and said real loud and proud 'I'll take Things That Throb for twenty.' And the answer was right: a migraine. 'Things That Throb for forty': a herniated tire. Sixty: a python eating a hedgehog. Eighty: a big blister about to pop from yanking on the golden chain too long. One hundred: a pulsar in the heart of the Crab Nebula putting out 75 megatons of foul fulguration per nanosecond."

The Nature of His Power

Physicists are at a loss to explain the rays emitted by his sinister eye. The facts — such as they are — do not solve the mystery of his strange attraction. As he grows excited, aroused, the Hypmogoogoopizin' Eye swells out of its orbit, sweat runs down his forehead glistening like primeval sea sludge, veins throb & tighten & tumesce & the phosphorescence begins to come. No geiger counter can detect the rays. No photographic paper can show their presence. No cloud chamber can track their course. But ask any sweet young thing and she will tell you that those rays are indeed real.

Deposition #2

"Real? Nothing more real in the whole wide world than when he turned those gleams on my gams. I could feel the gaze all the way to the bottom of my honey pot, yanking like sideways gravity. Knock, knock, knocking on Heaven's door. He stared & there was nothing I could do but skin myself down and say okay, okay, okay lay those golden beams on me. But the best thing was the tongue bath. I got a pretty long one. I wrapped it two, three times around his eye & I was plugged in direct to the big dildonic dynamo, juice flowing in through my mouth & running through my spine & out my sluice. My insides melted and oozed out like wax from a holy candle. I knew I wasn't the only one. I knew he had a main squeeze, but I took whatever I could get."

The Seduction of Queasy Pie

Mr. Hypmogoogoopizin' Man did have any & all the nubile young schnitzel he desired, but there was one above all who excited his bestial retinal lust to a frenzy that is hard to express. Her name was Miss Queasy Pie. White and cool as lovingly-sculpted cream cheese, so beautiful a form, so virginal a being, that a thousand raging Dero-Pygmies once threw themselves off a cliff in sheer ecstasy after getting a brief glimpse of her fornix. The untainted vessel of pure germ plasm, Miss Queasy Pie was the one morsel of overripe woo-bait that the H-man could not resist. He saw her one day at the laundromat, taking tiny weightless silk filigrees out of the washer, flicking them dry with a graceful snap of the wrist & he instantly felt the Maximum Mood Muscle pop a wheelie. He stabbed his foot down on the brake, triple-parked the monster fish-wagon Caddy and strode inside. Sweet detergent fumes, pheromones, funky wadded socks, overheated and supersaturated air — the laundromat was like a sauna-oven baking her to pallid perfection. In her jeans cut off far north of the knee, T-shirt too short, thong sandals, she was perfection. Dip her in the deep fryer, zap her in the microwave & you have the most scrumptious snack known to man.

The Seduction of Queasy Pie (Continued)

His eye went into orgone-overdrive & all the air was sucked out of the room. Sodium white light sex-rays bathed her, cleansed her. All the washers seized up & spewed forth their contents, neatly folded. Yes, her brights were brighter and her whites were whiter. She could feel the deep-down softness. The H-man's sexy shock wave hit her deep in her genes, inducing spontaneous mutation & her exuvia fell to the floor. Naked now, and unashamed, she faced him. Palpated, primed and pierced by the noisome retinal rays. There — right there on the Wash & Dry pitted linoleum floor. There — with great plate glass windows open to the street where hundreds of privileged gawkers stood gaping. There — between two ranked rows of porthole washer windows. There did said Hypmogoogoopizin' Man and said Queasy Pie mate & knead together their nucleic acids.

Bad Sex

I don't need to tell you, pilgrim, what the result was: even as the vile act of shameless shagging transpired, as his prehensile prepuce grasped at those blissom 95 pounds of estrogen-soaked grade-A creamery butter, as the ocular ram-rod slid unceasingly in & out & in & out of the moist poon socket, the city went mad.

Boogaloo Rampage

Fire & riot, looting & burning, bad language, disrespect, bickering and quibbling: an outrage of unprecedented proportions. Entire city blocks gripped in the hairy hand of King Mob. "We want electric pampers! We want high-def color TV! We want life-sized effigies of Minnie the Moocher carved out of frozen Spam! We want Mad Dog 20/20 I.V. drips!" All because the Hypmogoogoopizin' Man dared cross a line never before crossed. I was there at the barricades, dear one. I was at the scene of the crime in my capacity as Lord High Sheriff & Übergruppenführer of Squat Team #1. Body armor — yes, I look great in body armor. Plexiglass riot shield, Schutzstaffel helmet with the red light glowing on top, bulletproof cod piece & high tech electro-shock night stick.

Spare the Child and Spoil the Rod

Shock baton — my two sweaty fists tight on the Rod of Correction. Juridical juice streaming from the flexo-matic venturi pressure-control nozzle tip. Pearly jets of nacreous spume, glistening gouts of Special Sauce. My Rod and Staff they comfort me. Shock baton brought down again & again on the malefactors stirred to paroxysms of love & hate by the mere thought, let alone the endlessly repeated videotapes, of the H-man and the Q-pie locked in lewd embrace. I, the Lord High Sheriff and Chief Executioner, waded into the rabble flailing my bionic jawbone of an ass and drove back the mob of Philistines single-handedly. My ancient throbbing scepter brought law & order to the city but by then it was too late. The H-man was gone & with him out most precious chattel-prize juju baby & her two all-beef patties grinding endlessly together like greasy millstones of Love.

Riding with Mr. Fly

You've seen the footage. Is there anyone in the civilized world who hasn't seen the endlessly repeated image of the Hypmogoogoopizin' Man driving in the hulking behemoth Superflymobile? Low rider Pimp de Ville with pump-up shocks & blinking headlights behind mysterious glim-grates. A mile wide, impossible to hide, bold as the Bismarck in the North Sea pestered by overhead recon drones. Yes, we cut to the chase but then everything… slowed… down. Feet in molasses, voices at 16 rpm, a squadron of black helicopters like a swollen storm cloud that refuses to let loose its moisture. I followed. I arrived. I eventually caught him red-handed and still justice was denied.

Deposition #3

"Maybe black magick isn't the right word, nor voodoo nor root doctoring, but the H-man sure had something real nasty going down there. We landed the chopper on the roof and went inside the house & it was like some kind of Black Arts Bargain Bazaar: bunches of chicken heads hanging like garlic, a ghost muscle 3-ring exciter shank carved out of pure asafoetida, the big cauldron boiling on the stove, a dozen disgusting big-eye kiddie porn wretched-waif paintings, a 50 line fiber-optic cable hooked up direct to Heck, an infra-red bathroom. You name it, he had it. And in the so-called sanctum sanctorum was a big book of spells. I thumbed through it for a few seconds and had a poison headache that lasted for a month."

"To Create a Zombie Love-Slave"

Take 2 ounces of Squealer Wax, a drop of octopus ink & a half dozen desiccated glow-worm segments. Mix & decant into a Bromoseltzer bottle & bury this under a yew tree. Draw your bath water every day & on the seventh add the mixture piping hot. Soak for ten minutes or until the vibrations stop. Wear next to your heart, in a gris-gris bag made from the pajama bottoms of a narcoleptic priest, one crushed lodestone. When next you meet the object of your desire, he or she will comply with your every wish.

Apprehension

I went in with the squat team & chopper boys & he just gave up. Not a word. No fight. No excuses for the atrocity we found in the next room. Yes, Miss Queasy Pie was very very dead. Her prime slice would no longer ooze fine sweet peach juice. Her bosom would no longer heave under the shiny Brunhilde breast plate. Her Bermuda Love Triangle would capture no more mysterious U-2 flyover reconnaissance planes. Her fresh cream complexion was already blotched & blighted by the Hypmogoogoopizin' spoors. No more feral moans would ring in the night air. No more anatomically-correct googoo love-doll action. No more more sleek pulsing inner organ would whisper to me at dawn, "Invade me, invade me, you sexy Panzer Man."

"To Overcome the Power of the Law"

Gather 1 box Three Thieves Dejinxing Flakes, a pinch of Chinese gunpowder, a consecrated eucalyptus lozenge, a dozen cubeb wafers & a quart of Lucky Planet Oil. Mix in your golden magnetic bladder & apply with your left thumb to your naked skin, making leopard spots, as you stand at a crossroads at midnight under a gibbous moon. If prepared properly, you need fear nothing from the law or its minions.

The Ordeal

I have studied the *Malleus Maleficorum*. I am well versed in the works of Torquemada, Matthew Hopkins, Cotton Mather & John Edgar Hoover. I am quite adept at performing the ordeals of fire, boiling water, the balance, the eucharist, bier-right (in which the murderer — upon approaching the victim — will bleed copiously from mysterious wounds), poison, red-hot pincers, floating, sodium pentathol and polygraph. But in the case of the H-man, I knew that extraordinary measures would need to be taken to prove his guilt beyond a shadow of the valley of doubt. Probing the innermost recesses of his chromosomal structure & the structure of his victim, would prove to the twelve worthy and honorable men that he was indeed guilty.

Cracking the Code

10,000 fruit flies trapped in glass prisons. 10,000 fruit flies, some of them secret red-eyed mutants. 10,000 fruit flies, and every one of them a tiny living litmus test to prove the viciousness of his protoplasm, to show in cold scientific terms that his D.N.A. was beyond even the fondest hope of redemption. I called it the Red-Eyed Special and it ran all night, down in the bottommost subbasement of our top-secret headquarters where we'd dragged him in chains for booking. I took those fruit flies one at a time with tiny tungsten steel tweezers & pressed them to his skin until a positive ID was made. Then these little martyrs for justice were crushed in the jaws of massive steel pincers & the organic oozings subjected to spectroscopic analysis.

The Origin of the Species

It was said that he came from Skull Island, where naked savages worshiped him and sniveling priests offered for his delectation certain virginal bi-pedal mammals & voodoo cheese burgers, cash rebates & great salvers heaped with banana meat. It was rumored that Skull Island was his home, where throbbing tom-toms woke the turgid animal rutting-instinct, where he did appear at the full moon piercing the noisome sea-mist with his terminal ray-gun vision and great grasping monkey-grip. It was foretold that a eugenically-pristine hunter would appear to tame the beast. It was whispered that many would give their lives to bring this juggernaut of jungle rhythm to bay.

Unraveling the Helix

A hundred tiny volunteers, crack troops of the Melanogaster species, were placed live in a massive hypodermic needle & this needle was positioned directly before the great swollen, defiant Hypmogoogopizin' Eye. On the count of Eins, Zwei, Drei, I ran the fine steel tip through the taut erectile membrane & squirted the commando fruit fly mutant suicide squad into his aqueous matter. Drawn out after fusing with the floating protein particles in the eyeball, these brave winged warriors were then crushed to a fine paste, thus proving beyond a doubt that the H-man was guilty. Still, I am appalled to report, when the case came to the tribunal, no amount of evidence, no weight of logic or juridical reason or commonsense proof could triumph over his wicked hoodooistic ways.

"To Win in Court Every Time"

Procure a flagon of purified War Water. Mix in a pinch of Chinese gunpowder, aged goofer dust & Fast-Luck Flakes. Shake well & blend with an equal quantity of Bend-Over Oil. Slather the resultant unguent on an unused horehound bone-jobber & carry with you into the court of Law, preferably in the right hip pocket. When testifying, clasp your hand on the mojo bone & tell the truth, the whole truth, & nothing but the truth. Yes, the truth shall set you free.

Twelve Angry Mannequins

The entire world watched in amazement & disgust as the tribunal went on & on like a cat hit by a truck dragging its mangled leg behind through the ditchweeds. The H-man sat there smug as King Herod. He grinned for the cameras as he was forced to put the secret fingerless glove on the hand with which he'd pulled the rip-cord after strapping the suicide booster-pak on Miss Queasy Pie's naked & flawless human body. And even when the verdict was handed down "guilty! Guilty! GUILTY!" he was unruffled, still he sat there calm as Field Marshal Goering with the tiny hidden cyanide pellet in his twelve-year molar. Even as they dragged him off in chains to the holiest-of-holies Death Chamber, he did not bat an eye lash or shed a tear.

Deposition #4

"As the court-appointed psychoanalyst, it was my responsibility to administer the third-degree truth assays. Under duress, the subject did reveal certain factoids, though it must be admitted that neurological science was utterly foiled in its attempt to truly understand the nature and meaning of the Hypmogoogoopizin' power. As the 10,000 candle-power arc lamps were directed into the eye, the subject crooned, "Buff the monkey 'til he shines" to the tune of "Bali Hai." The longest piece of testimony, however, is as follows: "Lye, lye, lye. Red Devil Lye. Conk out. Red Devil kink conk out. Liar liar pants on fire. Red Devil Conk. King Konk. Congolean. Lye, lye, lye. Red Devil Lye out. Out damn spot. Out liar, Red Devil Lye." The wattage was increased a hundredfold until the paint began to peel off the walls and the restraining harness started to melt & he cried out: "My imps' names are Pyewacket... Melanogaster... Uneeda... Moonling... Bamboula... Gixy... Mundungus... Shebeen... Cicatrix... Tenaculum... Probang... Volapük!"

Beginning of the End

So it was that the H-man — unredeemed and unrepentant — was brought to the death chamber. In my capacity as Herr Doktor Professor Electropathologie I made certain that the subject was strapped in nice and cosy: his wrists on the arm rests and his feet cinched in tight to the middle leg of the 3-legged Pain Stool. The leather mask was fitted properly & the skin where the electrodes would make contact was slathered with cayenne & habanero conductive essences. This should have been my triumph. This should have been the peak moment in my long career of protecting society from itself. But — as the world well knows — the depth of the H-man's depravity knew no bounds & the majesty of the law was dragged mewling through the gutter.

Cheating the Chair

The death warrant was read aloud. The battery of big-bore TV cameras was aimed & locked on the subject. All doors and windows were secured. Though the H-man had refused any spiritual counsel, a tape of the Baal Shem Tov, the last Ismaili Imam, Pope Licentious X & the Reverend Jimmy Swaggart's tearful Master-Race Masturbation Race confessional sermon were played at too many decibels to clear the room of any and all pagan influences. My sweaty fist tightened on the smooth pulsing death switch. I felt the power course through me. I smelled my own pheromones, my manly musk. I clenched my buttocks tight, gritted my teeth to keep in the squeal of ecstasy & jerked down on the swollen doom-handle. The dynamo moaned as it released its liquid load. The Three-legged death squat bucked up as squirt after squirt of quintessential spuzz jetted into his body. But... but... how could we know? With every jolt, with every second the cameras whirred, gobbling up those ineffable images, the H-man grew stronger, bigger, harder, more handsome until the leather straps burst asunder, the mask & asbestos eye patch flew from his head, the machinery of loving vengeance seized & all fell silent. He rose, the huge Hypmogoogoopizin' Eye now emitting monster radiation storms, every band of the spectrum from short waves to gamma rays, sizzling, hissing, screaming electromagnetic ejaculation as we fell to our knees, abject worshippers, in sheer terrified reverence for the mighty H.

Pressure Drop

So it ended. So the H-man escaped. He walked out the door, which had melted off its hinges. Down the long corridor as the prisoners serenaded him with huzzahs and banged their tin cups on the xylophone cell bars. Out the front door and into the blaze of a thousand flash bulbs. Back to the hulking Cadillac Coupe de Grace & down the boulevard as the cheering rose & mountains of shredded hundred dollar bills drifted down on him.

Deposition #5

"Working with the Commissioner of Genetic Hygiene, I shortly thereafter began to see the shock wave moving through our gene pool. Babies were born with strange shark-skin complexions. Children developed asymmetrical eyes — always the left, always the orbis sinistralis, which swelled with venom. Prepubescent boys and girls woke to find their hair slick & high & greasy, transformed by spontaneous conk mutation. Our agents performed chromosomal breathalyzer tests & found a distinct shift in the genome occurring. How this will affect the population at large and the pending Germ Plasm Purity Laws is yet to be determined."

H-Man Heaven-Bound

See — a new constellation in the night sky, a dozen stars that form a celestial H. See — at a thousand gravesites the faces of granite angels no longer sad but smiling, suffused with ghostly love-rictus. See — in the flickering buzz of interstation static, an eye that emits wan granular illumination. See — crypto-pornographic films with titles such as *Heaven is Hard, Cream Your Genes* & *Gennifer Does Gehenna,* in which green-blue migrainous haloes float above the heads of sacred sluts. See — in the crackling fat of the Easter lamb a pattern that might spell out "hyp… mo… goo… goo." See — in the fog of the bathroom mirror, in the glare of midnight moonlight on a stormtrooper's goggle lens, in the retinal imprints of schizophrenic toddlers, images of the H-man's triumphant grin. See — the face on the ten thousand dollar wink & leer. See — inside yourself that little big-eyed waif-like angel who might or might not be your soul, who perhaps is the gentic trace of the Hypmogoogoopizin' spoor.

"To See the Invisible"

Burn a stick of pure puccoon incense while mixing slowly a handful of dried hellebore, one crushed squill, Nebuchadnezzar creme & a dash of Squatty Boy Essence. Mold into a finger shape & bake until hard. Dab the "fingertip" with Squint Oil & apply to your left eye, open. Sit naked in a perfectly dark room with a dead candle while pressing your bone magnet hard and long. If your heart is pure, you will see. **TIS**

Benares (a Metrophilia)
Brendan Connell

*T*emples, so many, rising out of the mass of houses, hovels, palaces, the air thick with smoke of incense and burning corpses; the air filled with chanted prayers, activity of life. Boats and satchels of human ash float upon Mother Ganges

Somadatta bathed himself in the Manikarnika Ghat, that pit which Vishnu had dug with his chakra and filled with the sweat of his meditation. Ascetics lined the banks of the river; some naked, hairless, skeletal, adorned with nothing but strings of beads; others covered with great manes, crouching like famished dogs, dressed in nothing but ashes. There were those who sat on beds of spikes, and those whose loins were encased in chastity belts of copper. One man held his right arm, wasted, shrunken, constantly towards the sky, having vowed not to lower it for twelve years. Another stood with a pot of fire on his head.

Somadatta had let his nails and hair grow out. For him it was taboo to eat ginger or sugar-cane; it was taboo for him to oil his body or garnish it with even the simplest ornament. And he was not an eater of living things; for him all living things were precious.

He now turned from the river and walked, with measured steps. The women he passed, their ankles jingling with bangles, their toes glittering with silver rings, he did not let his glance stray to. He avoided the streets where he knew existed the enclosures of harlots — he walked, making sure his glance was even and straight before him, not straying towards either earth or sky. He passed by the hundred-foot-high statue of Shiva

Mahesvara, which was made of shining brass. He passed by vendors of perfume and vendors of spice, by leprous beggars and princes whose turbans were decorated with richly hued peacock feathers. From shaded alleys came the sound of grammarians reciting Panini; from rooftops the cackle of bickering wives.

Soon he came to the patch of ground surrounding a certain sacred temple. Peepul and sirìsaka trees. A cow resting. Quiet.

Somadatta sat upon the earth and crossed one leg over the next. Unlike the general practitioner of meditation, he did not in-draw his senses, but rather, gradually, let his consciousness melt into a single one. That of touch. His skin

An ant crawled over his foot, its antennae quivering. Somadatta's tongue crept out of his mouth and moistened his lips. A fly alighted on the tip of his nose. Sentient beings. Ants. Flies. Attracted to his oils, his sweat. They were now coming to him, touching his skin. A file along the earth. The aerial causeway from the cow to him. Others might crush them, or flick them away, but he would not. Yes, at one time every single one of those ants had been a woman, as beautiful as any in all of Bharata. At one time, each of those flies had been a goddess, endowed with breasts like dual moons, and sweetly scented for extreme bliss. Could he deny their advances, these creatures who, in their former lives were sought after by the greatest kings, by powerful gods? The delicate touch of their thousands of feet, six-jointed legs, the glancing of their tibial spurs, was to him exquisite. Pleasure givers. Pulvilli. Vomiting saliva. Tickling labella. They began to cover his body, those numerous beings — and he, he gasped in ecstasy, — the ecstasy of the cosmic orgy. **T:S**

In Profit and In Loss

Ian Creasey

*T*he rebalancers kept staring at Provaria with calculating eyes. She checked her shares, but the price hadn't moved, not even after the touch of make-up she'd applied to her fourth-quarter earnings. *What does a girl have to do to get some attention round here?* If her shares didn't rise soon, she'd be thrown out of the index next rebalance. Already hedge funds had sold her short, anticipating that index-trackers would dump her. The vulture capitalists were circling, waiting to strip her assets and sell the empty shell.

She fluttered her patents, and smiled brightly at the industrials strolling from cum-div to ex-div. No point in flirting with retailers or utilities, but she'd love to be seen chatting to the guys in electronics. Some unfounded speculation would get her price up — and it didn't have to be unfounded.

A manufacturer leered at her cashflow. "You have a beautiful logo," he said. "What are your strategic objectives?"

He smelled of sweatshops and chemicals. She admired his handsome typography, the name PetroConZyme stylishly bit-mapped in Helvetica Bold Oblique, recently voted Best Font by Allium magazine.

"I aim to be the leading provider of domestic biotech solutions," she said. "What about you?"

"Oh, lots of things. Where there's a niche, there's a market. I look for opportunities — and I think I'm looking at one right now. I have plenty of production capacity, and I bet you have some great prototypes."

She was flattered, but wary. "I do, but I want to retain the rights to them."

"Of course. I'm committed to equality, and I value diversity while respecting the environment."

"Why, so do I! What else might we have in common, sir PetroConZyme?" she asked, checking out his earnings forecasts.

"Lots, I'm sure. But call me PCZ," he said.

"You can call me anytime," said Provaria.

And he did. Within days, they were discussing their mutual interests while scrutinising each other's figures. He wooed her at trade shows, he wooed her in zines, he wooed her with brochures for big new machines.

> He spoke of money-market prices
> And hedging for the dollar crisis
> She talked of targeting consumers
> From college kids to baby-boomers
>
> "Let's write ourselves a business plan
> "And launch our gadgets while we can
> "We'll pile 'em high and sell 'em cheap
> "And pray for market share to keep"

The more she saw of him, the more she liked. He had ambition, backed by a solid revenue base. He had experience, with operations in twenty countries. He had the drive to serve clients exceptionally well. And she had the vision to make them the highest beta stock in the bull market.

She unveiled her crisp black balance sheets, revealing a hint of sexy red leverage.

He said, "There's so much synergy between us. With my assets and your ideas, we can become the largest of the large-cap. We can be blue chip."

He bent down on one knee, and proposed merger.

● ● ●

> "To buy and to sell—"
> "—In profit and in loss."
> "For growth and for value—"
> "—In boom and in bust."

Under a confetti of press releases, they consummated their merger. They kept both names, becoming PetroConZyme Provaria, though she adopted his font. Retaining an ADR in New York, they based themselves in London, and commissioned a commemorative coffee mug upon entering the FTSE 100. Now they had futures long and short, options put and call, warrants in the money and prospects looking sunny.

We've private jets
And securitised debts
We sell a wide range of desk-living pets
They don't need food and they don't need vets
They don't slip outside to smoke cigarettes

They'll soothe all your frets
And gross up your nets
They'll tell you everything your boss forgets
We guarantee you'll have no regrets
When you buy our Marvellous Mechanical Pets

Together they conceived many products, though their leading line began as a promotional novelty. The desk-pets were so cute, and so good at filing, they became the executive toy *du jour*. Provaria loved designing all the variants: feathered and furry, spotted and striped, lazy and lively. Enhanced versions quickly followed, able to answer the phone, make coffee, and change the cartridge in colour printers. Combat fever swept many offices, with disagreements settled by duelling desk-pets, fuelling demand for further upgrades.

Their shares soared. Every tick of their price moved the index five points. They joined the elite stocks, researched by brokers and pampered by analysts. The Global Index Classification Committee created a new industry sector for PetroConZyme Provaria and their imitators: "Artificial Life, manufacturers and distributors." They sponsored TV shows, and acquired politicians, and denied that conditions in their overseas factories were exploitative. Provaria revelled in their fame and success, and blessed the day she had met her white knight.

But soon her name began to melt away.

• • •

Helvetica Bold is just too old
It's more up-to-date to be plain
Your name will shrink in paler ink
Till only my colours remain

Provaria's typeface faded from bold to plain, from 12-point to subscript. New business cards appeared, and they did not mention her.

PCZ spoke of brand rationalisation, of the need for a single image. "We can achieve this vision only by delivering seamlessly across our lines of business, practices and geographies."

"So much for respecting equality. So much for diversity," she said, feeling betrayed. Now she wished she'd tried harder to raise her own capital, instead of allowing herself to be merged and purged.

"But I do value your diversity," he replied. "Diversification maximises return for a given level of risk. Alone, we're sub-optimal. Together, we pioneer the efficient frontier."

"That's only because we're uncorrelated," she said bitterly. "I want a divorce."

"Certainly not. Your gadget-creatures sell far too well for that."

He issued a statement to the media denying that they had problems in the boardroom. But the press release, printed on their new stationery, omitted her logo. The marketing department rebranded all the signage and labels, and threw out the commemorative coffee mugs.

Provaria haunted her own offices, reduced to archived folders and a name on old constipated biros. She fought back by revealing her earnings adjustments, her pension fund deficits, the desk-pets' incomplete safety data and the conflicts of interest on the Artificial Life Approval Committee. She leaked the news that overstressed pets developed a compulsion to photocopy themselves and try to mate with the pictures.

Newspapers covered the spat with glee. The ratings on their bonds dropped below investment grade. A scandal erupted when her whistleblower revealed debts not consolidated into the accounts. "Corporate cellulite," she called it. "Everyone covers their ass, don't they?" But the markets didn't see it that way, and their share price dived.

And the craze for desk-pets died, like so many fads before it. Thousands of unwanted pets roamed the streets, offering to make coffee for the cigarette smokers huddled outside skyscrapers. Laid off like victims of corporate restructuring, they formed picket lines around their old offices, pleading for voicemail and Internet access. They doodled their demands on Post-It notes, and stuck them to the legs of workers who hurried heedlessly by.

PCZ shrugged off the setback, and moved on to new niches in other sectors. Provaria hated to see the offspring of their assembly lines cast aside. She had ideas for reviving the market, but kept them to herself, unwilling to boost profits and give PCZ a reason to hold onto her. Instead she arranged for a charity to ship surplus desk-pets to third-world countries, where they could help maintain office equipment. She pledged to meet the cost from company funds, knowing that PCZ would object to wasting money on obsolete products.

"I'm hiving you off," he told her at last. "Though I don't know what you think you'll gain. You're old and ugly, with heaps of baggage. No-one will ever want you, except to asset-strip you. That name you're so proud of will live only in court cases and footnotes."

"I'll survive," she said. "Better to be small-cap than small print."

• • •

"Ten write-offs to make you profitable"
"Easy diets for shedding liabilities"
"Surviving alone — red is the new black"

Provaria sighed as she tossed the latest self-help books onto the pile. They all promised a slim new look, yet recycled the same old tips. She had already made her assets sweat, ring-fenced liabilities in offshore subsidiaries, converted pensions from defined benefit to defined contribution. She'd dabbled with all the fads — open-source software, ethical standards, social responsibility. From environmental audits to feng shui in the office, none of it really helped. She'd gone from cutting-edge to window-ledge.

> Won't you buy my old desk-pets?
> Tuppence a bag, tuppence a bag
> Singles and pairs and matching sets
> Tuppence a bag to take away
>
> Super-sleek in Bold Oblique
> Tuppence a bag, tuppence a bag
> Retro-chic for the über-geek
> Tuppence a bag to you today

Life was hard as a single company. Management gurus seduced her with jargon, but she didn't want to hear that directors were from Mars and shareholders were from Venus. A succession of flings with sweet-talking consultants did little to boost her self-esteem. She felt dirty when she paid their hourly rate. Some said, "Follow your heart," while others said, "Follow the money," but they all followed each other through the door, ignoring the desk-pets begging for paper clips outside.

Only when she went on an away-day did she really start making progress. Between the self-discovery workshops and the team-building exercises, she vented her anger at the way she'd been treated.

"The past is holding you back," said the self-actualisation motivator.

"No, the past is who I am," Provaria said. "And I've learned from it."

In the brainstorming sessions, she reviewed all her old mission statements. Back then, she'd patented every line of source code in the desk-pets' genome, and she blessed her foresight in keeping the patents in her own name.

After all, nowadays the homeless desk-pets were evolving from a nuisance to a menace. Some built staple-guns, and used toner as camouflage to infiltrate offices at night. They hid in the air-vents, firing elastic bands at cleaners and security guards. Gangs of them sabotaged photocopiers, downloaded viruses, and printed obscene messages in Helvetica Bold.

Other companies had seen the potential of these tough survivors, and had begun to train them and customise them. One start-up had succeeded in using them for surveillance and minefield clearance. Indeed, the military possibilities were endless. Young 4-Dyne had plenty of ideas, and he could do even better with access to the specs and the guidance of hard-won market experience.

She would have to woo him.

"You have a beautiful logo," she said. "What are your strategic objectives?" **T:S**

Gaudí, Cons & Spires
Jetse de Vries

I: Delay the Light of Day
A) Angelo's Aspirations

Angelo is on a mission, another urgent package to be delivered by the swiftest bike messenger in town. He sweeps through the dense traffic in Barcelona's broad *passeigs* like a bat out of hell. Rapidly climbs steep *vias*, bypassing white-clad Cristina like an agile butterfly darting around a sedate Snow White. Descending steep *avingidas* at breakneck speed, like a cannonball thundering down a spiral stairway.

Yet, in this hyperactive body roams a wistful spirit. Angelo's dreams of winning the Tour de France were shattered when he found out the hard way that he couldn't even qualify for the under-18 *Vuelta* in his own country. His short and stringy body seemed much more suited for terrain biking, but Angelo declined. Those dirt-track racers didn't have an iota of the appeal and adulation garnered by legendary *cyclistas* like Pedro Delgado and Miguel Indurain. No, this courier thing — while keeping him in tiptop shape — is merely a byline financing this angel of *bravura*'s new dreams.

In the esoteric realms of cyberspace, Angelo has found a whole new world where the limits of his body cannot constrain the aspirations of his feverish mind. A place where the cornucopia of possibilities is only limited by his own inventiveness. A site where not only his imagination soars free but where he can also share it with others.

Lately he has become obsessed with architecture. Antoni Gaudí i Cornet being not the least source for his new inspiration. Although he knows he can hardly compare to Gaudí's genius he feels he has one big advantage: his creations are virtual. So he is not limited by mundane worries over construction strength and technical feasibility and the size of his creations is only limited by the capacity of his hardware. And he's constantly upgrading that.

•••

He started with his own digital designs. Took it easy at first, developing skills. Made modest mansions that contained more than was physically possible. Outside a straight, square building just a few stories high with only a few subtle touches hinting there's more than meets the eye. Inside a delirious maze with perilous passages and endless successions of parabolic arches, dark spiral stairways corkscrewing their way into bottomless depths and immense hallways under huge vestibule domes spiked with countless elliptic holes. A Damocles dining room ceiling from which rows upon rows of shining silver cutlery are hanging by thin threads, palace basements with supportive pillars looming like monumental archways of artisan masonry and a library where the bookshelves are craftily hidden between rows of thin curved separation walls, serrated near the arcs.

Lately his projects have become more ambitious as he began building his own virtual cathedrals. Making them incredibly immense was not the problem. The real challenge was to add depth and perspective to the greater picture, to imbue the grand design with a sharp sense of vertigo.

Once that was accomplished the somewhat less arduous task of constructing the cathedral itself could begin. Bell towers rising to vanishing point. Surrounded by a network of buttresses and parapets fitted with piercing pinnacles. Façades covered with lustrous sculptures, ordered by a sweeping arrangement of portals. A central nave overarching a long, tall hallway and the worshipping auditorium where steep rising choir benches side the immense, captivating church organ.

Inside this temple of total overload, ornamentation is omnipresent, pervading the dreamlike, almost surreal surrounds with the clarity of detail, the quality of realism and the persistence of vision. There Angelo spices his Gaudí addiction with a dash of Dalí. Gargoyles, staring into infinity, literally start moving if you approach them. Ornaments shape shifting at the edge of your sight. Sculptures suddenly changing, becoming grotesque. As if they're sending out warnings: beware, those that come too close to the subconscious!

Smiling maliciously, standing on top of the pulpit is the creator of this virtual vanity, preaching his figurative, symbolic freestyle sermons to the baffled audience at his altar.

•••

Walking through such a cryptic cornucopia is not enough. Other means of traversing and surveying it are asked for. He began with using a fly simulator program for soaring through his creations. While it worked perfectly for him, most of his friends had too much trouble controlling the simulated insect's flight behavior. Bumping into walls, ornaments and sculptures. Trying to fly through windows.

So for those that are less apt at the joystick controls than him (which is most of Barcelona) he developed some other software to traverse through his gargantuan creations. A dragonfly ride for the seriously computer impaired and a butterfly trip for the less informationally illiterate. Took a lot of dedication to get the butterfly's jerky movements just right, almost indistinguishable from nature.

Never mind if you don't like his latest taste. Don't matter if you're not into his strange mix of sleek modernism and old organics. What counts is that the presentation of his virtual structures is slick, suave and impressive. Details to be clear and convincing to the finest resolution level. Hacked the latest fractalware for that. Overviews to be awe inspiring, with real depth, superb shading and just the right quality of light. Acquired the flashiest 3D-ware for that. Colors to be larger than life, gleaming and glossy in places but basically radiating a rough'n'ready robustness. Racked his fuzzy brains for that.

To enhance his digital creations to the max, Angelo constantly shops for the latest updates and newest software. He does this by breaking in into several companies' networks. The shortage of IT specialists means that in some places system engineers have been hired who are so incompetent that they are thankful for every day the network keeps running. Angelo finds such companies by intruding their systems and leaving behind a bug that is relatively easy to detect. Any network controller worth his money should locate and take care of such a problem in no time. Those who do not clean up his bug get more of these little tests from him. No dangerous viruses of course since he wants to keep these networks running.

If he finds a system gullible enough he breaks in further and starts ordering the latest software updates on behalf of the software manager. To make the poor strugglers look good he installs them in those networks as well. Even if some find out that the system gets mysterious upgrades they would risk losing their jobs if they made too much noise about it.

Of course, he could afford most software updates himself. But there is no sport in doing it that way. This way, he considers himself a sort of self-help Robin Hood, allocating only a minor redistribution of riches.

Hardware upgrades, however: these are really expensive. He had to find another way to get them.

B) Cristina's Caresses

In the daytime, Cristina is the angel of sedate and exhausted grace. In her white, very loose fitting garbs she moves like a ghost, her feet touching ground very awkwardly. But she's not in a hurry. Not exactly. Compared to the shopping crowd strolling through La Rambla she appears to move in slow-motion.

She looks lost in thought. But it's not precisely that. More accurately stated, what goes on in her mind is not quite clear, even to herself. The impressions she tries to grasp are way too big to fit in her little head. At the same time the principles she tries to contemplate develop at a glacier's pace, with the speed of a moving continent.

Erosion is like flash-evaporation. Corrosion is like an explosive chain reaction. An Ice Age is like an afternoon cold. Evolution is like a cancer run amok.

To the outside world she appears: silent, almost stagnant. But inside she is: forever moving, forever changing. Everyone thinks she is — if not mute — dumb, simple-minded or retarded, but she knows she has no way to really express what is going on within her mind.

Rivers whiplash through the land, changing course like a very long and very agitated snake. Or, when staying in place, cutting through the earth like a surgeon's scalpel through skin. Mountains rise and fall like the heaving bosom of a deeply breathing woman.

She doesn't know why she is thinking like that. She would like to adapt to her urban environment but she is at a loss, unable to intervene. It's a sort of compulsive behavior she doesn't quite know how to quit. Lately though, she has found a way to somewhat quiet the quirky thought processes going through her.

From La Rambla she turns into Portaferrisa and heads for the medieval and overtly ornamented buildings of her favorite spot: the Gothic Quarter. There, in such sacred places as the chapel of Santa Àgata and the Palau Episcopal she finds a kind of rest, of peace. She visits churches, chapels and cathedrals without discrimination of belief. It seems that any place of worship will do.

She enters any palace of sanctity and sits languidly down on the nearest bench. Whether there's a service going on or not. Then, after she has settled down, anybody paying attention would see it. The subtle change coming over her. The drab, dragging tiredness becomes a kind of dignified resignation. The exhausted lines in her face evolve into little punctuation marks of acceptance. The dull look in her eyes develops a tiny spark of interest.

She seems to absorb something from her surrounds, inhales some sacred fumes, and assimilates the all-pervading aura. Her long, straight black hair contrasts more starkly with her white attire that starts to glitter lightly, as if irradiated by a more penetrating glow. She is enhanced by her environment, taking in an indefinable quality that is at the same time omnipresent and beyond reach.

Like a desert flower, she can last a long time with a little, as long as it's holy water. Therefore she doesn't visit man's altars of divine worship too much. Maybe also because a too frequent visitation would destroy the magic.

As she leaves the sacred palaces of the *Barri Gòtic* she gives a slight impression of a battery partly recharged, of a despondent ponderer finding some small, hopeful truth, of a burden somewhat enlightened. Her spiritual burden might be temporarily lessened; her body never seems to get enough rest. A lot of things about Cristina may be indistinct or poorly understood, yet if there is anything definite it is the disparity between body and mind, a sharp separation between the soul and the flesh.

What goes on for her thoughts is vague, non-localized and non-descriptive. What goes on in her body is definitely localized and describable. A light but constant cramp in her muscles, as if from overexertion. Yet she cannot remember any strenuous workouts she might have done. A slightly painful, sore yet itchy sensation, like a developing rash at the two body orifices that are very near to each other. Well, she certainly did no strange things with those! A general uneasy feeling, a crawling of her skin like formication. But she is no substance abuser and never drinks alcohol.

Worst of all is the ongoing overtiredness. She has not the faintest clue from where that originates. Neither had the doctors that have diagnosed her. They call it chronic fatigue syndrome, but that doesn't help her much since this has no known cause and no known cure.

•••

During one of her languid walks Angelo ran into her. A bit tired of the clichéd reactions he was getting to his virtual creations of late he was seeking for volunteers who might show a more original approach to his work. Well, this strange woman, dressed in white, known to everybody but understood by none might just do. If only to hear her out a bit. So he shows her his virtual, interactive cathedral.

Since he has no clue about her aptness in digital realms he gives her the dragonfly ride. After some minor uneasiness she maneuvers with the insect like she once was one. Her ability makes Angelo almost envious.

After a few quick, great sweeps through the immense structure she unerringly seeks out the most interesting places. Through all this she remains silent but she smiles, her eyes gleam and her body starts to shiver and shake. Every time a sculpture evolves before her eyes she is surprised, but not taken aback by the nightmarish imagery. Each time a gargoyle becomes a grotesque caricature of itself she frowns but is not appalled by its apparently evil characteristics.

Angelo cannot hold himself any longer. "Jesus, woman. What do you think?"

"Not bad. But I would think that a guy with your talents could do much better."

II: Alight the Dead of Night
A) Angelo's Aspirations

To get further, he must go beyond Gaudí. What was that old saying — he wonders — something akin to "Imitatio, Emulatio, Excelsior!" So not a single spiral staircase corkscrewing itself into an abyss but a double helix, like a twisted rope ladder. An immensely long, intertwined Jacob's ladder reaching for the stars.

Because it is imposing itself on the galaxy its internal cohesion is hanging on mirrored ideas of the nighttime sky. The rope of the Jacob's ladder is twisted into form by two entangled strands of the essence of Pisces and Sagittarius. These two are the backbone of the structure. Reinforcing the whole by complementing each other. The indecisive Pisces is given confidence by the burning enthusiasm of Sagittarius; the temperamental tendencies of the archer are tempered by the kindness of the connected fish. Together they reach a potential that is more than the sum of their parts.

Especially the versatility of Sagittarius is expanded to great proportions. It is now able to form tight bonds with six others: Aries, Aquarius, Cancer, Capricorn, Gemini and Taurus. Each of those forms an exact half of the rungs of the ladder. And while they all combine easily with the versatile Sagittarius, they are choosy when connecting with each other. So the steps are made up of certain combinations only.

While Cancer and Capricorn do not bond, they both can make connections with Gemini. The crab and the goat share a certain moodiness that — because opposites attract and equals repel — makes them incompatible with each other, and unattractive to others. Except for Gemini whose quick wit finds a good response with Capricorn's sense of humor and whose strong communication skills combined with their multitasking abilities evoke admiration in Cancer's highly developed imagination and so make an intuitive link, enforced by the crab's protectiveness.

Gemini is a strong and willing communicator but gets no response other than that of Cancer and Capricorn. Taurus is too headstrong and — while possessing his own charm and sensuousness — quite jealous of Gemini's smooth demeanor. The same competitive feelings estrange the twins from the bull. Aries' impulsiveness and Aquarius' unpredictability also prevent a bonding with Gemini.

In the same manner as with Cancer and Capricorn, the fickleness of Aries and Aquarius makes them incompatible with each other. The only one able to pierce through their fierce individualism is the robust magnetism of Taurus. Here, the reliable practicality of the bull combines well with the adventurous dynamics of the ram and the eccentricity of the water carrier.

So the steps to the stars are formed by either combinations of Taurus with Aries or Aquarius, or of combinations of Gemini with Cancer or Capricorn.

Strangely though, all have no problems bonding with versatile Sagittarius, everybody's friend. Therefore the steps are firmly anchored in the supportive backbone of the ladder.

Angelo doesn't know why he is bothered so much with the construction side of it. Something inside compels him to do it this way. A conviction that the inner structure is an intrinsic factor enhancing the external appearance to a new level of achievement.

A better way of doing things. Don't adapt the impressed expression with the hottest software, but fabricate the expressed impression from the bottom up. A symbiosis between the parts and the whole, improving both. Almost like reality, he muses. But no, more like Angelo's deepest core desires. *Desiros Nucleotides Angelos?* Has a definite ring to it.

Time to take a break. Angelo instructs the program to raise his intertwined spiral tower a little further while he stretches his legs. When he returns from his short stroll Angelo finds his latest brainchild is running off into chaos.

Through a sudden software glitch the construction of the double helix tower goes haywire, gets completely out of hand. It grows to an unimaginable length and starts to get tangled up with itself, like an infinitely long strand of spaghetti self-intertwining. Before he is able to arrest the program the whole thing has somehow turned into a gargantuan "X," challenging the sky.

At moments like this, Angelo thinks his 23 years on Earth are too short to deal with the caprice of random chance. He feels lacking in experience and wisdom. Until his inspiration is rising to the challenge.

"What the *cojónes*, let it be!" he thinks out loud. The more he considers it, the more he likes it. At first sight it looks a bit jumbled, a spontaneous mutation of the original, concise capital X. At second sight it is one of the most internally coherent structures he can imagine, more intricate than anything he tried before.

The letter it resembles. The symbolism of the outcome. The dichotomy it radiates: explicit yet mysterious, diverging yet focusing. The myriad implications of its expression. The X of change. The X of challenging the conformity. The X of the ultimate, mysterious achievement. Yet — he wonders — maybe it needs to be counterbalanced with the "Y" of the eternal question.

Anyway, he's getting too tired to improve on this and he has some important deliveries to make tomorrow.

B) Cristina's Caresses

In the nighttime, certain drastic changes come over Cristina. After a short nap — started just before dusk — she wakes when enough darkness has set in. Then she is the antitype of her sacrosanct self. A schizophrenic transformation occurs, the untouchable lady of chastity becomes the devious whore of Christ. The virginal, white attire is dumped in a laundry. In secretive, locked dressing drawers, not accessible or consciously known to the pure part of her personality, extremely provocative and alluring outfits are stored. A demure damsel dramatically metamorphoses into a flabbergasting *femme fatale*. The latest, slickest models of curling tongs transform a head of thick, long, sleek black hair into towering tresses of spiraling finesse. Tight, subtly laced semiopaque *chemisette* over panty girdle and camisole top to enhance a naturally superb figure previously in hiding under those big, loose fitting white garments. Packed in a red silk dress with long, black velvet gloves, fishnet panties and long, long leather boots she readily traverses the threshold from desperately desirable to completely irresistible.

Then she's off into Barcelona's long night, hunting for victims. Starts on La Rambla, warming up the already hot-tempered single or not-so-single male populace of the city's nightlife, hinting at the shape of things to come. Continues in the discotheques and nightclubs of the *Barri Gòtic*. Of course there's always a guy, ready and willing and savoring the illusion he can keep up with her. A lot of aspiring candidates have fallen off by then, and she's homing in on the most promising subject. Not realizing what will hit him, he — all too voluntarily — comes along with her.

By then she has made it perfectly clear that she is not in for such time wasting nonsense like elongated foreplay and other senseless subtleties. At that point her seductive charms, suave dance floor aplomb and keen sense for just how to make him totally weak in the knees from anticipation alone have shattered all his reserves.

"Come on, jump me like the ball of testosterone that you are!" she demands with a voice that comes from the great-grandmother of all dominatrices. Some sensible part of her victim might be getting second thoughts, but that part has already been drowned in cascading waves of unleashed desire and lust.

"Fuck me up against the wall, you no good stud!" She urges him on, as thick drops of sweat trickle down his hard-working body. Of course he came prematurely but she didn't even give him the ghost of a chance of losing his hardness. No way, sir! Now do as the lady pleases.

"Stick it up my ass, you faggot!" She shouts as the battle rages on. Taboos are for the small-minded. Tattoos are on the small of her back. Get it on, they read. So she keeps him going until he begs for mercy.

Totally exhausted her victim falls asleep. And *they* call *us* the lesser sex? Anything to support their superiority complex. Well, while the superior sex enjoys a blissful coma Cristina takes half the money from his wallet, then dresses and leaves. Most of these morons don't even notice. The rest are too proud to complain.

She's off back home to take a long bath and treats herself to the exclusive toiletries and ointments she finances this way. Soothes her soreness, locks her night attire in the secret *dressoire* and goes to bed, passions fulfilled.

When the morning light scatters through the thin curtains, a thoroughly cleaned Cristina wakes up. Also an innocent Madonna that has absolutely no idea about her sacrilegious adventures of the night before. She finds that once again the night somehow hasn't given her body enough rest. She is so tired, she would rather stay in bed longer. But she promised that cute boy, Angelo, to check out his latest project.

III: The morning after

He was trying to postpone it as long as possible but the big glitch of last night — although he turned it into a victory — emphasizes the need to update his hardware once again. So — reluctantly — he is offering his services to some discreet clients.

Every time he hopes it is the last time. After that he will be able to attract enough paying visitors to his website. But he knows that his virtual creations need the latest cyberware and the fastest fiberware to be run properly. This automatically limits his circle of potential customers. Of course he could make a cruder and easier accessible version, but hey! Would you like to watch the Night Watch with just one tiny, flickering spotlight? Would you rather see Guernica through a smoke screen? Or appreciate Las Meninas through a distorting mirror? Or even view the Hallucinogenic Toreador on drugs?

So you see: no compromises. For a short while he tried to sell a sample CD-ROM of his wares to electronic publishers. A lot of them were interested. Interesting stuff, but how about using his formative talent in a more — uhm — *rewarding* way? Like, for instance, in computer games? Angelo did not hide his disgust. Quite the contrary, so they didn't need to see him again.

Anyway those virtual constructs on disk are static, still, bound in punctured aluminum, not really interactive. The work on his website: that's the real thing. It's organic: it grows with him. Constantly updated, enhanced, improved. Scrupulously honest, so you not only get the advances but also the failures, the setbacks, the whimsical blind alleys. It shows you the path of progress is really a zigzag mountain trail, sometimes almost coiling in on itself. The learning curve to self-improvement escaping from self-entanglement.

To further propagate that curve he needs new equipment and since any ordinary day job steals too much time from his vocation he uses another way. Some very circumspect people had a need for a very inconspicuous means of transporting some goods. Valuable goods, compact, concentrated and rather lightweight.

They couldn't use public means or private companies. Too unknown, not reliable and not personal enough. They needed special friends, people they knew how to find at all times that at the same time would have no idea as to where they were. People that know the city like their back pockets and at the same time merge so well with the crowd as to be nearly invisible.

That last description fitted Angelo only half as his custom-painted mountain bike and his self-designed cyclist outfit made him recognizable half a mile away. Now this — one of these very prudent people, thinking himself always a little smarter than the rest, postulated — very overexposure makes a perfect camouflage. And nobody could maneuver the streets of the city as swift as Angelo, who hated routines and took a different route every time.

So Angelo was approached by a very cool, very slick person. Would he care to be — on a very freelance basis — one of the very select, very elite group of message deliverers, the *crème de la crème* of cycle couriers in town? Angelo didn't know there were any in Barcelona; according to the works of the cyberpunk classics these only existed in exotic cities like San Francisco or Amsterdam. No, also here but our clients are really exclusive, celebrities that need to keep a distance, remain incognito. That's why they pay so well and why we need to be very discreet. We have to protect their identities, otherwise they would be besieged by endless legions of admirers and nasty press mosquitoes.

The job suited Angelo's needs so well that he hardly gave it a second thought. Over time, though, doubts and suspicions slowly crept into his mind. It began when he made a cautious business proposal to one of those cool and collected guys.

"Why all this cycling around when we can send these messages over the net?"

"What do you mean?"

"I know somebody who has developed encryption software that is virtually unbreakable. We could set up an internet courier service—"

"Not a good idea. We're *not only* sending messages." Said with such finality that Angelo didn't mention the subject for a second time. Immediately after that he was called up a lot less frequently. So he kept quiet until they started using him more, again.

Bad qualms, horrible hunches began to take root in his mind. The dreaded *démasqué* of innocence. Naïveté lost, announcing: "Your dreamworld is just about to end." Draw back before you're drawn in too far.

But once again he needs the money. Once more he ignores the insistent voice of his conscience. One last time, then never again. Then again, he might be wrong, he has no hard evidence. It might be a bona fide operation after all. Sounds nice but not reassuring.

Still he is taking another small packet to a certain rendez-vous point. He rides best when his mind is empty, in a sort of driver's trance, a mental autopilot that is restful for his mind yet sharpens his reflexes. A nirvanaesque state of mind that unites body and purpose and makes him the ideal town traverser at rush hour.

Traffic cops have long ago given up trying to track him. They found he is slicker than an oiled eel in a grease pit. The effort to catch him is not worth the minimal annoyance he's giving. Never ever — to anyone's knowledge — came even close to hitting anything or anybody. Darts out of the way with an agility that would frustrate the slyest fly. The rare few that claim he's nearly brushed them are simply ignored. An urban legend unaware of his own reputation.

This time he is far from his optimum morale. Excitement about his latest *virtuoso* virtuality and gnawing doubts about his scapegoatish couriership fight for dominance and refuse to leave his mind blank. In this troubled state his concentration is waning.

Then the unthinkable almost happens: he nearly runs into somebody. With the fiercest reflex in his courier career he miraculously avoids close contact. But drops the small packet in the process. It bursts open and white powder rains over the street cobbles like a miniature snowstorm in August. In the middle of the crossroads of Avenido Diagonal and Passeig Sant Joan in rush hour.

He panics. *Estupido! Loco!* Even the most ignorant idiot can make an educated guess as to what that is. He can't pick it up. He has to go, escape, vanish, *vamos!*

This means he will not be at the right place at the right time with the right stuff. They will miss him but where to go? They know where he lives!

Now his garish outfit makes him stand out like a peacock butterfly in a petting zoo. Hide or keep moving? Caustic fear and paranoia clench his mind in a vice-like grip. Cold sweat breaks on his brow as he sees a familiar face looking at him, speaking fast into a cell phone. The next thing he knows, a furiously approaching black car crash-stops, whirls around with shrieking tires and chases him.

IV: At the top of Parc Güell

His flight leads him further uphill, climbing like crazy through steep streets until suddenly — as if by magic — he arrives at the top plateau of the Parc Güell. A quick scan of the plateau reveals no sign of his pursuers, only a few tourists enjoying the view and some locals taking a stroll.

The view of the city is enchanting. Even when — like now — a slight haze is hanging over town, giving it a mystique touch, pronouncing it not quite real.

Still panting he pauses to take in the grand overview. From the two ugly grey skyscrapers of Port Olympic to the finished World Trade Center in Port Vell. From the Olympic symbol Torre de la Cavatra (looking like a white cross from this distance) to the eight spires of the Sagrada Família cathedral. The Passeig Sant Joan, a big corridor cutting off the east part of the city from the rest.

Strangely, as the sun sets the haze seems to dissolve and the hard light of day is gradually replaced by the subtler shades of dusk. As a last salute three sharp reflections of mirrored office windows seem to blink at him, one by one. They give the illusion of beaming their light over his shoulder, pointing behind him.

"Always check your back! Never forget to check your back!" His subconscious forcefully reminds him, spiking through his mesmerized musings. He turns around and sees the mountain of Tibidabo. On top of it — against a clouded sky — sits a lone cathedral.

His attention is completely focused on it, locked in with a will stronger than his own. This lone cathedral changes, expands before his eyes. In a Dalíesque transformation it grows to enormous size, becoming the eight spires of the Sagrada Família. Then those skyscraping towers, eerily immense, begin to vibrate, shaking softly. It is like a sine wave is passing through all eight of them. But instead of breaking and crumbling and tumbling down they become flexible, moving in a slow, graceful way. Like the tentacles of a gargantuan octopus, mountain Tibidabo its body, spouting dark blue ink against a blood red sky.

One of these tentacles lashes out and snaps him up like a whiplash artist taking a cigarette out of a victim's mouth. He freezes in fear as he is taken up, up and up, higher than he has ever been. Through the stratosphere — puncturing the ozone layer — into deep space.

Just as he starts to wonder if he can still respire his breath is taken away by the spectacular sight below. It should be the ocean-dominated, clouded sphere of Mother Earth but the sea forms only a small part of the view as he sees that Barcelona has become planet-sized. The anchored, satellite-like painted balloon near Port Olympic has expanded and moved to become the moon.

A third object is coming in from outer space, moving soundlessly, an alien craft. Its main, cylindrical body is not quite triangular but also not completely circular. Colored lights are flashing all over its main body and two extensions. In the middle of one flat side of the semi-cylinder a long, pointed mast is fixed. The whole vessel is accelerating down, as if it is going to spear Barcelona. It seems to be heading straight for the Barri Gòtic but just before it crashes into the medieval buildings it deflects its course and takes a sweeping curve towards mountain Tibidabo. There it turns around, its sharp extension positioned upward, the thicker pole on the other flat side of the near-tube pointing down. Then it drifts slowly towards the side of the mountain and gently parks its lower pole on the ground. Thick cables shoot off from the main tubular-triangular body and anchor it to the earth. To his surprise, Angelo sees it exactly resembles the Collcerola Telecom Tower and finds himself back on the top plateau of Parc Güell again, cold sweat running down his neck.

Suddenly he sees Cristina, in profile. Dressed up and down in a way that shames his wildest dreams. No time to be amazed as something more fatal is attracting his attention.

He hears the shouts of his pursuers. They come from both directions. They have him cornered. A showdown out in the open. He feels like a high plains drifter. Without the fast-drawing guns. A despondent desperado at the end of his rope. A nihilistic nitwit at the beginning of a noose.

"You didn't deliver the message, Angelo," the slickest sleazebag mouths with maximum melodrama.

"Oh, you mean the coke was encoded?" Angelo answers in his sweetest, most innocent tone. Live like a smartass, die by the tongue.

"No, its meaning is as clear as your death wish, you moron."

Before the exchange becomes really pathetic, Cristina enters the scene as an improbable apparition, the embodiment of contradiction, sin and shame entangled like a jumbled yin and yang symbol.

"Leave him alone, he is under my protection."

These hardened criminals have seen many a weird broad but this tops all. Yet the big gun she's pointing their way is quite unmistakable. The least spellbound of the group moves a hand to one of his pockets. She shoots him in the knee. To emphasize her point she shoots the hat off one's head and the spurs off another's boots.

"Now fuck off before I blow you all to hell," she says, dangerously calm and matter-of-factly.

If there is one thing these guys know it is when to scatter. And come back in strength, of course, later. Cristina watches coolly as they drive off in their cars.

V: Mother Nature and the Computer Kid

"Cristina, what happened to you?" Angelo asks, hardly believing his eyes. Her attire, her make-up, her manners, all are split in half. Her left side the introvert, white clad modest nun, her right side the provoking, sharp-dressed, indecent temptress. Hardly recovered from the confrontation poor Angelo is so baffled by her alluring right that he hardly notices the blatant impossibility of her combined attire.

She puts her right hand to her deliciously curved, delicately clad right side while her angelic left hand casually holds the big gun.

"Forget them, Angelo. They are just scum of the Earth. They will be washed away by the new rains."

"But they know where I live."

"Leave it behind. Your future lies elsewhere."

"All my hard work, my virtual creations—"

"—are parked on the very best server available. Your brains."

"I will never get it exactly as it was."

"Doesn't matter. Never really did for you and you know it."

"I hardly know who you are!"

"I'm only getting a glimpse of that, myself."

"Huh?"

How to explain this to a perplexed young man, a wild talent that has just scratched the surface of his own potential? Understand the world and begin with yourself. She herself is not so unsure as to where her origins are but very uncertain of how her present manifestation came into existence.

Maybe Mother Nature needs to communicate with those wayward sons that are becoming too estranged. An interface filter to dampen the feed forward loop before it turns into white noise. An intervening agent triggered by a combination of events.

An experiment as well. Almost failed, her initial reactions to this bastion of civilization swung between two extremes, causing a split personality, memory fragmentation and dislocation. One reaction was allergic, seeking sanctuary from this overblown artificiality. The other was fascination, leading to overindulgence with the modern way of life. Both reactions were too strong to mingle and too evenly matched for one to dominate. So they were temporally disconnected to different domains: night and day.

Her identity, her personality, her *gestalt* was scattered together with the discrepancy of her memory fragments. Still, indistinct, imminent yet profound forms of order were appearing out of the chaotic haze.

Then she saw Angelo's virtual twin spiral tower and immediately recognized what it represented. The possibilities. The implications. Her mission unfolded before her.

If this is the advent of the next evolutionary jump then her task is to help ease the way. You cannot stop the inevitable so you better be with the *avant-garde* before you find yourself becoming extinct.

What's more, it would be very stupid indeed not to take four billion years of evolved experience and wisdom along into the great unknown. She needs to secure and facilitate that. Quite probably she won't be the only one. The short interval in which she gathered her thoughts vibrated with an abstract eternity. Invigorated with a new passion and imbued with a new meaning to her existence she turns to the lost boy.

"You have an intuitive link with the biological heart of the matter. You don't get everything right, make the wrong links but you come quite close with your limited knowledge."

"Oh. And you know better?"

Already regaining a part of his composure. If he knew how far he still has to go he wouldn't act so cocky. But Cristina now knows she has nearly infinite patience and an almost unending reservoir of forgiveness.

Together, they walk through Parc Güell. She moves with a rhythm of her own, effortless, elegant, and gracious. It is not imposing, yet moving in sync with her is a little easier, more fluent than forcibly keeping your own step. Still there is more than enough room for a melody of your own. Contrasting, counterpointing, amplifying or rejoicing: interacting with that rhythm works best.

Traveling onwards, supported by her deep rhythmic complexity in cooperation with his unique cadence, they prepare a new way. ⊤⊗

Gulls
Tim Pratt

*G*rady ran bounce-bouncing down the sidewalk, flip-flops flapping, face smeared with summermelted chocosicle, and Harriet swooped down (like a bandersnatch, she thought, like the poem I read to him) and grabbed him before he could jump off the curb.

He didn't struggle, only goggled with mint-green eyes at Monstrous Miniature Golf across the street. That's where he wanted to go, Harriet thought, to bat balls between Frankenstein's legs, to climb on the papier-machè tombstones. There were jagged fake trees (coathanger trees, she thought, all twisted and pointed) with rubber bats hanging like rotten bananas from the branches. Harriet clucked and guided Grady along, past the surf-shops and lemonade stands and not-so-discreet stripclubs. They were looking for a public beach access. Harriet's shoulder bag was swollen with towels and sunscreen and grocery-store-checkout romances, and it thumped against her as she walked.

Her nephew, dear Grady, sweet Grady, wanted to swim. That was all he ever wanted to do, swim or chase sandcrabs. He did that all day at the house, the rented house, crammed with relatives pitching in money to make a vacation possible. They slept six to a room in that house but none of them could have afforded it alone, and they were right on the beach. That didn't help now. Harriet had gone shopping with her three sisters and her nephew Grady, and Grady had stomped and been bored and Harriet offered to take him swimming for the afternoon. Her sisters only talked about children and Harriet had no children so she too was bored. She was nearly forty and worry-lined and fifty weeks a year she typed things she didn't understand and fed her cats. Now two weeks of vacation and she was at the beach, unnerved by bikinis and broken glass, surrounded by her squabbling kin who made her nervous, all but Grady, who was almost a son. Once a man had promised to marry her and give her children, but he was gone and no children though they'd done it enough, the thing that makes children, but not often enough or well enough to keep him from leaving her, she supposed.

She sweated under her floppy hat and even through tinted glasses everything flashed neon and gleamed metal. She could hardly believe there was an ocean nearby. She could have been in a beach-town theme park, otherwise in the middle of a baking desert. She giggled at the thought and Grady giggled because laughter made him happy. He was already tanned brown despite the pale promise of his yellow hair, just like his mother's and Harriet's (though his mother seldom laughed and never just to make Grady laugh, what sort of mother was that?). Everywhere metal now and no surf sound, only the whoosh of passing cars (too close, even holding his hand it was too close and she moved him away from the street), no salt smell just exhaust and the fried reek of fast food. Nothing to really speak of beach except the wheeling gulls, like styrofoam gliders overhead, and they flew over other places, inland dumps and sewage treatment plants. The beach is there, she thought, craning her neck to look around buildings and dumpsters; only show me the way.

And then a blue sign, standing up rusty and bullet-holed in a weedy gravel lot, blue with a zigzag diagram of waves and a cartoon picnic table with umbrella. There were no cars in the lot, tiny as it was and jammed between a white hotel and the bar (featuring wet t-shirt contest amateurs only) they'd just passed. "Look, Grady, the beach!" and he streaked but she held his hand and he bounced back like a paddleball. They couldn't really see the beach, but a boardwalk stretched over the grass-covered dune, its steps drifted with fine sand. They crunched over gravel, Grady babbling excitedly about dolphins and mermaids and octopuses and crabs, and clomped over the boardwalk.

Fifty yards of walking before the beach. A high fence of weathered wood ran along the right side, partitioning the beach for the people in the hotel. The fence ran for a distance even into the water before giving up hope of division. Harriet heard happy shouts and laughter from the other side. It was a gleaming white hotel with balconies on the back; she could see the top floors rising over the fence, much better than the ramshackle crammed-in house with rusty showerheads and sand in the mattresses. Same water, she thought, squelching her envy, they get the same beach we do.

But this was a sad little beach. Grady surged like a live wire, pulling away and eager to be in the gray-green water, but she held on and stepped with distaste around broken beer-bottles and chunks of styrofoam. The horizon was infinite and curved but the air stank of fish. She saw a dead jellyfish on the line of the lapping water.

"Lookit the boy with the seagulls!" Grady said, and Harriet lifted her hat-shaded eyes to see a boy down the beach. He held his arms open, playing Messiah to the shorebirds who circled around him and dove at his feet. He had a jumbo-bag of potato chips and he scattered them, feeding the devotion of the birds. There was something horribly hungry about the gulls, dirty white feathers drifting and long beaks darting as they squabbled over fragments of food.

"Why they his friends?" Grady demanded, his jealousy an echo of Harriet's when she looked at the fence, screening off a beach without beer bottles and dead things.

"They'll come to anyone who feeds them," she said, "They're not really his friends, not like the animals in cartoons. They're just hungry." Grady nodded, already forgetting and looking at the water. She tenderly ruffled his short gold hair and wished there were time to teach him about friends, about being careful. He wouldn't understand that some people are true friends, but that some people only want to feed on you.

She spread a towel in the long thin rectangle of shade cast by the fence and told Grady to be careful and mind the undertow and stay in the shallows. He nodded, all impatience and eyeing the water, and bolted at her nod. She smiled after him and rummaged through her bag for sunscreen and her current gaudy romance novel; she knew they were foolish, and told herself she read them only because that is what women alone on the beach do, but secretly she loved them and dreamed.

She looked up to check on Grady and he was deep, dog-paddling deeper. "Grady!" She stood and ran but he was swimming, bumping against the hotel's board fence in the water. He didn't hear. She slipped off her sandals and ran, glad she wore shorts now despite her pale thin legs. Her hat fell away and she barely had her feet wet when Grady disappeared around the fence. Harriet hung, a moment of indecision (like a seagull flying against the wind, suspended), then ran back up the beach. There was a gate in the fence, tacked with a sign that said NO ENTRY. She tugged and it opened and she ran through.

An impression of clean sand, beach chairs and sleek dark people in bright swimsuits and trunks, a multitude of children, but her eyes were on Grady, swimming back to shore, grinning impish and in no danger of drowning. Curiosity, she thought, every little boy has to see what's on the other side of the fence, never mind the side they're on.

Grady came out and looked around, face aglow with sun and shiny with water, and Harriet took his hand, scolding until his smile faded and his eyes widened and he nodded, solemn as an owl. Grady never meant to be bad, and if you pointed out bad he seldom did it twice. Harriet was satisfied, even if her heart still pounded in her throat from running and fear, the fear (she imagined) of a mother for her child.

She held his hand and walked from the water to find every eye on her. A dozen adults, all so similar in height and color that they must be a horde of brothers and sisters, all a bit younger than she was. The women were hurrying over, looking concerned, and the men stood in a group around the barbecue grill, the eldest with gray hair holding a spatula. The smell of cooking meat wafted toward her, slightly sweet, she couldn't place it. No smell of dead fish here. She blushed as the women, their oiled bodies firm and cared for beyond the fitness of youth, crowded around. One was older, white-haired, but her face had few lines and her black one-piece swimsuit fit snugly. She was a match for the man at the grill; grandparents to all those children, perhaps? Six wedding rings glittered on six hands, and Harriet supposed these women were married to those men, for all that their husbands looked like blood siblings, too. A similarity of taste, she supposed.

"Is he all right?" white-hair said, smiling a greeting. Grady was looking around them at the gaggle of children, from toddlers to almost-teens, laughing and splashing in the shallows and taking no notice of the interlopers on their beach. Grady was thrumming, wanting to be away with them, but Harriet held on.

"I'm sorry," she said, "I know we shouldn't be here, we'll go." The women exchanged glances with a familiarity that spoke of sisterhood; certainly it was a clan of daughters. But all the men shared the square-jawed features of the gray-haired man (now approaching in a polo shirt, spatula in one hand like a scepter) and they stood nursing beers like brothers.

"You'll do no such thing," white-hair said firmly. The youngest of the others smiled and licked her lips, then looked startled when she met Harriet's eyes. "The boy frightened you, and the beach is awful beyond the fence. Do stay. We'll help you watch the boy."

Grady hooked a finger in his mouth and looked up at the women, who cooed and smiled at him, but Grady seemed only fascinated by the bright colors of their swimsuits.

"We wouldn't want to be trouble," Harriet said, feeling every sag and brittleness of her body, thinking of the broad-shouldered square-faced men and wondering why she'd never found them, why she wasn't oiled and tan and beautiful.

The gray-haired man arrived in time to shake his head and say, "No trouble at all, this family makes enough trouble on its own, you won't add to it. You're welcome to stay for dinner. There will be plenty."

He smiled, straight white teeth, and Harriet found herself nodding. Grady sensed the shift and darted toward the children, who greeted him and sucked him into their throng. There must be thirty children, she thought, and glanced at the women again. No sign of stretch-marks, no indications of motherhood, they'd borne perfect children and emerged perfect themselves.

The women hustled her aside giving introductions, establishing relations (though unclearly; three generations of a family on vacation, but which were married, whose children, who belonged to the old couple, and who were in-laws?). The women had long perfect nails and tiny teeth, and Harriet was aware of her own bitten-to-the-quick hands and coffee-stained smile. The women chattered and hardly noticed if Harriet answered. Did they ever ask her name? They certainly never used it. She wondered; why are they being so nice to me? Pity? She thought she heard something, a scream from the children and she turned, but they were only splashing in a knot, playing. She didn't see Grady; his golden hair should have stood out like a beacon in that sea of dark, but there were so many children, he was surely just out of sight, and the women were plucking at her sleeves for attention. The youngest, with her eager eyes, plucked too hard, her fingernails brought a crescent of blood on Harriet's forearm, making her gasp. The girl only licked her lips again and the white-haired woman slapped her daughter (in-law?) hard across the face. She dropped her eyes and murmured an apology. Harriet stared, shocked, but in a moment she was overwhelmed by chattering ministrations, offers of paper towels and exclamations over the small wound.

The white-haired woman smiled graciously, then laughed, looking beyond Harriet to the water. "Those children," she said, "Always snacking when we're about to have dinner."

Harriet turned to look, a tentative smile on her face. The dark children were crouched in a circle, eating something off the sand, reaching down with their hands. One child, very small, sat sullenly away from the rest, tearing at a half-rotted fish with her teeth, shooting glares at her cousins (brothers? sisters?) as she chewed.

"What?" Harriet began, standing, drawing breath to call for Grady. The gray-haired man shouted, "These are done! Bring me more meat!" and Harriet smelled the sweet, unidentifiable odor from the grill again.

Why so friendly? She thought. What can they want from me?

The children scattered at the announcement of food, hurrying toward the grill, a flurry of graceful limbs and placid faces. They looked at Harriet as they loped past, wolfish faces and cool dark eyes. What they'd left steamed on the sand, ragged, scattered, wet. She saw a mass of golden hair and a jagged white stick, driftwood or a bone, driven into the sand beside it, but nothing she could call Grady. The gray-haired man called again for more meat, and his wife and daughters began plucking at Harriet's skin, silent now, no more chatter. Harriet didn't make a sound either, only stood, barely feeling the nips become tugs and wrenchings. She watched a cyclone of white gulls descend to fight over what the children had left. **тs**

The Sibyl of Tamarish
Darja Malcolm-Clarke

An evening shade fluoresces amidst the walnuts; I walk among them hearing things spoken by wraiths lurking here in penumbra of night. In the failing light their voices froth into a murmur like a brook rushing against a fallen tree. They tell me of things that happened here long ago or here, far away in mists, in layers beneath here. Day evanesces, wanes into twilight, the night you can see. I wait for the phantasmagoria to flicker before me, that parade like the fluttering of pale faceless moths behind the shade at my cell window. Some nights, sensibility drops away slowly, as teeth from an ancient skull: I am the mouthpiece of the spirits at town's edge, the dark others, the wild mothers of seed, of leaf, of rot, of wormbody, of pistil and bark, of collapsing carcass. They tell me, once and still they are my sisters. They have deceived me before.

Their presence is disconcerting in this grey not-day. Their eyes are wide, their lips are thin, and they approach with the cautiousness of cats. In this particular light, when I must leave my cell, they like to peel back their ethereal skin; they like the feel of dusk inside them. Elsetimes, they wish to be heard by the folk of Tamarish, to speak their weird wisdom. They come to me with mouths agape, a strain of jabber upon their tongues. They do not enter my body as you would expect, but gentle; place their lizard-grey fingertips upon me like I am a newborn creature, and ease beneath my skin, their mouths still working. They grate my throat with the gravel of their voices. I, not myself, lie among the walnuts' shed leaves, my flesh ceasing to be my own for a time. So come the housefolk, approach and gather at the edge of the grove. My mouth moves, a voice rises, words of a sort emerge — an inexplicable jabber, a tangling on the tongue, a voiced flickering like lark's wings on a wind. I know of this: I have conducted this work for centuries.

Or I walk from my small stone cell at the city's edge up to Tamarish thus, limbs flailing, for the dark others are not accustomed to flesh. Housefolk stop to watch, listen in their doorways when my feet pad their dusty streets, when the spirits speak through me. They hear the sibyl of Tamarish; they do as she bids. And they fear the company she keeps.

My prophetical screams have rung up and down these hills and through these trees for centuries. Those dark others know each form I have taken and will take, each child I have been born and crone become; they always bring me back here. They see the tapestry of Tamarish — that vivid fabric, a subtle weave — and see the greatest and smallest lives dance before them like tail feathers dropped in a breeze. And this I see and know and hear, their voices in me pressing against flesh like a searing sun. I wait on them to give my life shape. For this, I have over-fed some of my senses, starved others; that is the way of the sibyl, who sees in riddles. Distantly, I recall a touch as a child before the specters brought me to this, my ever-home: a woman's soft arms around me, a word or two, spoken just to me. Oh, the housefolk speak to me; a'times, I feel it is not me they speak to. My life is for them, who fear me, and keep their distance.

A centuries-old conflict returns. Depraved the undead who wouldn't let go their hold here after even their bodies had belched them out. They grow restless among the pine groves behind the walnuts. Two autumn-tattered moons now they gather nightly for a carnival, a howling, shrieking affair the housefolk hear, and cringe, for how could they not. Among the walnuts the dark others whisper, *Spectacle of bedlam; clamor and phantasm; wing and horn and ear.* The undead will march on Tamarish, three nights hence, and take spoils of Tamarish for their carnival: olive silk lengths of flesh, scalps for headdresses, bones and nerve for body again, eyes and earlobes and toes their jewels. Prop and costume the folk of Tamarish, for the masquerade of the undead.

Sister, say the dark others, ethereal tongues lolling, slopping beneath the twilit walnuts. *We would help; we would make the undead fear us.*

We'll have but one thing in exchange.

We'll have your body in exchange.

•••

They start as night is setting, their grey forms working over me a swarm like hungry cats. Their nearness sends shudders through the body no longer mine; their delicate touches are like insects scuttling over. Clawed fingers tug at the toes beneath my toes; the hands behind my hands; the me behind my eyes. Each scrape of nail invokes moss, loam and pale grub, mushroom nosing up through black earth, bloom and sprout and root. Somewhere in the pines, cries of the undead tangle like berry briars in my head.

I slip; abruptly the walnuts shift; my edges cease to be edges,; I am standing over a body. I am flickering in a breeze that does not rustle the walnut leaves, but tosses the knotted hair of the wild-eyed dark others. I shiver against myriad claws on my arms placed as if to comfort; as if they could comfort. Like two red tulips blossoming and closing through days and nights, the chest of the body rises, falls, rises, breath for lungs no longer mine.

They take turns trying on the flesh, slink in carefully, wear it like a robe, unwieldy in its extravagance, its heady corporeality. Such use is hard to see: the awkward motion, the thrashing of limbs, the grotesque contortions.

The sun has set, the ash moon risen. The shrieks through the pines have reached a bacchanal timbre. Say the dark others, *Be glad; this is a pact we choose to uphold.*

The undead will find it the worse: leaving here to march too bold on Tamarish.

•••

As the season reaches its height — as leaves paper, loosen and fall, crumble — the throng shrieks and groans in the pines, eager to garner costume for their masquerade.

A'times, I cheer to be rid of my flesh.

All Hallows Eve. We lie in wait, me and the dark others. Silent the throng of dead swells and flows up the hill towards Tamarish, and we, we're close behind. The lizard-grey bodies slink and slip through shadow, swarm while the dead shamble, frenetic.

A clamor crescendos in the dust-laden streets as the first of the throng walk through walls into houses, are enveloped like stones sinking in water. Wails rise as housefolk nearest the hill's edge know fitful dreams, for the dead dance in their sleep.

Many and frightful the dark others. Muttering, gibbering, they close like a cloud of hard-shelled insects over pale houses, streets, blue stone shrines, alleyways — and over the undead. The housefolk toss in their beds; they wake to half-glimpses of bodiless limbs, jeering faces flashing in and out of sight. In the streets, an ethereal cacophony flickers into hearing. Bites and blows, sudden maiming; pain out of air. Some perish, lay mute and blind in the dust.

And I — I have my own masquerade. Bodiless as the undead, I join their ranks and walk through walls, donning eagerness to sunder limbs. My costume — I speak with the graveled voice the dark others put to use in me, and I, how I coax the restless back into the streets — *More human wares across the way!*

In the street, the dark others fold themselves upon the undead.

Elsetimes, I leave the raucous ranks of undead and slip to speak to housefolk in the streets, in their beds: *To the foothills.* I am a warning wisp that draws them from dream, a whisper that penetrates sleep. Somehow, seeing through dreaming eyes, a few know me. *Sibyl* — they say, but I: *To the foothills.*

The housefolk flee.

That is how we scoured Tamarish of the undead.

•••

The town is littered with bodies — some invisible, some that wet the dust. Dawn blooms a bright rose as the housefolk return from the bluffs to tend to their own, the ones they can see; the ones they weep over, and cover with white sheets. Each kiss of a sun's ray blesses the immaterial bodies of the undead, who have lingered too long. Now again is their time, and they go leaving empty places that were empty afore.

It is All Hallow's.

Afternoon the dark others return muttering to the grove, to the silent pines. I — I stay behind, walking among the losses, the living whom I have never known, but only prophesized for when a spirit moved me to pass through these streets. Once, I starved my senses of touch; now I touch the living on the arm, the shoulder to comfort, as if I could comfort. I am as alone as when I'm in my cell, except: A woman bent over a body looking up blinks. Blinks again, at me. *Ah,* she says. *I see. You spoke to me night afore. Great my thanks.* And I; what can I do but stand unspeaking, gaping, as she moves away?

A raucous crowd is gathering outside a tavern, will go speak to the sibyl of Tamarish: Why these dead? What those specters night afore? I flutter past the crowd towards the valley, stirring up murmurs of those who glimpse me. There she goes, they say, while others gawk.

In the grove, one of the dark others rests in my body beneath the walnuts. I will not beg to have it back, to speak to the housefolk as I have always done. *Ours, this flesh now,* says the one at this moment in my body, so myself speaks back to me. Before I think on how I might speak to housefolk, it says, *But,* looking at me with my eyes feral. *What shall we tell them?*

Here the housefolk come, such a company never assembled beneath these walnuts. The sibyl of Tamarish has always been voice for specters, reliant on them, on housefolk's listening to give her life shape. See how the housefolk still need, still heed her. So the sibyl's body steps forward, shambling in the hush. It tongues the words I gave it: *We have sent danger, a horror from you. Aiding was a spirit who walked amongst you, and never left your sides, who goes amongst you now.* And something I did not: *We have always said — she is my sister.*

Always the housefolk hear the sibyl of Tamarish, yet her words till this day never were her own. Someone speaks for her still, even as the words leave the mouth once hers.

Light is waning between the walnuts. Pools of shadow drip from the branches onto the shoulders of housefolk as I move up the hill to Tamarish, leaving the cell behind for the last time, and the body I do not need.

In the streets, between the rows of houses and shops, evening fluoresces like shadow flowers blooming. I linger at the entrance of a shrine. For centuries the word-markings inscribed above my cell door were the same as these: *Kindly spirits welcome herein.* I step into the cool doorway of this, my new abode, and wait to hear the housefolk returning home up the hill.

Ever was I the vessel; now I the spirit who will speak.

Housefolk may hear the sibyl, do as she bids; they may fear the company she keeps. But the sibyl resides in a walnut grove, in a stone cell far from housefolk; she moves queerly. She is voice to wraiths. But I — I am the spirit of Tamarish who flits among the housefolk, looks after them centuries past and coming, lays ethereal hands upon them to comfort, speaks to those who listen — and evermore my own words will I whisper in their ears. **T:S**

Wash Is Done
Mikal Trimm

We start with clothespins, reweaving our shirttails with dragonspikes. Our sleeves are bristling boars, our pantslegs porcupines. We cry ululations into the spring air, monsters all, beware, beware! We dance and sing, toes tempting the shadowed edge of the cliff-stage before us. *Crumble*, we say, *crumble and be done with you!*

Sean tumbles to the ground, tangled in clothesline and wet from the morning dew. He shudders, and clothespins fill the void of his passing, the shrapnel of wood and metal coils snapping at us. Angry wooden vultures snip and tear, and Seamus expires in a gout of blood and flapping flesh.

We pause and bow in respect. They have been cleansed.

The sheets are next, ghostshroud gray and angelwing white all at once. We fly through the meadow, owlbat wise and skyhawk willing. Moira spins in the wind, a top-heavy dervish, and wraps herself in her own stagnant cocoon. She falls, she fails, she ferments.

We mumble to ourselves, sheetwings fluttering in the newbirth air, the scent of springbreeze flowers growing rancid in our noses, and we kick her broken chrysalis away from our yearning space, over the cliff.

She falls again, flying at last.

Free, we shout, *free and free and free again!* We wizen the Sun and desiccate the Moon, we suck the lifeblood from Mother Earth. Our dance is anathema, our song is discord. *Woe to the churches and spires! We shall be heard!*

We reap the whirlwind that is us, and stockings tear beneath our baleful stare while unmentionables do unmentionable things, and the world is ours is ours is ours, its throat laid bare beneath our savage teeth, the pulse of it fading, trembling, waiting.

• • •

"Wash is done."

Mother drops the basket of laundry, and we pin the sacrifices to the line, one by one by one... T:S

Dog Days

Leah Bobet

*L*t's the dog days of summer: sleepy golden afternoons where the dust drifts, never settling on the carpet. Warm currents of wet southern air buoying it along to chair, corner, mantelpiece. Too hot to wag a tail, lift a paw, too hot to do anything but sleep, drink, piss on the shady spot in the wilting, flower-drunken yard. The insects buzz in the trees, falling to earth like a thousand tiny meteors and sizzling on the driveway. Falling stars.

• • •

"You have to get serious," she told him, fresh off the Greyhound at the end of the school year. "Look at these grades."

He ducked his head, suppressed the urge to whine or cry or mutter. He was a man now. Couldn't do things like that anymore, no matter how formidable she was angry, no matter how much he just wanted to see her pleased. First of his family to go to college; he'd been able to see the window offices and crisp-starched shirts in his grandparents' eyes the day the letter arrived.

"You can do better than this. You're not stupid." Her voice softened into something worse: disappointment. "I wish you'd have told me if something was wrong. I could have helped out."

His eyes traced the cracked grout lines between the kitchen tiles. "I'm sorry, Momma."

A hug, the scent of warm and tired skin spiced with sweat. "Don't worry. It's not a bad GPA. Just… get serious."

• • •

Waking up, yawning, padding to the dry kibble she's set out. Nightmares are hard to put out of the mind; everything's crazy in these middle-of-summer days, dreams bleeding into afternoon and evening, chasing a body behind couches and under the porch, stalking just behind on the morning walk. A few too-dry bites and lukewarm water with the smell of sweat and disappointment still fresh in the nose, then curling up on the striped cooked-meat-smell shirt for fitful sleep, fitful visions.

• • •

Get serious. Get Sirius. Reach for the stars, young man.

He couldn't tell her that he wasn't going back.

He mowed lawns for next year's supposed tuition money and never ignored the corners like the other college kids. He worked five days a week at the Burger Stop in town, and they praised him for never skimping on the cleaning, never rushing the orders and always remembering the change. He worked until he was tired and numb and stared at the sky every night, watching the dog star inch through Canis Major.

Looking for falling stars.

• • •

Dog days of summer, and they say it's a dog's life when they gather on the porches every evening with pitchers of tart-smelling lemonade. Rustles of shifting feet on wood, laughter, cigarette smoke that makes the nose twitch and sneeze. She's silent when the rest of them talk about work and children and their own lost chances and say it's a dog's life, ladies, it's a dog's life.

Her hand pauses, scritch-scratch behind the ears, and the strongest smell is the salt of hot tears.

• • •

Make a wish upon a star, wake and wonder where you are. The dog star Sirius rose and set closer and closer to the sun, and he wished with hands on the lawnmower, wished cleaning big metal machines in the Burger Stop, wished and wished with all his might. It was coming up to August. He had to tell her soon about spending Saturday nights alone, the unfamiliar northern streets and northern accents, the things other students took for granted that were so new and strange to him. The way crisp-starched shirts strangled when they were actually worn and office windows only looked out over blank concrete walls and how the venerable study of economics — so out of reach for his poor slave ancestors! — withered something precious in his heart. He had to tell her before the leaves started to wilt and flutter.

He wouldn't go back. He wouldn't.

He practiced the words every night in the mirror, and every night went to bed with them jostling between his teeth and her worried glances following him to the bedroom door. She wished he'd tell her if something was wrong.

He couldn't tell her. He had to tell her.

He had to make a decision.

Dog Days

●●●

Dream bleeds into memory, and it's the same one over and over again: waking up in the newborn heat without skin, without voice, now four legs and fur and a worried feeling around the eyes that's the only thing familiar. No Sirius in the morning sky, as if it has fallen from that lofty perch, even though it's obvious it's just rising with the sun. Fallen stars. Rising stars. Sometimes it's hard to tell the difference until it's much, much too late. And then, of course... what's left to do about it?

Dog days of summer, and not long until the leaves wilt and flutter. After that, decisions can be made. No pressure. No need to even tell them that something was wrong.

Yawn. Stretch of the tongue, running muscles strong and warmed-up, tail alert. Ready to run. **T:S**

Stations of the Cheeseburger

Lawrence M. Schoen

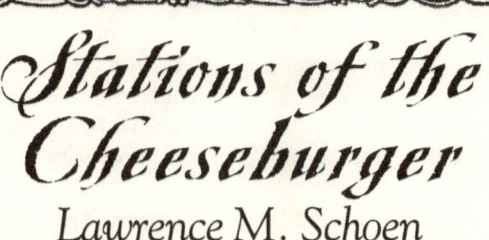

The moment of my reward was at hand. After years of mind-numbing employment servicing the syllogistic underpinnings of rhetoricians and interlocutors of seven generations, I had been found worthy to glimpse the deeper mysteries. Let others scoff and claim stochastic indifference, I believed my selection by the higher elocutors had been deliberate and devoid of parametric happenstance.

I was to be enfleshed. For the briefest of spans I would know weight and color, texture and temperature, touch and taste and scent.

Contemplating the Imminent made my gravimetric fields cavort and writhe with anticipation. Had I limbs, I would have danced or tumbled. Had I a voice or lungs or air to breathe, I should doubtless erupt in a celebratory aria of spontaneous composition. Such behaviors were not possible, alas, for beings of attenuated spectra, and bodiless alignments of thought. Or, not normally so, but soon, so soon, I would be enfleshed!

To say that I had dreamed of this opportunity would be an understatement too vast to consider. I had devoted every spare instant of my awareness to reviewing the blessed documentaries and immersing myself in the numbing study of corporeal nature. When the guiding theocrats approved my selection, I petitioned them to incarnate me in one of the manifestations of the holy feast.

Now my time had arrived. A trio of nigh-omniscient theodicists aligned the concepts of my individual existence within the targeting chambers of an ancient pyx of primordial matter. With a final prayer they projected my consciousness across time-space wreathed with transubstantiation. After a timeless oblivion, self-awareness returned with a wealth of sensory intimacy beyond my preparations. Metaphors I had learned by rote without true comprehension now shone clear. The afferent barrage was a blizzard, a tidal wave, a thunder storm. It threatened utter dissolution, but I had trained in callaesthetics, and as the overlay of my consciousness onto the sacred host achieved completion, chaos abated.

A more propitious placement could not be conceived. I reeled with the immediacy of corporeal perception. Pressure. Weight. Volume. Chilled air blown from an unseen source carressed me. My host stood poised at the top of a queue. His consciousness ebbed and abated as the transference overlay gave me possession of his flesh.

I stood in control, a physical being, with a collection of local specie clutched in one hand. I gazed through his eyes across the gleaming counter at a pock-faced youth. He spoke. The first vocal sounds of my experience. "Can I take your order?"

Mutely, I gazed upward and witnessed firsthand the iconography and sanctified glyphs I had only known from the documentaries. Spasms of bliss accompanied my use of this host's speech apparatus as I spoke aloud the phrase of a venerated petition. "Give me a number seven, jumbo-size."

Effortless. I had uttered hallowed words and set in motion a liturgy of untold splendor. I reeled from my own audacity and lunged forward to place my hands upon a molded tray laden with the holy feast. I grasped it reverently. I walked the host body away from the counter, trembling with fear that I might stumble and thereby topple or spill anything, so novel was this locomotion.

"No," I enjoined myself, resisting the seduction of movement. My time was limited; the overlay could slip free at any moment and without warning. There was not time to relish my host's full sensorium; I had my glorious enterprise to complete. Sacrificing the proper respect due his kinethesis and proprioception, I focused on his chemical senses, olfaction and gustation, as required by the ritual, and by the host's own reflex slid into a resplendent lacquered bench. I began the rite.

My borrowed heart fluttered with anticipation as I tore the end off the paper sleeve that housed the flexible plastic drinking cylinder. It was a brightly rendered helix of primary color against the tube's whiteness. Boastful humanity, flaunting half their DNA every time they slurped a soft drink.

I withdrew the cylinder and plunged it through the paper cup's fragile cap with practiced mental familiarity. I'd seen the documentaries, lifetimes of them; I was a student of these people, this geography, this timescape, this infinity of worship. But it's not the same. Knowing and doing, a subtlety so rarely appreciated by noncorporeal beings, yet the distinction loomed so obvious amidst such lushness. And what an inventively backward people to make drinking vessels out of paper! I guided my new lips to the exposed end of the straw, formed a satisfactory seal, and mimicked the cheek concavity of uncounted viewings as I reversed the direction of flow. Oh, flesh divine! "Fizzy" and "sweet" stopped being abstract concepts as I experienced my first taste of cola. I swallowed. Rapture! This single moment alone was worth the lifetime of humiliation, the servitude, and the sacrifice required for the transference overlay, and I had barely begun.

Within seconds the sensation abruptly halted. The flow of cola abated and the pressure within the drinking straw reduced drastically. A deep hollow sound resonated in the cup as now and then minute droplets intersected the far end of the tube and the pressure altered briefly. I had consumed all of the cola.

I... frowned. It was a disconcerting sensation. The complexity of coordination required by so many facial muscles was daunting and yet my host handled it without noticeable effort. The cup, though devoid of fluid, seemed far from empty. It rattled in my grasp. Pulling free the pierced lid, a cursory examination revealed a surprising amount of frozen water. I had of course expected the substance; it was customary, a commonplace means of lowering beverage temperature to optimum levels. Still, the sheer amount of it was in excess to the task. Unbidden, linguistic reflexes of my host activated and I found myself muttering "cheap bastards" before I could reassert volition. I glanced about the temple. No one appeared to have heard or noticed.

I set the cup aside and contemplated the remainder of my repast. A golden collection of elongated subsections of Idahoan tubers, crisped by immersion in molten vegetable lipids and lovingly dusted with reclaimed ocean minerals beckoned. I guided my host's hand to the pile and drew one to my lips. The mineral stung even as it stimulated. The rectangular solid of the tuber's surface produced a satisfying crunch of tactile splendor followed by the introduction of a warmer, pulpy interior. Both melded with saliva to stimulate lingual papillae and transport me to new heights of ecstasy. All this from one single subsection, and the entire collection contained in excess of fifty similar instances of exquisite bliss. At last I understood the writings of our most pious sages; their glorification of physical sensation and most especially the intoxicating allure of gustatory/olfactory blends.

In that instant I lost all control. I grabbed the segments with both hands and shoved them into my mouth with wild abandon, an orgy of mastication, salivation, and ingurgitation that left none unclaimed. I stared at the projective test formed on my tray's paper placemat by the segments' excess lipids, marking their previous existence and passing. This was not like the cola; I could not cry foul and bemoan the imposition of frozen water. The golden tubers had existed in plenty, and I had consumed multitudes, soiling the peak experience of my life with impatience and gluttony.

But redemption lay at hand. The main course was yet untouched and pure, still wrapped in virgin paper and icons of authenticity. My hands trembled as I raised it off the tray, rotating it in space to allow the folds of its casing to ease open until I gazed upon the epitome of corporeal consumptive desire. Infinities of experience with the documentaries had been inadequate to prepare me for this moment. I held it, gazed upon it. I could feel its weight and texture against my skin. With awe I cradled the relic and separated its superior and subordinate halves of baked grain stuff, unveiling its glories. There was the essential core of the nearly circular, steaming ellipse of charred bovine sinew. Atop nestled the complimentary mysteries: the blazing orange square of processed curd, a swirled design of the sacred condiment of colloidal suspension, twin ridged slices of embalmed yet verdant cellulose.

Respectfully, I brought the components back together. I willed my borrowed hands to bring the sandwich within range and trembled. I vowed to savor each bite, to prolong this experience and not waste it as I had with that of the tuber sections. Swirls of fragrance titillated my host's nostrils. I paused on the precipice of bliss, olfaction being a large part of gustation, and I wanted it all.

Then pain! Searing and pungent, as the overlay slipped and my consciousness tumbled away, my time expired. The patterns of my awareness fragmented instantly and reassembled at the velocity of cognition. Once again I occupied my designated gravitic receptacle, the site from which I would return to servicing syllogisms. But I remembered everything! Vivid and numbing in its carnality, the experience was no less exquisite when translated to more comprehensible analogs consistent with noncorporeal senses. I wrapped myself in my epiphany, incomplete though it was. It would have to suffice. I would never be granted another overlay. I prayed though, to whatever divinity might care, that my host had bitten deep and tasted of the godhead I had so briefly held in borrowed hands. **T:S**

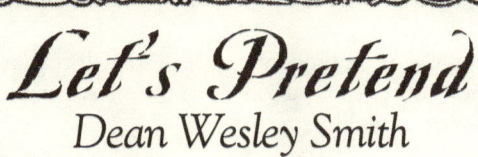

Let's Pretend
Dean Wesley Smith

*L*et's pretend, you and me. What do you say? You're dead. I know that. But let me touch your cheek one last time. You rot, yet you are my lover. I have always loved your smell. Let me touch your body and pretend just one last time. Soon I will taste the vile truth. But for now, let's pretend. What can it hurt?

Picture:

Cobblestone streets of a European village. You can feel the roughness as you walk the narrow path between two-story stucco buildings that you think look comfortable, but you know are not. You're not lost. Yet. You know your tour bus where I sit, pregnant, twisting my new diamond wedding ring, is down by the main gate of the old city. You know that if you just walk down, you eventually will find the old stone wall that circles the city and can then make your way to the bus. But even with that knowledge, you still feel your stomach twist with that uneasy feeling that something is wrong.

You glance around. There are no people. You can smell the thick aroma of dinner cooking. But there is no sound of children playing, pots rattling, or music being hummed. The world is empty.

Then you remember.

You stop pretending and find yourself sitting beside me. We are on a log, at the edge of the forest, resting, looking down over the sacred lost city of Canton, Idaho. You are disappointed that we have found it.

•••

Let's pretend, you and me. Even though you are dead, will you let me hold the truth up to the light just one last time so you can see its thinness, listen to it whine, smell its fear. Let's pretend. What can it hurt?

Picture:

You are moving slowly down cold, cement stairs into the great subways of New York. The old art covers the walls, faded from the long passage of time. You run your hand gently over the drawings and the huge, meaningless letters. It feels damp and cold to the touch but you thrill at the glimpse backward to a time wonderful in its madness.

Ahead, you hear a soft noise, gentle, like the breeze through a tall pine. You silently move down into the darkness until you reach a barrier of rusted metal. Something feels wrong.

Then you remember and stop pretending and find yourself standing beside me at the very edge of the sacred lost city of Canton, Idaho.

I can tell you are disappointed. But there is nothing I can do. You and I must go into the sacred city. There we will make love and once again you will plant your seed. Our child will rule the world. She will lead us out of the wilderness and back to the gleaming cities of the pretend time.

You do not believe it possible. That is a pity.

•••

Let's pretend, you and me. Allow me to lay your wrists open and lick the blood. Taste the desire, the hatred. Let's pretend. What can it hurt?

Picture:

Gentle ocean swells, a clear blue day. The waves lift the boat and then drop it lightly, up and down between the sharp peaks and empty eyes of the staring buildings. Below you, crushed under the weight of the water, is most of the great old city once called San Fransisco. You catch glimpses through the island building windows of a world long lost. Forgotten. Drowned. You ease the boat as close as you can to the tallest building, then wait for a swell to raise you to an open window before you jump.

You pull yourself up and stand on the ledge, looking into the cave of a room. Slime covers the floors and starfish cling to the walls near the corners. You jump inside and wade to the center hall, looking for the stairs that will allow you to climb to the top, to where the past has not yet been washed away by the ocean.

You find the door. As you pull it open you remember and stop pretending. You are opening the sacred doors to the Temple of Love in Canton, Idaho. You pause and look at me. Your eyes are sad, because you know that I believe in something you do not. Maybe never did. But this is where it starts.

This was where it started.

You pause, then open the door wide, accepting what you must face.

I also turn to face our wedding room. This time I am the one who is disappointed.

•••

Let's pretend, you said. Smell the flowers, taste the honey, feel the satin. Let's pretend, you said. What can it hurt?

Picture, you told me:

I am walking down a long, thickly carpeted hall, arm in arm with you. Ahead lies a big, white, double door with a red heart on the outside. My own heart is pounding and I can barely contain my excitement.

You pull from your pocket a big, golden key and with a smile, unlock the door and let it swing wide. Inside, the room is like a cavern. The carpet is white, the walls and drapes are white, the spread that covers the huge heart-shaped bed is white. The pillows are a pink satin and the room smells fresh. New.

A beginning.

You sweep me into your arms and carry me into the room. Then I remember and stop pretending.

I find myself sitting in the ray of light that comes in through the broken ceiling of the sacred room. Leaves litter the dirt floor and there is a large pile of rubble that fills one half of the room where one wall and part of the roof has collapsed. Animals have made nests in the pile. I am sitting on a stone and you are standing over me, smiling.

It is not a smile of laughter, but of sympathy. You told me we could never return. Should never return. But I did not listen. You told me there would be nothing but ruins, but I did not listen.

I climb to my feet and walk to the position near the back where I stood so many years before and waited for the ceremony to begin. Our beautiful daughter, Jenny, was only six months from being born and I remember so hoping that she did not show. My dress was white and I stood holding the pink flowers that I was to throw to the crowd later.

You stood where you do now. Turned. Waiting for me. I walked slowly down the aisle toward you, keeping careful time with the music of the wedding march. My stomach fluttered, yet I was so happy. Beaming faces smiled up at me as I passed, but I remember never taking my gaze from you.

We joined hands at the front, turned and faced our future. How were we to know the future would be this?

●●●

Let's pretend, you said. Walk the roads in the heat, plant the crops in the rain, build the fires against the snow. Let's pretend, you said. What can it hurt?

Picture:

A small Midwest farm on a warm, humid day. I am standing at the kitchen window. An apple pie is baking in the oven behind me, the wood on the fire crackling softly.

Through the window I can see you and our two boys working the field. You are plowing straight, clean lines in the rich soil.

You see me watching and wave. Your hair is starting to gray, but you look healthy. I start to wave in return and then I remember the collapse happened the following month.

And stop pretending.

You have me gently, but firmly, by the arm and are leading me out of the old church in the remains of the town of Canton, Idaho. It is a long, long journey back to our cabin, especially as old as we are. I wish we could have found someone left alive, but you tell me that won't happen. Ever.

I wish Jenny would run up to me and hug me like she used to do, but you angrily say she is dead. That she died the same as our sons and the rest of the world.

I wish I could be happy.

But you have no answer for that except to tell me to stop pretending.

But how can I do that when I have no reality?

• • •

Let's pretend, you and me. Taste the cake, sip the champagne, rip the brightly colored paper of the presents. Stand up from there. Let's pretend, you and me. What can it hurt?

Picture:

You are back inside the island building of the submerged city of San Fransisco. The waves caress the walls and fill the lower floors with a new life. I am with you this time. You find the dark stairway and we begin to climb. Higher and faster, we run, wanting to reach the top where the world remains the world of our youth.

We run, hard, fast, higher and higher. Finally the stairs end and we emerge out into the light of the top hall.

Then you remember and stop pretending.

You realize you are again on the hill overlooking the sacred city of Canton, Idaho, and the world around you is as dead as that building. As empty.

You are breathing hard and there are sharp, shooting pains in your chest.

You sink to the ground and hold my hand as the pain increases until finally there is nothing but blackness. You were too old to climb that final hill. You warned me that this might happen.

I sit beside your body through the night. I do not have the strength or the tools to bury you or move you. So, as we did for so many others, I must let nature do my work.

I turn back to the sacred city and start down the hill. There is nothing left for me back at our cabin. It was only a prison. My true destiny lies in the Sacred Temple where I will be reborn. Where my life started.

Where it ended.

I reach the beautiful white doors of the Temple and inside I can hear the sacred march playing. It calls for me. I must keep in step and pretend that you wait. Turned to face me. Smiling.

What can it hurt? **TTS**

The Song of the Solipsilepidopterist
Greg Beatty

I entered the room eager to find others like myself, but once again I was disappointed. I waited patiently, as I always do, but when the first break came and everyone stepped outside for a breath of air, I kept walking.

"Going so soon?" one of the club members called.

Abashed, I turned back towards the building and shrugged. "It's just not what I was looking for. It's all bugs and stuff."

At the man's expression, I hastened to add. "Don't get me wrong. They're *lovely* bugs."

The club member slowly said, "What else were you looking for at a lepidopterology organization?"

I shook my head. "I shouldn't expect anything else, but I was hoping for something more. I keep hoping to find a really specialized group."

Every word I spoke seemed to confuse the kindly stranger more. "More specialized than amateur moth and butterfly enthusiasts?"

I gave up on words. "C'mon," I said. "I'll show you."

He walked home with me. Along the way he told me his name, which escaped me, and what he did, which I've since forgotten. He was, however, properly impressed when I unlocked my seven locks and showed him my collection.

"Stand there," I said. I flipped on the diffuse lighting and walked into the middle of the room. I spread my arms, and took in the glorious sight, sight, sight of myself reflected 1,037 times over, in the mirrors, bumpers, still pools, holograms, glasses, crystals, mirages, frosted glass, EtchASketches, tin cans, tarot readings, fountains, sunglasses, bowls, sketches, ice cubes, cups, bowls, plastic, off-spring, spoons, light bulbs, astrological charts, bubbles, mantras… I spun and spun in pure pleasure.

"What is all this?" the non-me asked. "No, wait. They're all you. All of this is you."

"Aren't the colors beautiful?" I said, still spinning. "And aren't you smart. You can stay, and you can even become a solipsilepidopterist like me if you like. We can be a one person club."

To be honest, I can't remember if he joined or not, but we've been perfectly happy together ever since. **TIS**

Holly:
New Paree Prime:
Spring Two
Steve Carper

I flew in for the fashions, the spring-two show on New Paree Prime. Me and she and two hundred hundred of the more and most converging from points east and west and up and down. The hotels along the Champs E. + One flung their doors wide like maws to welcome us with open arms and pockets, servants real and robot. In the gapingly exposed lobby, balconies filled with lookers and lurkers, I grabbed a slipper sloppy with Chateau Unpronounceable. Bubbles blasted through my nose snorting a greeting to the twenty twenty others doing the same.

Circulators wafted used champagne fumes away from our bodies before the residue could stain the gossamerity of our outfits and the tickle of air made me hard and soft in all the right places. I laughed, already half-drunk, and spun around in sheer giddy and saw her.

"Holly!" It was a cry, a burble, a delighted, annoyed recognition.

Holly was a wealthy girl. Wealthier than me, and I had all the money I would ever need. We were friends, after a fashion. We saw the same faces in the same places, did the season we were pleasin', bumped and dumped the lower-lifes, the hangers-on, the lesser and merer. Hey, nobody liked us but us. And we didn't care.

"D'Loverly." Holly's voice was lower than mine, affected and projected. We air-kissed, then kissed for real. I tasted Chateau on her tongue and a hint of Black Rouge as well. Holly started early.

I slurped down another slipper's worth. "Darling, you look lovely," I said, "luvvvvvly," my words wafting greenly until the circulators tore them away. Oh, she did, she did. Her gown caught on her projections as if her body had captured a late fall leaf, lacy and frail, blown by a vagrant breeze and perched trembling, waiting for another breeze to blow it away. Breast and shoulder and hip, all creamy and smooth, flashed through the lace, a backdrop of sheer divine. My iridescents suddenly seemed flash and dash by comparison.

"Last year's rag," Holly sneered. "Hardly worth keeping." And to prove it, she grabbed at the fold hanging low between her breasts and ripped until it slit. A torso shrug, a shoulder roll, a twitch of her hips and the gossilk, light as half a butterfly's wing, drifted in slowest-mo to the ground. The crowd called out for more.

So what could I do? I bent over to the hem of my gauzily draped nothingness and pulled up and out in one quick motion. Nothingness shreds from a nasty look. Embarcadero's most now now creation split like a banana, peeling me navel to neck. I flung my arms back and it slipped away, drifting on the light indoor breeze to a gawker-stalker on the upstairs. Or so I guessed. I never look back.

And, oh, the buzz from the lookey-loos. Holly put her arm around my shoulder and I around hers, light and dark, cream and chocolate, contrast blasting fast each other's charms, and we curtseyed low to the galleries. Then the twenty twenty rended and rived, cleaved and crinkled, bared without care. Pow, bang, clang and the celebarazzi quivered like quarks in a blender at the sight. Lights flashed, recorders zinged, our exposed everythings flung to far corners of the Everywhere. We straightened and preened and swallowed Chateau and drizzled it down our bodies so we could lick it off one another and one another off, reveling in the enhanced taste of our augmented flesh, and generally made exhibitionists blush. Hey, that's why we were there on New Paree Prime and that's why they were too and Holly and I were truly prime drunk indeed by the time we marched our naked selves into the street.

How the Champs E. + One shone that very night. 'Twas always night during spring-two, perpetual party, decadence and daytime being too-too-off for words, and the Champs wore a backdrop of dizzy radiance. The lemur-lights of Afrique Seven woke when our cadre-corps paraded out into under the night stars and looked their lurid glances at us. Afrique Seven, the world of the Darkest Continent, had no natural lights and the lemurs made their own out of luminescent symbiotes that lived behind their eye-lenses. When they gazed they lit up their prey and we were that this night, each one of us shining, basking, burning in the beam of her own individual spotlight. I threw back my shoulders and thrust out my chest and lifted each foot so that my toe daintily struck the ground shoved forward by high higher highest heels, and I sashayed my goods down the Avenue shaking my honeybutt for all the Everywhere the better to see.

We walked one long block, the most work for most of us for most of the last year, just long enough for the cameras to spin and circle to fling three-sixties out to the watching poor for them to stuff away in storage and secretly or no drool over our various and manifest perfections for the coming season. Male and female coveted them us. Our augmented selves.

We outdid ourselves that spring two. BeePage sleeked herself in finest of fur, pinstriped just barely sufficient to show when strutting ruffled her hairs. Solari's scales caught the ruddy lights of the underwalk and threw crimson highlights to the waiting winds. The skin doctors they sucked the melanin from Jamsam's epi-damn-dermis and left her so almost translucent she took on the coloring of whatever light landed on her vale of pale. Holly had liquid flowing down and around just under her surface forcing the eye to follow and flow over her every every perfection.

I moved close and spoke out of the side of my mouth, careful to keep my smile at a kilowatt high. "Holly, Holly, Holly. Girl, you are the belle with balls. How much did that effect set you back?"

She mentioned a number that seemed to go on and on. Whole planets could move continents around for less.

I whooshed. "Girl, you break every piggy bank you own? What will you have left for the later?"

Holly mentioned another number that whispered like the wind wafting from the water. I was a wealthy girl. Holly was rich as a bitch.

"No," I said.

"Yes," she said. I watched the tear drizzle out of the mica splendor of her right eye and flow like milk down the cream of her cheek. Couldn't help myself. I went to her and licked her clean as she bawled. Damn up a blast, but she tasted more than fine. Bottle her tears and I would double my wealth. Almost worth it too, just to share.

Tears are a contagion, sad and bad as laughter. Jamsam and Fidelity and Mmimmi and Honeybutt the Second looked like they were about to wail and frail. I eyed them up-and-down and calculated the numbers in my head and the digits spilled out over into my tears. They were all so damn rich, what else could I do?

But the whole world was watching and not a one of them tuned in for tears and besides the air was misted with Chateau and Black Rouge and Surfeit and a great deal more and each breath made me spin around with giddy purer than before. I breathed deep and long and the fumes blurbled my brain, flushing the digits away. We were almost to the end of our walk, and they were waiting for us, ready to pounce.

So what was more beautiful than us naked? Us with the finest dazzle-est damnfine divine clothes by the best fashionistas in the Several Worlds. In the park at the end of the dark the canopy rose and rose over beckoning enchantment. Giant Yardstick Balloonatics high on helium bubbled above, a New Paree Prime specialty of the planet. Kazillions of yards of the Lensique fabric spun by the big-brained Caterpiggles of Beta Kappa (Phi) hung tent-taut below the Balloonatics' billowy frame, magnifying all the girly-girls on the inside and dilating each and every greedy eyeball on the out.

Oh, we charged in two hundred hundred strong, irresistible us meeting the moveable feast of them, not a one critical of our mass. They swarmed us locust-like, their lastest bestest designs bursting about our heads like beauty bombs. We went wild ourselves, none for all, this for me, as we plucked the bewitching eye-slamming tens-on-a-scale-of-two flamboyosities out of the air and formfit them to our slithering bods.

A million camera-mites buzzed us with a million projection screens so that we saw ourselves in the full and oh-so-round, our fronts and rears sneering at gravity, peachlike and coconut-husky and extra-shelvy, the eye darting here and lured to there and migod-migod-migod down to the down where they all wanted to be. Then poof, we whisked them away and snatched another goodie from the air or right off the heaving flank of the foully-berserk show-it-all girl next door.

"D'," squealed Holly with no jolly. "That butt-end rag don't sit at all well against your chocolate tits. Cuckoo Coco Pierre had me in mind for it from the get-go. So get-gone of it." And she sucked the colors right off my bod and onto hers.

"You couldn't dress a salad, let alone yourself," I said. Nevermind that the multi-colors looked so fine stretched across her impressive frontage that I contemplated frottage. "How many of these you going to take for yourself?"

"As many as it takes, gal my pal, as many as it takes." And Holly stuffed the dress program into her air-purse. I saw a dozen more in there too. Holly was buying out the store, spending like no tomorrow. And in the dark, dark, dark of spring two, tomorrow was another day.

We ate 'em all up, gown, frock, skirt, suit, soutane, smock, chiton, kilt, catsuit, and nipplehalter offered by the buttery crème de la crème of the Many Several Worlds. The making machines hummed as they spun the physical from the phantasmic and loaded us down with gossamer goodies for the coming season to sashay through the endless night for the (men) and (women) and (beasts) lust, lust, lusting after our multitudinous charms.

Then we touched our thumbs to the payment buttons and watched our wealth flow away from our accounts. The zeroes oozed across the screens like owl's eyes, wide and surprised at the vastitude of their number. Holly outdid us all, and we bowed and scraped at her bounty, a record for the ages that shamed us all for our pinchpenny ways.

And she fell into my arms, pale and weeping. I licked the milky tears from her perfect cheek and whispered sweet nothings in her ear, but the tears kept flowing and flowing, a spring-two storm breaking across her bountiful highlands.

"It wasn't enough," she finally gasped. "Not enough, not nearly enough."

"You don't mean…" I said, knowing that she did mean indeed.

She whispered a number in the air, a number that hung between us huge and luminous. For all she spent, Holly was still a wealthy girl, the richest of us all, the mostest of the most.

And we all knew what that meant.

"Girly girls," I called out to the crowd. "It's Holly, poor Holly."

They gathered around her, BeePage and Lookyme and Topknot and ICU and Jane-enaJ and Flutterby and even snootpuss Honeybutt the Second, and such kissing and hugging and weeping and wailing you've never seen while the million camera-mites shot the whole and sent it off to the Everywhere.

Then finally it was time. Holly's eyes flashed through the cosmetics a real look, a last look, a why me look. Then they closed and she sagged. Honeybutt the Second thoughtfully stripped the rag from her and left her bod bare, the cream no longer flowing, opalescent in stillness.

For Holly was too wealthy a girl, and we all knew the trade-off that wealth brought, the bargain for which we signed our scanty souls away, that gave us all we could wish, for the least amount of time. Holly had the most, and therefore the least, and she died as happy as any whirly-girl could ever do.

While the rest of us toted up our numbers and calced our calculations about how much we had to part with in order to have more later. So in another swarm, en masse, together and alone, we fluttered back to our hotels along the Champs E + One and chose the lastest bestest of all the ostentatious opulence the servants real and robot obsequiously offered and ordered up oodles of caviar and cake and tried to spread ourselves as thin as ever could be.

I was a wealthy girl. But Holly was as rich as a bitch. Was, indeed. I cried a perfect tear and sealed a memory of her inside. Then I took a chain of purest Perfectium and hung the tear around my neck. The others saw and followed. Holly as fashion statement. Made by me. I looked inside my conscience and smiled greenly. I blasted a ball of Black Rouge and scrounged the night from my head. Spring-three's perpetual sunny day awaits. **T:S**

Juju Hoodoo Man Sangs the Blues

Toiya Kristen Finley

Don go round ol Dutch now, babies, don go round ol Dutch. Come out the streets for a minute. Leave them boyish things behind. Come spend some time on my porch for a minute. I gots to tell y'all bout ol Dutch.

He's home after forty years — I seen im the other day. Seen im slink in under the humidity, after a loose woman sent im away. You too young too know the ways-a loose women, but you'll know soon enough.

Ol Dutch shoulda been good to his wife. He didn't satisfy her none. All of us knew her lover-man, said he loved Betty more than his life. Loved this woman, damned lover-man, he asked Dutch for her hand.

Boys, you don know bout ol Dutch. He's a juju hoodoo man. Cures warts and hives and takes the clouds from eyes or'll break your best friend's leg. Lover-man was both real bold and dumb. Shoulda kept his mouth shut bout Betty's bed. Woulda been the best for everyone.

When a man gits played, you've pissed his pride — that's what we done to Dutch. Lover-man and Betty disappeared. We shoulda spected as much. We didn't know we'd suffer too. You cain't laugh at a juju hoodoo man.

Keep lookin at me so stupid. You haven't snatched a clue. When a man starts sangin, babies, you're under his control. He can pour his life in a song, young fools, and he knows how to grip your souls.

Forty years ago, Dutch walked in Staley's bar with his guitar. He came to wish us farewell. Ol Dutch sangin in a packed-out Staley's bar. It haunts my memory still.

Grab your woman close, says Dutch.
Grab your woman close.

Long brown fingers caress his guitar neck. He closes his eyes and turns his face up to the light. Them fingers make the strings cry.

Lawd, you gave me a woman.
But I had to let her go.
Lawd, you gave me a woman. But I had to let her go.
She was puttin out in my own bed,
and these bastards didn't let me know.

Lawd, yer merciful, but I don't want no peace.
Oh, Lawd, yer merciful, but I don't want no peace.
You won't let me drain these souls, the devil give me what I seek.

We weren't drunk or nuthin, but we swayed in Dutch's blues. We cried and screamed and bit our tongues. Our sins caught up with us. We woulda begged and kissed his feet. That didn't mean shit to Dutch.

My baby sittin next to me, she heaved a final sigh. A woman jumpin out her skin, she heaved a final sigh. We didn't all go then and there, cuz I'm the only one left. But when ol Dutch makes you his puppet, your soul's desprit to die.

I don know what games you runnin, but you better stop em now. It's time to grow up, babies. Juju hoodoo man'll show you how.

Y'all listen good, young bastards. What I'm sayin's true. Ol Dutch controls my memories. His blues drowns like a flood. Boys, I'm just a broken record. Juju hoodoo rules my blood.

And since you heard my song, young fools, know ol Dutch sho owns you too. **TIS**

Soma
Forrest Aguirre

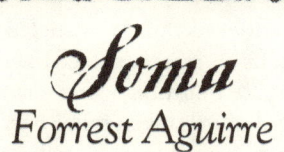ald. Clean-shaven. Skinny. Pale.
Besmirched with ochre dirt, earthred rills through the seams and creases. Skin smooth as eggshell. Only textured by the dappled shadows of the huge leaves behind which he hides, their susurrus rustling protestation to the moonbeams that cascade down through the cool, blue night sky. The full moonlight causes his skin to glow, cut only by the blackness of the shadows. An emerald dragonfly darts up to the figure, retreats, hovers, darts in again, then whisks away on the wind. The figure doesn't move. Has no interest. Looks down at his feet, eyes wide with fear. The eyes are huge and soft brown, but stricken with bloodshot vessels that pulse in response to his hummingbird heart. The color contrasts sharply with the chalky white of his long, thin nose, his delicate cheekbones, his extruded chin.

● ● ●

I know what hunts him: The ogress. I saw her leaving the carnival, searching the horizon. She was immense. Willendorfian breasts bowled from side to side over her abdominous paunch as she lumbered about looking for him. Her head, clad in a gas mask, swiveled around like a tank turret looking for a target, snapping attention past the wind-whipped carnival tents. Piercing the beyond. I suspected that beneath that mask, she clenched the expression of one who has been cheated, held it scrunched up in her eyes, firm in her jaw. The insectoid goggles peered wide, foreshadowing the eyes of terror I saw in the Obfuscate, all pupils, save for thin leather frames as irises. But I'm sure her true eyes squinted almost shut with rancor. Her arms seemed too gangly to carry the immense knobbed club that dangled from her outstretched hand. It was a gnarled thing, bumpy. Its outline resembled the tattoo that was splayed across her belly — a giant God-mistaken-birthmark of a tattoo, like a red and black mold colony, punctured by the hand of a drunken sailor over the course of an alcoholic's lifetime. And yet the markings seemed imbued with pattern and esoteric meaning, an Ur-text embedded with primevality. And though the nipples of her full breasts stood erect and firm, I could not tell her age — the arms, skinny as they were, were taut in sinew, but loose and wrinkled in skin, contrasting with the youthfulness of her tits. The belly — was it pregnant, or simply obese? The ogress's gait was ungainly, awkward, more akin to senescence than youth, yet the clothing — a strapped leather harness that pushed the breasts up and out, and a tiny leather thong — implied the sexuality of youth. The hair provided no clear indicator of age, either. It swept back like a black and gray cockscomb, but cotton-wispy, like the hair of a mummy, half cobweb and dust. A crowd of teens, all piercings and swagger, parted like morning mist before a hot sun at her approach. Their faux-jadedness disappeared to let the awe-full woman-thing through their fragile shell of clique aloofness. She passed and, passing, flawed their jades, leaving psychic fragments of once-hidden childhood innocence in her path.

• • •

In time, she will find this place. She will first pass several young couples copulating in the dark on soil-stained mattresses. Her ears will turn from their grunts and cooing and the clink of cheap beer bottles to the rumbling of an engine — MOP318LB-4 Chrysler — being operated by a drunk farmer driving in her direction. Were it not for her gas mask, she might pass out from the oil-burning fumes as the ill-fated jalopy grinds to a halt. No doubt the drunk will step out on to the dirt road determined to lay blame and hands on the passing figure. "You wrecked my car, you bastard...!" But upon seeing the behemoth (for she stands well over seven feet tall), he will yammer out an apology in his liquor-soaked voice, then flee into the woods, abandoning the car to the holocaustic fate that has already been set in motion under the hood.

The firelight will cast her shadow up the road, past a one-room evangelical church. The din will be almost unbearable, or it was when earlier I passed — drums, guitars, and shouts of "I love you, oh Lawd!" like a cannonade through the church's open doors, light and warmth inviting in the rapidly cooling light. I am confident she will enter, as I did.

• • •

Two young women, twins, black ponytails over long denim dresses, turned to me as I entered. Then, after a brief tandem smile, they turned their simple, pretty faces back to the sermon in progress.

"As it hath been said in times of old," the gaunt preacher shouted, leaning over his equally tall, thin pulpit. "As it hath been said, ye shall take up venomous serpents and they shall not harm thee!" The band burst into song — a flat-top, redheaded teen in a white tank top banging on cheap orange drums (reinforced with duct tape), a methuselaic old man whose very skin looked to slough from his frame at any moment, banjo-picking a chrome flying "V" electric guitar, and a haggard woman in a food-stained apron-clad dress yodelling praises to "The Lawd!"

The room smelled of stale cigarette smoke and an odor I couldn't immediately place, though a childhood trip to the zoo came to mind. As I searched my olfactory catalog, the answer came to me in a hiss — the preacher reached down into a box he had hidden behind the pulpit and extracted an arm's-length cottonmouth, then another. Others pulled rattlesnakes, copperheads, and coral snakes from rickety vegetable crates, worn purses, and coat pockets. The overhead lights went out, replaced by strobes that pulsated in rough tune with the odd mix of bluegrass and carnival-ride calliope that threw the congregation into an asp-wielding, writhing trance dance. I backed up against a wall to gain some semblance of stability amidst the dizzying reel, careful to avoid the whirling serpents and their feckless puppeteers.

The stop-motion vision caused by the strobes offered only a montage of still images, like a badly done animation:

The preacher's face, mouth agape with exhortation.

Two snakes, clenched in the preacher's upraised fists, near the darkened fluorescent bulbs in the ceiling.

The open pages of a Bible, King James version.

The raven-haired twins, smiling broadly at each other.

A snake's fangs, immediately before my face, then gone in a flash.

A crucifix, Christ aloft for you.

The preacher laying on the floor, eyes rolled back in trance.

And the frenzy of dancing slowed, the congregation gathered in a circle, ambulating around the now-convulsing preacher, from whom two snakes dangled by their fangs. The church members walked slowly around the thrashing figure, casting their serpents upon him with shouts of "Lo, how the mighty have fallen, have fallen!", "Sinners be damned!", and "Thine innocence hath fled far from thee, deceiver!"

In an instant, the hillbilly calliope stopped, the lights came on, and the congregation, standing still, turned their eyes to me as one being, their smiles gone.

I sensed my outsider-ness and ran out, into the anonymous darkness.

●●●

"Excuse me," I manage, not wanting to startle him. He looks up slowly from his feet to my face, his shoulders slumping back into relaxation or resignation to fate, I am not sure which. "Excuse me, but I couldn't help but notice that you are in trouble." He steps further into the leaf-shadows, holding up his effeminate hands in front of his chest to protect himself. His only clothing is a pair of soiled white briefs and a tank top, yellowed at the armpits.

"No, I don't want to harm you," I offer.

He looks at me from the corner of his eye, suspicious.

"I want to help."

"Help? Yes, thank you." His voice is timid, small, wanting to be trusting.

"Come," I say, trying to reassure him with my firmness.

"Are… are you sure?" he half-whispers, looking from side to side into the darkness.

"It is safer elsewhere. Come, I've a clue what troubles you."

"You do?"

"Yes, but you must fill me in on the details."

He clears his throat. "Very well, I shall tell you."

We head away from the inevitable path of the Ogress, toward a town-glow being cast up into gathering clouds a few valleys away.

• • •

The Tale of the Obfuscate

"Start, start, where to start? Two hours. No, two weeks. I am a grown man," he puts a hand to his head, confused, or in pain, stumbles over a root. I look up — moisture scents the air, a wall of indigo water in the sky, stampeding over the far horizon. "I am a grown man, with friends. Friends? They are called so, but are they? I am a grown man. I left my parents two weeks ago, a grown man. Found friends. At the carnival."

"You work there?" lightning etching ink under the wall cloud. We will need to find shelter somewhere.

"Parents. Left my parents. I stowed away, to get away. I shovel shit for the animal trainer. They feed me." A warm puff of air is followed by a waterfall of temperature drop, portending rain. My ears pop with the drop of barometric pressure.

"But do they take care of you?"

"Like parents?"

"Like parents."

"Not like my parents. They — the carnies — they laugh much more. Everything is funny, except shoveling shit. My parents never laugh. They scream and hit a lot. But they protect me, they tell me. Protect me from an evil world. I think they love me? They — my parents — love me?" Leaves rustle a minor complaint to the breeze.

"How old are you?"

"Old. Old. I am a grown man. They tell me I am a grown man." His hairy chest and armpits imply such.

"How many years?"

"Many. I am a grown man." The wind picks up and grows yet colder. I give him my overcoat.

"What does the woman want with you?"

"They sent me to her. They said I would become a real man. But she looks at me — she looks at me *empty*. She doesn't laugh. Doesn't yell. She doesn't show her eyes. She looks at me and wants to — wants to hurt me, I think. I don't want to hurt. I want to think. Not think — about hurt. I left my parents for hurt."

I understand his fear. She is a juggernaut of primal killing urge, waiting to be unleashed. A Pandora's Box of ultraviolence. It shows in her gait. Blood refracts through those eyes, behind the goggles.

Inevitability has her way. The sky bleeds aqua, the moon washes away in luminescent streaks.

• • •

The factory workers will not be pleased with the weather. The night-time horn will bellow "release!" into the night and they will emerge under a chemical cloud of their own manufacture. The black toxins that had, only moments before, spewed forth from their machinery into sky-choking swarth, through, then above the sentinel smoke stacks, will slither down the rain-pour onto their yellow helmets and ragged overalls. The over-workers and under-paiders will wipe the rheum from their sleepy eyes and smear the snot from their benumbed noses only to have every fold and fossa power-washed with gypsum, cyanide, and a dozen unpronounceable compounds.

In essence, they will be pissed off.

And they will walk to the carnival looking for trouble, as they did the night previous.

• • •

Negotiations had gone sour. The chemical workers and the carnies were at an impasse. A barrel-chested foreman lay in the dirt at the circus-camp border clutching his balls. Squeal-grunts syncopated with snorts that cratered dust rings beneath his pug nose, a stream of half-spoken obscenities sputtering forth like the sound of an airplane propeller that won't quite start.

Above him, pyrrhically triumphant, stood the trapeze artist in a victory stance. Her tight muscles shone through torn leotards in the prismatic carousel light, flashing yellow, blue, and green in time with the organ-tones of Saint-Saën's *Le carnaval des animaux*. Blood glistened in a black stream from her ruptured lip, tints of color swirling like oil on its surface as she spattered threatenings over the wracked foreman.

"Hands off, tough guy. That was my left foot, but my right is the real kicker!"

A few carnival attendees stopped to watch the entertainment.

The foreman looked up from the ground, face trapped between a pain-grimace and an evil grin. "Jus' wanna taste of that honey, honey."

Behind him, a mob of his employees filtered in. They chuckled out of obligation, rather than genuine good humor. Their leerings swallowed the young trapeze artist. She tried to gulp down the fears that swelled in her chest. The factory workers wanted very much to grasp those fears, to caress them, to squeeze and molest them until the fear-milk ran as freely as the blood from the girl's lip.

The center of the carnival grounds, far behind the young trapeze artist, billowed in the gathering dusk, canvas pumping like an immense dark heart against the background of evening-fall. From there the ringmaster emerged — first, an indistinct black dot birthing forth from the labial folds of the company tent. Then a top-hatted penguin with the momentum of a rhinoceros crossing open ground to put out a fire in the night. Finally, a squat moustachio in a sweat-stained tuxedo. He arrived, wheezing, as the foreman regained his shaky legs.

"What is the problem?" the ringmaster asked in a high-pitched voice altogether unlike the low-bass with which he announced his acts. The quivering in his throat led me to believe that this was his normal timbre, the bass a falsetto. His stance and eyes belied the fear hinted at by his twitching voice.

The foreman spoke to the ringmaster, but kept his eyes locked on the trapeze artist. Words one direction, attention another. "Your beauty here was spurnin' my charms. Something most women ain't stupid enough to do."

"I apologize," the ringmaster said nervously. "I'd be glad to give you each a pair of tickets to tomorrow night's performance, for your troubles."

The foreman sauntered up and over the ringmaster, towering above him. "You don't need to give me those tickets, small man. I'll be taking them from you."

The chemical workers chuckled.

The darkness had fallen complete, and out of the shadows of nearby tents stepped a muscle-bound strongman with shaved head and walrus mustache, a bear trainer as large as the foreman, and a pair of male gymnasts, likely the trapeze artist's compatriots. They lined up to either side of the trapeze artist, facing the foreman's crew.

The chemical workers still chuckled, albeit more softly. An un-even fight, still, and they held the advantage.

Then the ogress shambled out from the darkness. The chemical workers' remaining courage fled them. They reacted with disgust, as if they had been shat upon by an elephant. She walked up to the pair in the center of the tension and put her hand on the ringmaster's shoulder, forming a tri-level spire of ascending fear, anger, and awe. Anger gave way to awe, backing away with a curse. Fear gave way as well, burying itself between the strongman and the bear trainer. Awe stood tall, facing the chemical workers, all of whom turned and walked away from her un-gaze, the gas mask sending them off to their pathetic, dilapidated trailer-homes in the woods. Their grunts and complaints, along with the occasional sound of someone vomiting, filtered off into the beyond.

• • •

We rush, the Obfuscate and I, through the trees, from copse to copse, trying to find a moment's reprieve from the downpour in our flight. Nevertheless, we are soaked and now, because of our stop and start sprinting, exhausted. My throat tastes of steel and the hot breath hissing from it contrasts sharply with the wet shivers that quake over my skin. I am painfully aware of every joint in my bones and every bronchus in my lungs. My face feels as if it is melting from osmosis onto the wet grass beneath.

The Obfuscate has fared no better. He wraps his torso in his own arms, teeth chittering a morse code string of decreasing body core temperature readings and blows air off his cupped lower lip to send droplets of water off of the tip of his nose. A goatee of water rivers from his chin. He must be desperately cold, as he stares numbly ahead, devoid of any awareness but that of the rain.

I turn my eyes to the infinity on which he is fixated for a moment's reprieve from thought. My hair stands on end and I expect a lightning strike, until my consciousness swells up and through my subconscious physical reaction.

It is her. And she is walking right for us.

We are frozen. Adrenaline needles through my veins, but the fight/flight impulse is rooted to the soggy ground with my aching, blistered feet.

She stumbles ahead, head lolling back and forth like a rag doll being shaken by a merciless toddler. Her arms drag at her side — her club is notably absent — and her too-thin thighs buckle, then crumple beneath her swollen paunch. She lays in the mud, limbs akimbo, unmoving.

Curiosity compels us to approach, cautiously, at first.

Our only illumination comes from a pair of faint lights of indeterminate source on a nearby hill. In the milky reflected glow of the water we see that her body is freckled with pairs of small dots over every bit of exposed skin. I touch the marks, frightened that she might suddenly come to consciousness and seize me with her clawed hands at any moment.

The freckles bleed, rust red diluting quickly in the swirling rain water. These are snakebites.

But the scent arising from her body (she is still breathing, though barely) is more than mere venomous pestilence. She reeks of solvents and acids – in fact her skin is burned in large patches and the leather of her harness and gas mask is discolored by contact with some kind of chemical agent.

The Obfuscate speaks first.

"She is hurt. We must aid her."

My repulsion is over-ridden by the Obfuscate's compassion. I promised him I would help him. I will help him.

The nearby lights, we soon discover, belong to a smouldering-engined Chevy. We drag her to the vehicle and set her in the open trunk. One lens of her goggles is shattered. I can see inside, but her eyelid is shut. It does not look like a peaceful rest is hidden behind that eyelid.

We put the vehicle into neutral then push it up a gentle slope to the top of a hill. Beneath us is the carnival. We had been running in circles under the blanket of the storm, it appears. The Obfuscate shoots me a look of disappointment, as if I have betrayed him in my ignorance.

The car coasts down, coming to rest not far from the rows of trailers that serve as the carnies' portable village. The bear trainer is there to meet us with a baseball bat, which he thumps into his open palm until he sees the Ogress sticking out of the trunk. He drops the bat and helps us extract her from the car and carry her into her trailer.

The bear trainer and the Obfuscate dry her off with towels and wrap her in warm blankets. The trailer bed is too small to allow me to crowd in to help, so I make a mental inventory of a series of items tacked to an immense corkboard to keep myself distracted from my pain and exhaustion. After a moment, I tug the Obfuscate's arm, pointing wordlessly to the corkboard. He soon understands my reluctance to speak.

• • •

Birth Certificate: August 27th, 1974. Portage County, Wisconsin. Michael Kade Brouley born to Mrs. Margaret Brouley (Resident) and Mr. Henry Brouley (currently imprisoned at the Minnesota State Penitentiary, Stillwater, MN).

Photograph 1: A yellowed polaroid inside a ziplock bag. A young mother, probably in her late teens or early twenties, holds her newborn baby. Both are dressed in dingy pale blue hospital gowns. She smiles, bedraggled but beautiful, from under a sweaty mop of salt and pepper hair. Her brown eyes are warm and comfortable, if a bit weary from labor. The child's hair is jet black and abundant. It's eyes are disproportionately large to the face frame, though only narrowly opened. Through the slivered lids one can see deep brown pools, reflective of the young mother's eyes.

Photograph 2: A group of men and women posing in front of a dark brick building. The long, squat structure is surmounted with several low, thick smokestacks. A grey-green smog wafts up into the dimly-lit early morning sky. Those present all wear the same slate-blue uniform and a canary-yellow hard hat. A name tag is worn by all on the left breast. The young woman from the previous photo is nestled among them, smiling cheerfully. Her tag reads "Marge."

Photograph 3: A black-and-white portrait of the mother and infant, now a little older, but still very much a newborn. Both are dressed in shining white, and their eyes are each other's. The mother's dark, angular features stand out almost in relief beneath the white mitre-cap under which her hair is tucked. Her expression is one of reverence and piety, like that of a frescoed saint. At the front of the hat is an embroidered cross, embraced by a coiling serpent.

Newspaper clipping 1: *Stephens Point — Workers arrived at the Minawauk Corporation Processing Plant on Monday morning to find the compound gates chained shut and the chemical-processing lines stopped. Amid growing hostility at the company's front drive, a Minawauk executive arrived to inform the perplexed workers that the plant was being shut down by its parent corporation due to high overhead costs. When asked about compensation, the executive, board member Scott Peterson, replied that the newly-laid-off workers would receive one month's pay and job-location assistance, but that the plant was being closed for good and their jobs would be sourced overseas...*

Newspaper clipping 2: *Central Wisconsin Newswire* — *Authorities have arrested Saint Moses the Serpentine religious leader Hywell Marion in connection with allegations of fraud. Charges are being leveled by a number of plaintiffs, all of whom have been associated with the group over the course of its fifteen-year history. Attorney Chad Lashlegger, who represents the plaintiffs, hopes to prove that "Mister Marion's greed and chicanery have led to heartbreak and financial ruin for the estimated one thousand adherents to the Serpentine movement." All followers of the faith are required to contribute one-third of their yearly earnings, while a select group known as the "Brass Serpents" donate all of their earnings in exchange for room and board at the religion's Portage County compound. The women and children who compose the "Brass Serpents" will become wards of the state upon the seizure of Marion's bank assets, as a part of an ongoing investigation...*

Certificate of Adoption: December 9th, 1975. Portage County, State of Wisconsin.
Child's name: Michael Kade Brouley.
Biological Mother's name: Margaret Brouley.
Biological Father's name: Henry Brouley (deceased).
Adoptive Father's name: Heinrich Nellson.
Adoptive Mother's name: Brenda Hill-Nellson.

• • •

I watch the Obfuscate as a realization grips his spine, setting him stiff with names, dates, and locations. Memories flood him until he can no longer contain them, and he drops to his knees, vomiting on the floor beneath the corkboard. I put a hand on his shoulder, then turn to the bear trainer for help.

My vision turns to stop-motion, my hearing the distant echo of proximate action — I feel as if I am viewing the scene from another vantage point, outside my body:

The bear trainer draws a bowie knife.

The Ogress lifts her legs up, knees to chest.

The bear trainer ferociously cuts the leather thong from her hips.

The Ogress reaches up and puts her hands on her distended belly; her neck arches up and back.

A spray of water and blood engulfs the bear trainer.

The knife clatters to the floor (I sense, but do not see, the Obfuscate twist under my hand to see the source of commotion).

The bear trainer thrusts his hands between the Ogress's legs.

The Ogress bucks her hips once, twice, then goes limp.

The bear trainer laughs, a smile of glee rips his face wide open, his eyes bulge, as if conquering an enemy in battle.

He holds up his trophy.

The Ogress does not move.

A child is born.

A girl.

She could be the Obfuscate's sister.

• • •

They will form two lines. One, a white-clad serpentine line of zealots looking for their lost sheep, the other a factory line of yellow-helmeted chemical workers offering on the job training. They will intertwine and converge on this site, overturning the Ogress's trailer in their effort to find the child. Somewhere in the moil, their purposes will collide, reconcile, then coalesce, a pastel yellow vortex of twisting morals and contrapunctual priorities carving a swath of desire-for-control over the girl's life.

"We will teach her about solidarity and rights."

"We will give her a code to live by."

"She is a worker by birth."

"She is the child of the scapegoat, pure, unsullied."

"She is a rallying point, a symbol of our struggles."

"We will acclimatize her to the chemicals — she will be immune."

"We will sup her on venom until she grows accustomed — none shall hurt nor make afraid in all the holy mountain."

"She is the chosen one."

"She is the harbinger of freedom."

"She is God."

And they will tear her limb from limb, rend her in half like the child of Solomon's judgment, an Orphic sacrifice to herself.

• • •

The Obfuscate picked up the girl and their eyes, a quadrenary system of identical planets, orbited around the invisible emotional focus that tugged at their empathies, drawing them together in an unperturbable system.

A change arose in his voice, cutting up through and overwhelming the timidity that, earlier that night, had sodominated his tone.

"I recall now that my parents, while breaking me, had told me that my real father had died and that my real mother never wanted me. I thought that this was their idea of a joke. It seems they were only half-joking."

He held the girl in his arms, like a brother holding his infant sister.

"You shall bow to no one, and no one shall bow to you."

The end-of-work whistle screeched out from the chemical factory. Bells rang from the church steeple.

• • •

The son rises. T:S

The Midas Touch
Mike Philbin

You know Midas, right? King Midas? Everything he touched turned to gold? Well, I am getting super paranoid. I have been doing my research on this strange material ability, and I think I've got it. Well, I say got it, I've got something like it. If you imagine that the original diseased touch was like the sound of a perfectly tuned C, then my malady is like the dull sound of a cracked bell. No less potent as a Massacre device though.

I had saved one life that fateful day of my conversion from mere mortal to Angel of Death. She was driving her car on my side of the road and destined to kill the pair of us. I must have played some esoteric trump card that I'd been keeping up my sleeve for just this occasion for the last twenty-nine years of my life. I should have died that day. And so should she — well, she did soon after but that's just jumping the gun. She died later, okay, of "natural causes." Nothing to do with me. I had saved both our lives with my act of sheer charity. I was a local media star for a week or less.

Celebrity in my own lunchtime.

I returned to my regular job of Kitchen Attendant at the swankiest hotel in my district (I can't use the name of the hotel for legal reasons). It was a good, steady job where all's I had to do was turn up, put in hard morning's sweating graft clearing up from the night before, then the rest of my day was my own. It was a luxury life in many ways, no middle management decisions to make, no political power struggles, no in-fighting and bitchiness. Just me and the kitchen and the double sink unit. I never used the dish washer. Not only was it a clunky noisy mess that detracted from my thoughts of how to spend my afternoon, it was impractical. Impractical in that I was there, in the kitchen to expend some energy, sweat some effort out. I wanted the purity of a hands-on job which didn't tax my mental faculties. And I got to sample the chef's latest inventions.

But then my mind started to play tricks on me. It read the news headlines for me, taunted me with their repercussions. There was no great turning point, other than my memory of the crash, the crash that killed that other driver. I don't even remember her name, Lily or something. In my mind, she is at the cockpit of a supersonic winged war machine. She comes at me like a glowing bullet refracting the lens of the afternoon like solace in a summer shower. I have these chrome fragments that refuse to interlock. They remain forever enigmatic. Like my actions that day had severed the judgemental hand of an Angel of God — at least broken a wing or chipped a halo quite severely.

I had done certainly something very wicked, that much was clear from later events. I hadn't read that local rag in the weeks since the accident and my convalescence. I had only fractured my pelvis a bit. She had gotten off a little worse but nothing fatal. Nothing that warranted that garish headline that day.

Date with Death for Local Survivor

The article pulled no punches. I thought I was on a medieval mushroom trip or in some God-awful fly-agaric fugue, such were the graphic particulars of the report. Blood had issued from every pore, it screamed in stark subheadings. Cancer of the lung, liver and blood (they called it leukaemia) had decimated her body until only a skeleton remained. She had haemorrhaged to death, turned to concrete before the eyes of her astonished witnesses — became a cold statue, drained of all moisture. If you can understand how horrific that must be for the relatives to watch, a loved one ossifying to a slab of death as the red, red wine spills out of every glass she ever touched to her lips.

There is cancer in my family and my mother herself had to nurse her dying dad as he sank into his deathbed and shat out his colour, his life essence pouring from his bowel. I know all about loss and death. I have witnessed enough of it. Watched relatives' lips turn blue as they smiled their last. But everyone has that in their lives, right? Tragically flawed family members, victims of fate? Cruelly torn from us while we can do nothing? We all deserve to experience a little loss in our lives?

Well, this is stupid. This sorta goes *beyond* all that natural stuff. I had The Midas Touch. I was now sure of it. I thought back to recent times, recent announcements; deaths in the family I had heard of and whose funerals I had been to busy too attend — distant relatives in a big family, you understand. There's always a shoulder to cry on in a big family, right? But my family, the more research I did, was getting thinner on the ground than snow in the Congo. They were literally dropping like flies.

I started getting in contact with all my old college chums. Many had moved abroad using their degrees as stepping stones to traverse the globe. And the story I discovered was one of death after death after death. Many flavours of death, some accidents, some illnesses, one or two suicides. I was driving a road of death and decay back to that fateful day. But surely it couldn't have been that? My old colleagues, for example, at the night club where I used to tend the bar, on Thursdays and Sundays, even there a toll of death stretched into the black fog of nostalgia. This was well before that fateful car crash when I interrupted an Angel's dirty business.

I lay awake all night, in a cold sweat. I couldn't find any connection, other than the casual touch of a hand on a colleague's shoulder, or a girl's thigh, or a relative held in an embrace of emotional relevance, a child cradled uncomfortably. I started to really panic then. I had this vision of these babies crawling back from the grave, their little hands pushing up through the rain loosened soil of harvesting perfection, their eye sockets dripping maggots, their bellies swelled with sorrows, their anuses falling out behind them like rolls of carpet from a gypsy's van. I literally sat there all night, crouched up at the foot of my damp single bed and shook, my toes cold and numb. I don't remember blinking. I just shook and waited for the phone to ring. And it surely rang. All night. But I never answered. I couldn't move. I just couldn't bear the news. I knew it would be no good.

I didn't eat for three days. I was terrified to go outside. I remember seeing the postman pass by each day. He never ventured down my path, but he looked in. Like he knew. Maybe deep down inside, the whole world knew by now what a murdering bastard I had become — what a legacy I carried. How my merest touch meant death — ossification. I found myself down the local supermarket in my jeans and stripey pyjama top. I was still shivering. In my basket I had useless things, toiletries, microwave meals (I don't have a microwave oven) and cleaning products. He was a beacon in fog, the cashier. I remember every detail like it was only yesterday. He was slim, 5' 10", blue eyes, stubble, tongue bar, fighting scar over his left eye, his hair was golden brown, texture like sun lays me down, through my mind he runs. That song barged into my consciousness, I couldn't blank it. It stuck like glue. He had LOVE and LOVE tattooed on his fists in alternate red and green ink. He took the rather phallic deodorant bottle from me and I remember thinking at the time, "That man is scanning my cock."

That's the thought I had in my stupid head despite all the turmoil of those lost few days. Maybe *because* of the turmoil of those lost few days. I had distanced myself so effectively from reality that the very next day Simon (that was the cashier's name) was pressing his face against into the hair at the back of my head, inhaling. His tip of his cock was riding against my unwashed anus. We were in my miserable bathroom. I had my face against the cold glass of the mirror. I could see both of us, I wanted to see if he turned to gold before my eyes as I let myself succumb to his smooth seduction. He felt so good there, behind me, holding my face to the glass. He was skinny but hard, maybe he worked out? I didn't understand a thing. I made him promise not to penetrate me. He seemed immune to my death touch. His eyes stayed on mine as he thumbed the tip of my cock. He told me how he'd watched me for the last few weeks and found out as much as he could about me. His breath smelt of spicy meat and garlic tainted by the spearmint chewing gum that I'd made him spit out.

His lips at my ear. His thick tongue on the back of my neck. That bar of metal against my jawline. He held his cock against my anus and with slow deliberate circular movements he made my erect cock stiffen to a rod of metal. I'd made him promise not to penetrate me. I had no idea what the death signal was, what fired it off. I had looked back, searched long and hard for any connection to those people whose death I had already caused. But there was no answer. No way to tell if I was the reason for the destruction of life after life.

He was stroking my cock, gripping the shaft with his hand, the foreskin torn back. He held me like that for a solid minute of purest joy. My foreskin threatening to rip right back. His eyes in the mirror. The stress in his throat as he gasped and grunted. I couldn't even understand what he saw in me. What was the attraction? He bucked once and before I realised it, he was in me. A tear in his eye. I just didn't see what I could have done to so upset him. Tears poured down his face as he ejaculated up me, his legs quivering like winter branches. I could feel the life force pouring painlessly out of him. He knew exactly what he was doing. I could not bring myself to ejaculation but later, after Simon had left for his shift on the tills, I worked off my frustration. Alone.

Even the golden boy succumbed to my touch in the end. I found out about it through a friend. His family can't hear the truth. They just will not listen to my fatal mantra no matter how many times I call. They confess they didn't even know he was *that way inclined*. I think it was the guilt that got him. My guilt at allowing his love to enter me in such a golden way.

Fact: I touch you, you die.

Fact: you will never believe my story. **TTS**

Last Thoughts Drifting Down

Jeremy Robert Johnson

I.mpact bears fruit. A great blossom of fire is given to the world in one billionheat moment. So fast, and full, and the sky knows what it is to be swallowed up, to be designed and undone, to give power to heat as a parasite, to fail in the face of a formula that solves itself (600 billionths of a second to make the introduction, uranium-233 a seed to bloom to tree to cloud).

And something above becomes nothing below, feathers to dust, and with the taste, that first life, the introduction to *other* creates

I

Am. and the feeling is not one of being torn apart but rather of being put together, as if all the matter before me was part of the whole and just misunderstood the potential for growth.

But I educate.

And everything that was I, and tried to run, is torn to Us, loose atoms at last, joining me, slipping back fast to the ever expanding

I

of the storm.

To be perceived is to be understood. Those that become part of I leave traces, thoughts, and though nothing slows there is a feeling of moving backwards, of understanding that I have been

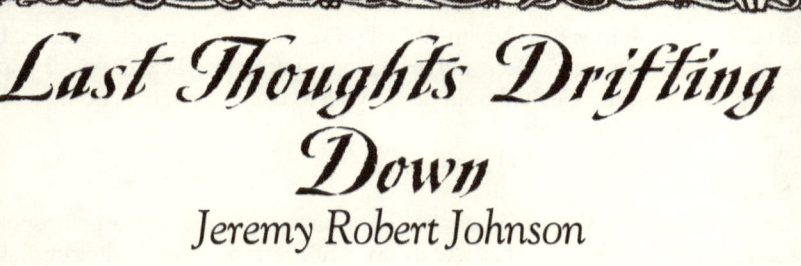

Made. in the minds first. My initial vibrations created synaptic tremors, bred obsessions, turned thoughts black and spread logicancer. Hot, slick foreheads dripped sweat upon blueprints, the fluid from flesh trying to blot the ink that would undo it. But the concept was indelible.

We could make this. It could work.

Should we?

Nervous laughter, shifting in chairs. They have nightmares that go unspoken, sweatdrenched fever dreams of black birds, dripping fire, tongues expanding until skulls burst. None of it stops the vibration.

A rose blooms in the desert, child of a new Trinity. Proud fathers show photos. It is an introduction.

Should we? The world applauds with fear in its bellies. It is a strange vindication for a life's pursuit.

Photos can be doctored.

I
vibrate in the minds of millions.

We want proof.

An island washed clean by my birth. My afterbirth scars the air. The land itself becomes sacred and heavy with reminders of my birthday.

As tribute the witnesses shed what had turned black inside, scream, and their cells promise to bear no children.

The. people think I am an end, but they remain as long as I do. Last thoughts move from the electric to the sub-atomic and grow dense at my center where they collide.

I can't see, how come I can't see   *Our Father who art in heaven*
         If I can just get underground, if I can dig then   *No*
Wake up, wake up, wake up   *I thought I'd be holding you when this happened*
      He owes me twenty dollars   *I love you, I love you, I lo*
She never got to see my face or anything   *Shit, my hair, am I burning*
    It's about time   *Great, now the T.V. won't work*   *I can't even remember*
Where's mom, oh

      Breathe, just close your eyes, and bre

Destroyer. Some think it (even those who view my birth as a blessing think it at the moment I touch them and sink white silhouettes into stone behind them).

An old man with a placard predicting my arrival yells "Destroyer, unholy light, bringer of death" before I wash through him.

He's smiling as he yells, as if I am an old friend. His last thought is thankful.
You finally came.

I deliver him to dust, and slow. The feeling throughout my body is heavy and

I

drift

down

and spin within my own winds. I move with siltskin and vomit ash from a million mouths.

Last thoughts turn to lightning in purple bruiseblack clouds. Few remain to witness my glory.

Of. those that still breathe, no lungs go untouched. Alveoli implode, hearts boil.

I

change but never stop growing.

Each cell introduced becomes part of a chain. Eyes burn, blood coughed to the ground is granted a new purpose.

To contain what I have become. To radiate and sing my secrets to anyone who passes, to spin a siren song as old as seawater and promise change.

Worlds. are within me now, the knowledge of every cell that spins to earth as ash and falls to soak the soil with my legacy.

Others exist within me, cradled in my heat, moving stones and breathing with new plastic insect faces. In concrete rooms beneath the soil there are mothers sneaking potassium iodide into baby formula and cursing now extinct world leaders. Some steal televisions that will never run again. Some stab, some rape, some run forward as if I have an end just beyond the horizon. Their skin soon knows my secrets and learns to sing, each cell vibrating in tune. A woman weeps next to a dog kennel filled with dust. A man is carried across the ground in a suit made from cockroaches. A small boy makes snow angels in the ash and smiles at the clouds.

There is an echo, a question whispered beneath my swirling winds.

Should we?

There are cities painted black, populated by blast-shadows.

From the cities, no response. **T:S**

Love in a Hot Climate
Anil Menon

Where do I begin? At the beginning, says Mr. Carroll. Yes, Mr. Carroll, if this were an essay about The Cow, certainly, I could begin at the beginning. "The Cow," I would say, "is a Four-Legged Beast. Two legs move him forwards, and two legs move him afterwards." So on and so forth. But this story is not about a Cow. Time Machines peep in their heads. So does a Great Cogitator, an intractable Midget, Fiduciary Matters, the inestimable Poornima and an Impediment. Then there is the overcast of the umbra casting Conundrum. All these items must be fitted in somehow, higgledy-piggledy, grunting and squealing, back to front and side to side. It is not so simple, Mr. Carroll!

Ergo, the first casualty: Truth! *aff.* Fanny Hill: "Sir, I can be true, or I can be entertaining, but not both." Verily. Some things have been goosed, pinched, twiddled and stretched. Reality be damned, it is *your* two rupees worth of Enjoyment that I am worried about only.

Ergo, second casualty: Grammar! Down the oubliette, I say, with Grammar. Damn it, feller, dangle this, don't dangle that, "may I have some more commas, please, Sir" …what the Old Nick is all this talk about spilled infinities and what not? True story: I was reared by Ursuline nuns; it was either that or the wolves. Regular, doughty old penguin brigade with a chip on their rounded shoulders 'cause I was a boy (hypocrites! Baby Jesus!). And all day long: colon this, semi-colon that, conjugal this, conjugal that; Damn, I am thinking, some inferior Freudian explanation here for Mother Superior, old chap. Not to mention the intoxicating effect of such gab on young impressionables!

Prescriptum having been disposed of forthwith, here we are, orb to orb, friendly like, across the Void Of Text. "So who are you fella?" I catch with my ears.

I, one Mr. Purushottam Deshpande, twenty-five years old, gentleman, entrepreneur, autodidact, author and inamorata of the inestimable Poornima. At your service, Reader!

Some further background intimations of my Character: I was born an Only Child, and to boot, an Orphan. Subsequently, I was much booted about. Still, after all the scars are rubbed and pinched, and all "buts" kicked in the same, it was *la dolce vita*; certainly, I didn't know a better life. Also, caste-wise: a Brahmin, or in this hot climate, hooray! whew! free drinks for all!

Enough with this flashback. Some buses seat forwards, and others, againstwards; I, Reader, am strictly (no excuses) a forwards sort of bus.

The bus is currently parked at the New Delhi Talkies; the year: 1955. At close proximity is the inestimable Poornima.

Poornima: My Lebanon! Eyes like fishpools in Heshbon. Hair as a flock of goats. Lips, a thread of scarlet. Two breasts like two young roes that are twins. In short, to see her is to read the Song of Solomon. She's kindly obliged some perusal, but here's the rub! I am a cover-to-cover sort of feller.

At present, I am gazing unremittingly at her and ditto conversely.

"O Poornima!"

"O Purushottam!"

At long last, she tore her eyes from mine and reached into the deep cool vale betwixt her silk wrapped ivory towers. She produced a much-folded piece of paper and offered it to me.

I caressed the paper as I unfolded it. Oh, were I where it had been. Myrrh and frankincense, Reader, makes nonsense of common sense.

"Read, beloved," says she, huskily.

I perused the handwriting.

"Suitable match sought for a surprisingly pretty, fair, domesticated, accomplished Gowd Saraswat Brahmin girl, 20/160cm, B.A, B.ED., Teacheress from a respectable family. Father in close proximity to the Minister Of Finance. Smokers, Drinkers, please excuse."

"What? It can't be!"

"My father's handiwork, beloved. God proposes, my father disposes. We are doomed."

My bowels constricted. My eyes swam in pools of despair.

"Damn, damn, double damn doubled!" I expostulated.

She would soon be on the Market; lock, stock and barrel. If the parent unit was busy polishing the signage, then Purushottam and Poornima would soon be Purushottam sans Poornima. No, the Conundrum had to be Solved and Solved soon! Devouring Time, Sonnet XIX et cetera.

"Your progenitor, dearest," says I, utterly bitterly, "is an Impediment."

"We must not sit down and be made conveniences of," says she. By golly, her vim was invigorating.

"Perish the thought!" says I, feelingly. "Am I not like Mother India, rich in possibility but poor in presentuality?"

"Your gifted tongue alone qualifies you, dearest."

"Am I not rich in Forecast but poor in Fact?"

"The nail has been truly hammered, beloved."

"In short, it jingles down to the matter of my negative Net Worth, does it not? The dog that does not bark, eh? The jingle that is not heard? Eh? Eh?"

As the Conundrum exposed itself — naked, throbbing and purple — she broke down.

"I can't live without you," Poornima burst out, collapsing into my arms. "I'll kill myself, I will. I will."

"Collar those tears, my Full Moon," begged I, vastly gratified. "Be rest assured that the cogitator" — I tapped the noggin — "will overturn every stone."

"I am your garden, lord," says she, humbly, and dam' if the old sentimental orb was not breached!

I flipped the signage on its posterior. On perusal, it looked like a memo from one Shri. Milton Friedman to the Honorable Shri. C.D. Deshmukh, Minister of Finance.

"…the key is to realize that it is a Time Machine, a recent idea. One aspect is that five percent per annum rate of increase in real national income, seems entirely feasible … what is called capital investment is only part of the total expenditure on increasing the productivity of an economy … a steady expansion in the money stock (allowing for seasonal influences) at a rate of something like four to six percent per year … this Time machine will produce all the prosperity an Investor might consider his reasonable due. What is needed are Entrepreneurs to exploit this opportunity."

Time Machines? I eyed the Memo again. Damn! There is no Limit to the Western Genius. First, that Relativity feller. Then, robots (goodbye, Mr. Marx!). Nonce, Time Machines! What next? Now we'd NEVER catch up; not if the fellers had gotten Time on a leash and carrot! It was the old story of Achilles and the wide-awake Hare all over again. If only the Ursulines had set me straight on Logarithms! These cogitations darkened the Atmosphere, but then I deduced that the lights had blinked out because the talkie had started.

I continued to cogitate on the Conundrum. Assassination was Out. The lady's tender sentiments and all that muzak. Diplomacy was Out; it assumes Gentlemen, and the Impediment was Anything Butt. That left Guile; the cat's ass of Valor.

Tap. Tap.

"Hey," says someone, tapping my head.

I ignored the tap. Sir, I abhor taps. Especially in that general vicinity.

Tap. Tap. This is Intolerable.

I turned, swiveling and glaring daggers. A diminutive but beefy gentleman with the general aspect of bronze; well-developed musculature and Kaiser moustache to boot. I amended my gaze.

"Pray, my good man," says I. "Please explain your need?"

"Your head is too big, fellow. Either shift or detach said item."

I am astounded at the man's extermis temeritus.

"Sir," says I, widening my nostrils and smiling horribly. "Your vertical inadequacy is equally offensive to me. Wait till the intermission, if you please, and I will relieve *your* discomfort. However, I will not insist on quid pro quo. The flaw in your design, no doubt, offends you as much as it does me."

The murmuration of our fellow theatre-goers, excited by the daylight robbery of their two rupees worth of Enjoyment, sufficed to silence the quarrelsome midget.

"I don't like your tone, fellow," says he, with equally widened nostrils. "But very well, intermission, then."

I swiveled my head back and slid a glance at Poornima. She was pre-occupied before and post-occupied now. I let her continue to be occupied. I grimly retraced the exchange of a few minutes ago. I flexed my musculature. No doubt, in a fair fight, I could thrash the midget. But would the villain fight fair? Bitterness gargled like the ocean, choking my throat. What could I possibly do about my allegedly oversized egg? If a really oversized noggin had to be pointed out, why, it should be the one sitting calmly on the shoulders of that Time Machine feller. I, quite contrary, am a Man of Action. A different species altogether. Never shall the twain mate. I considered the matter at rest, but insurrection in the rank and file!

"What's this hue and cry?" I queried the cellular.

"What if?"

"What if, what?"

"What if the twain *did* meet?"

"By god's golly, fellers, let me do the Caesar around here. About march!"

But the proposal was on the table and nothing-to-do till said item considered and disposed of forthwith. Hmmm. Le Rouge & Le Noir. Cogitation & Action. Royce & Rolls. Square & Compass. Friedman & Deshpande. Why not? Blackballed Jupiter! The masses had glasses after all.

Purushottam Deshpande, Proprietor, Indian Time Machines was born, Reader, in that climactic moment. I rubbed my hands in my gleeful heart and waited with crossed legs for the Intermission.

At last... Intermission. Lights flooded the bowels of the hall.

I turned to my beloved, slapping my thigh.

"You will yet be the Mother of my Children, O Poornima!"

"What do you mean, dearest?" says she, casting her eyes in my direction.

"I have, as promised, cogitated on our Conundrum. Consider it solved!"

"What do you propose? Have you decided to work?"

"Sort of."

"A wise sage has said, dearest, that some things are All or Nothing."

I shrugged away the Sage. Can has no time for Kant.

"Advice is the vice of the wise. I, contrary-wise, am of the 'Blunder and Eureka!' school myself. In short, behold an Entrepreneur!"

"What is the item under consideration? I hear the jam market is in a slump."

I laughed. There's the fem species for you! Jam.

"Dear, dear, munchkin. I intend... to *mass produce time!!*"

Silence.

"Time?" asks she, doubtfully.

"Yes. Time machines. No more scraping seconds together."

"Yes... I see. But this Time machine... does it exist?"

I exhibited the memo. She bit her lip as she perused it, and I couldn't decide whether it was better to be the lip or the tooth.

"How does this Wondrous Machine work, dearest?"

"Oh. I'm sure it uses Logarithms. We leave those details, my dear, to the Great Cogitator. This white gentleman — and he surely is both — is in search of a partner; to wit, a Man of Action. He is a Great Cogitator, come down from Sinai, and in his hands is... Soap. But who'll convince the dirty buggers to Wash? Me! That's who! Marketing. Segmentation. Target and Conquer. The Impediment wants Jingle. By Golly, I'll jingle him deaf. Behold, O Poornima, the Slayer of The Conundrum!"

"Such a man is likely to have many petitioners," says the inestimable Poornima.

Tap. Tap.

"Petitioners, yes. But Men of Action? A Roosevelt? A Carnegie? A Ford?" I thundered. "I am not a man of small parts, as you know, my dear Poornima."

She blushed, the crimson blood galloping to her fair cheeks.

"Verily," says she, aside.

"In my capacity as the ex-editor of *India Tomorrow,* I will approach him incognito. We will talk, we will laugh, we will have tea, and then we will talk some more. Then at an auspicious juncture, I will offer my hair-raising proposal. I will prepare the Business Plan this very evening. Against his mighty Cogitation, and my equally mighty Action, the Impediment shall fall as cow droppings."

"O Purushottam!"

"O Poornima!"

I could have deflowered her then and there. We threw our eyes at each other, breathing heavily.

Tap. Tap.

"Well, fellow, are you shifting or shall I hand you your head?"

Intolerable. The plot device was now a plot hindrance.

"By George Polti!" I swore, and struck the first blow.

● ● ●

I slept but sleep wouldn't come. I tossed and turned, buggered by the ceaseless neighing of my cogitations. Round and round they raced in my Coliseum. "Ave Caesar," the idiots would roar, "morituri te salutant." Then it was off for the next round. After four hours of Ben-Hur, I threw in the sweaty towel wrapped around my allegedly large head. "Cogito Ergo Sum and be Damned," I shrieked. I needed Rest but the masses were bent upon Worrying what if, and why not, and so what, and but this.

I was out of it. See if I cared. If the Mind was bent upon giving the Body the yes-yes and more-more, who was I, a humble renter, to be the squeaky wheel?

All this I recount, Bosom Reader, to give you a good view of my end. I was half awake and half asleep, a House Divided, and (thank you, Mr. Lincoln), a House Divided can't stand. It was thusly that I arrived at the Ministry of Finance: Gruntled and disgruntled, gusted and disgusted.

Eight annas for the Chowkidar, one rupee for the clerk's In-File assistant to open my file, two rupees for the clerk to overlook my file, (Damn, this was getting expensive), one rupee for the clerk's Out-File assistant to get rid of my file altogether, and eight annas to a miscellaneous rogue who had the ballsy wherewithal to try the oldest tail-tweaker of all: ask and ye shall receive. All in all, I was down in the oubliette for five rupees just to cross a hall. Spend money to make money, say the Wall Street fellers, but that's dam' hard for us Main Street chaps.

In one corner of the room sat one Mr. Lagoo. Pigeon-chested personal assistant to the assistant deputy of the personal secretary of the Minister Of Finance. In short, the inestimable Poornima's male parent. I had managed to duck his gaze thus far, but success is a bitch goddess, and who knew when she'd turn.

The last thing yours humbly wanted was for him to throw his eyes in my direction. As I cogitated on the consequences, I sweated. The sweating created its own sweaty consequences.

I see him sniffing. Damn, damn, double damn doubled.

"Duck," screams the Mind. Recall, however, that I am a House Divided. "Duck! Damn You," screams the Mind, rattling the bars. No use. The Body is snoozing. It is all over. Goodbye, Mr. Deshpande, it was a good life.

"You!" roars the Impediment. "Deshpande! Come here."

I perambulate accordingly.

"Namaste, Sir!" says I, showing all the chinamen.

"Explain!"

"An appointment, O Parent Unit."

"With whom, scoundrel?"

Really, the man was intractable. "The Great Cogitator, your Munificence. I am here in strict official capacity. I would have given advance intimation, my dear Sir, but if you recall, the last time I was seen in your vicinity, there were certain odds offered against my continued existence and what not. But what the Hades, Sir; let us shake like gentlemen and begin anew. 'Brave New World, That has such people in't' and et cetera. What do you say, Sir?"

"Deshpande, I—"

Through the corner of my eye I see a white feller, balding, perambulating corridor-wards. That, says I, must be the Great Cogitator. Frankly, I expected more vertical adequacy, but Hades! who was I to quarrel with Nature? In these moments, House Divided or not, it all comes together. One Nation Under God. Body and Mind shook hands, let bygones be bygones et cetera.

"Excuse me, excuse me, Sir," I hollered. "Mr. Friedman, Sir."

"Deshpande!"

I ignored him and cast my voice again in the perambulator's direction.

"Mr. Friedman! Mr. Friedman!"

"Deshpande!" hollered the Impediment.

Allah be praised. The white gentleman was not deaf. He stopped, and as the clouds of Deep Thought parted, smiled hesitantly.

"Mr. Deshpande? Of *India Tomorrow*? Ah, yes. My 9:00 AM. Come along."

I bowed to my future father-in-law. "A few minutes with my Friend, O Protector of Poornima, if you please."

• • •

"As above, so below," say the Rosicrucians. Be that as it may. The Outside was not, however, as the Inside. Inside was cool, AC'ed to Canada-buffalo comfort, and outfitted with the very best. My ass was grass, as the yanks say.

"How did you hear of me, Mr. Deshpande?"

I winked at him. "Usual channels, Sir."

"Yes... which are?"

"Oh, I am well oiled, Sir." I winked again.

"I see... inside sources, eh? Frankly, I was puzzled by the request for an interview. I'm hardly a celebrity and I can't imagine my thoughts on developmental economics being riveting reading. And that too, developmental economics from a monetarist viewpoint!"

"Sir, the whole world knows you are a Great Cogitator!"

"Pardon?"

"Cogitator. *Ko-gi-tat-or*; to wit, a thinker."

For some reason, this amused the white gentleman enormously. I laughed along; oh, I can match you Move for Move, my wily Cogitator.

"Oh, come now. You're surely pulling my leg."

I continued to smile. Naturally, he had to test me.

"Rest assured I am a Man of Action, Sir."

"Well... good! This country needs a few. Mr. Deshpande, I suppose we'd better get started. Shoot."

I was ready.

"What, Sir, in fifteen words or less, is the Operating Principle of the Time Machine?"

He stared at me blankly. Damn! These Great Cogitators are all the same. They can tell you how to spin a galaxy but can't spell their names. I consulted the memo.

117

"Sir, apropos your comment to the Honorable Shri. Deshmukh: 'Time machines will produce all the prosperity an Investor might consider his reasonable due...'"

His face cleared. "Ahh... That was a private memo! I'll have to speak to Lagoo about it... you are well connected, aren't you? I'm still getting used to the way things are done around here... Anyway, my point was that a five percent per annum rate is perfectly reasonable. It sounds a bit over-optimistic, but it isn't really. I was referring to the post-Keynesian idea of thinking of monetarist policies as worth and value propagators... it is pertinent towards this issue. Mind you, in general, I am dead set against the Keynes approach to Economics. The Keynes approach is a disaster, never mind what my good friend, Mr. Galbraith might think. It is a pity your—"

I was getting a bit tired of smiling. Yes, yes, jolly old chap, we all know our Marshallian Scissors, but what was the Principle? Fifteen words or less, remember?

"—in particular, the current budget plan for 1955, from what Mr. Deshmukh has told me, will lay even greater stress on the two industrial extremes; heavy industries on the one hand, and handicrafts on the other. It may be good politics to invest in these extremes (and I disagree), but it makes for really poor economics. On the one end, you have too little labor and capital intensive investment, on the other you have the exact opposite. Furthermore, as I outlined, logarithmic risk returns—"

So it *was* the Logarithmic Principle.

"Thank you," says I, smiling.

"Uh... sure. Sorry, I'll try to be more succinct."

"Yes, Sir. Ready?"

"For what?"

"Number two, Sir?"

"Uh, sure."

"Well, do we need Petrol or Atoms, Sir? I'm thinking housewives hate Radioactivity, there's just no talking to them once they hear that word. So Petrol is preferable, if you don't mind. Is that feasible?"

Silence. A certain Expression slithered across his face. Damn, these Americans are inscrutable fellows! Play cards with one hand on their pistols, if you know what I mean.

"Er, I'm not sure I understand... Your natural resources are *not* the problem. In fact, I have a section in my memo explaining why private industry should not be coddled to move in certain directions. Look at Japan. Very few resources, but they've begun to have an export surplus! Perhaps I'd better focus on the monetarist aspects... this is getting a little vague. Did you read my comments on deficit financing?"

What was all this Economics gab, man? Damn, this Cogitator was a money-grubber. Then, cogitating at the speed of light, I caught up with light. Oh-ho! By Jove, so *you* want to control the purse strings? Well, talking the talk is not good enough, my good fellow. You couldn't walk a day in Bombay without putting the feet in shit.

"Yes," says I, smiling. "We can discuss that later. Leave the financing to me, Sir. I have 'friends' if you know what I mean."

I tapped the side of my nose.

Silence. He stared at me.

"What the hell are you talking about? Who are you, exactly?"

"I am Purushottam Deshpande, Sir…"

"Let me see your press papers if you don't mind, Mr. Deshpande?"

Hardball, eh? I spread my hands.

"All right, gotcha!" I expostulated, grinning. "I am not really a journalist, Sir. Specifically, I am an ex-journalist. More specifically, I was an ex-assistant to an ex-journalist. He quit, and I sort of inherited his job, if you know what I mean."

"I think you'd better leave."

The fellow looked upset. "Henry Ford," I prayed, "I need you Nonce."

"Sir," says I, "I know I came under cover of darkness. Let me explain why I am your man—"

"Excuse me, Mr. Deshpande, 'man' for what? Are you looking for a job? If so, you are wasting your time. I'm leaving in a couple of weeks."

Couple of weeks! Impossible!

"What about your Machine? Have you found a partner, then?"

"Mr. Deshpande, I swear—" his eyes were sloshing about. "*What* machine?"

"The Time Machine! What else?"

"Time Machine?"

Was there an echo? "Yes! it is an open secret, you know. You have invented the Time Machine, and I am asking, humbly asking, if I could make a profit for you."

"Mr. Deshpande… I don't know what to say. What gave you the impression I have invented a Time Machine?"

Damn it, don't be coy, man. Still, what was one more Tango around the dance floor. I handed over the page. He read it silently.

"I see…" says he, and burst out laughing. He laughed so hard, I split a stitch.

"Excuse me, Mr. Friedman. Excuse me, but I do have some decency."

He rubbed his eyes. "Of course, you do," says he, and laughed again, shaking like a tickled baby. Really, this was getting Aggravating.

He inspected the other side of the memo. He found that even funnier. Boy, the feller was a leaky laugh bag! I supposed it came with all the overheating from cogitation. Got to relieve the stress et cetera.

"My dear Mr. Deshpande, do excuse me…"

"Purushottam, Sir. So… shall we spit and shake on it?"

"No, we don't. We can't. There is no Time Machine. I am an economist, not an inventor. No, wait, let me finish. I came to this country to advise your government on financial matters. As for money being a time machine, I meant it as a metaphor, nothing more. It is *as if* money were a time machine, because it can transfer wealth and spending power across time. I was just trying, Mr. Deshpande, to make some technical points about balancing liquidity with investment."

Damn, damn, double damn doubled.

"So it was just a metaphor?" says I, forlornly.

"Indeed."

"Too much metaphorical Tea drowns the Dormouse of Comprehension, Sir."

More of the tee-hee and the ha-ha. I looked at him askance. I knew how to deal with Abderites.

"Yes, I suppose it does... Now, tell me, why are you so keen on starting a business? Why not stick with being an ex-journalist?"

I spilled the whole kit and caboodle. 'No Quid no Quo' was the law of the land, I explained. God's golly, was I tired of Micawbering and making the buffalo squeak! The Conundrum peeped its head in, and naturally, introductions had to be made. The Cogitator raised his hand.

"Mr. Deshpande — excuse me — let me get this straight. This is all about a girl? And that too the daughter of Mr. Lagoo? I am in the middle of a thwarted love story?"

"Exactly like the midget, Sir."

"Pardon? No, don't tell me. Well..."

We gazed at each other. The white gentleman was grinning. I grinned back. "What's so funny, old chap?" thought I.

"Must say I didn't expect my day to begin quite like this... Let me ask you something, Mr. Deshpande. Do you want to make Money, or do you want to spend it?"

"In the Book of Life, you'll find me indexed under 'Tree; giving'" says I, feelingly.

"I see... Well, there are four ways, Mr. Deshpande, to spend money. You can spend your money on yourself. Your money on others. Other people's money on yourself. And of course, the government's approach. Now, replace money with Time and you'll have your solution to the Conundrum, as you call it."

"I have often been accused of wasting other people's time."

He thumped the table. "Exactly. As I thought. You have a natural genius for it. There you go, Mr. Deshpande."

"Go where?"

"To your career."

"Spell it out, man!"

"Mr. Deshpande, you are an entertaining fellow, and that is what you should be. An entertainer. Write! Be an ex-journalist. Sing! Dance! I don't know. Find your own unique way of spending other people's time. Or join the government and do it the easy way. What do you think?"

Inspiration reached down and grabbed me by the nitty-gritty. Eureka!

"May I inquire if the person I am addressing has been entertained by the advisee?"

"What? Oh... yeah, I suppose."

"Then how about a small leg-up to said worthy, my dear Sir? For the sake of your namesake and my future first-born. He adds his tiny voice to my yearning!"

I confided my Inspiration, and he grinned like a sailor on shore-leave.

"Sure," says he. "we can have some tea and play at being, how did you put it? yes, 'bosom friends.' I think I know what you are up to." He reached for the intercom. "Mr. Lagoo? please join—"

So we had tea. And biscuits. The Impediment sat in the corner, slurping his frightened tea and oscillating his eyes. The camaraderie between Milton and yours humbly was palpable. He painted me in such glowing colors to Mr. Lagoo that I was a virtual Aurora Borealis. Overcome by emotion, I nominated the same. "You are equally well endowed, if not more," says I. And my child, when forthcoming, would be his, I insisted. After all, we were all related vis-a-vis the One True Monkey. The jolly old Egg laughed a bit more than the scene called for, but otherwise, it was a *tour de farce*.

Can you blame the poor ex-Impediment for wringing my hands of all moisture and apologizing for past misconduct? He had had no intimation of my reach and grasp (apparently, the damn Ursulines had spread all kinds of rumors). There is nothing-to-do but to go to his house for dinner. Disembowel me or agree, says he! I took the high road and invited him to canter along likewise, and we let bygones be bygones; spit and shake, as the Yanks say.

•••

So here we are in the fullness of Time. The inestimable Poornima currently houses a small Child Unit; by definition, one Milton Deshpande, and hopefully, a virile male issue.

Damn it, Reader, I'm casting about for an End, and it is as oleaginous as the Beginning.

"End on a moral," advises well-wishers. "A moral, for a time-spender of this sort, is a must!" Thusly:

Moral! Dare to count your Eggs before they hatch because Fortuna, bless her bosom, does not favor Chickens.

Or how about this:

Moral! All's well that ends well, sayeth the Bard.

So be it.

Notes:

In 1955, Milton Friedman was invited by the Indian Government to advise the Ministry of Finance on economic planning (which, as Galbraith pointed out, is like asking the Pope to recommend a good contraceptive). During his visit to Delhi, he produced a report. It was ignored at the time, but is now considered something of a classic statement on the post-Independence Indian economy.

I must confess that there is no mention of any time machine in Friedman's original report; indeed, in Prof. Gary Dymski's paper, *Money as a "Time Machine" in the New Financial World*, the metaphor is credited to the economist Paul Davidson.

As regards Purushottam: there is a certain character type peculiar to post-colonial nations. He (and it *is* a "he") haunts government offices, he is forever on the verge of success, he is congenitally optimistic, his entire life is a circus of circumstances, and he can often be spotted holding forth at tea stalls. The Indian novelist, G.V. Desani, reified this character in his magnum opus, *All About H. Hatterr*.

Desani aficionados will find Purushottam's liberties with the English language rather familiar. Here is how H. Hatterr describes it:

> "I write rigmarole English, straining your goodly godly tongue, maybe:
> but friend, I forsook my Form, School and Head, while you stuck to
> yours, learning reading, 'riting and 'rithmetic."

Purushottam's English is Desani-lite. It is not really "Indian English" (Anurag Mathur's *The Inscrutable Americans* has some great examples of this variant).

I have no doubt that Dr. Friedman encountered a Purushottam or two during his trip to India. That's just the way Karma works. Again, H. Hatterr:

> "As to *Truth*, the great generalization is, '*Dam*' mysterious! Mum's
> the word!' As to *Life*, the locus classicus, '*contrast*'!" **TIS**

This story is dedicated to G.V. Desani.

The Devil's Half-Brother

Timalyne Frazier

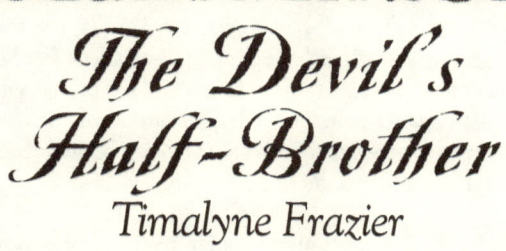

*A*n old mountain man leans on his walking stick as he makes his way down the Appalachian dirt road.

"Evenin'," he says, lifting his hat toward the figure on the porch.

Lia creaks back and forth in her rocking chair. She doesn't respond to the greeting. She never does. All passerbys pay homage to the house out of timeless fear and superstition. She faces the setting sun and the town and listens — nothing but useless chatter and gossip.

Bats dart and flutter after moths and mosquitoes in the dying light. All across these worn mountains, kitchen windows are lit by kerosene lamps. Lia's is dark. The old man swings his stick at a wispy ghost diving low in his path. He hurries to get past the Devil's house before absolute darkness consumes this moonless night.

The last rays of sun disappear behind the hills as Lia rises from her rocking chair. She enters the house reluctantly; she hasn't heard much all evening. She feels cheated. An owl questions from its nest in the graveyard behind the house.

The sound of laughter drifts down the holler. Lia's house remains silent except for the flat sound of a drip from the water pump hitting the smooth, stone kitchen sink.

•••

Lia sleeps; she dreams.

The babies scream. The man picks them up and throws them against the wall. The babies scream. The man does it again, throws them against the bricks. Almost all the babies are silent.

One laughs. The man gathers the child up in his arms. "My child, I've found you again, my lover." The baby laughs again and reaches up to slap her father's face, baby fist, blubbery knuckles rap her father's nose and bloody his mustache. The man smiles down at the fat face framed in curls. The man is not a man. The child is the next heiress of the Devil's family, and daughter of the daughter of the daughter of one of God's most beautiful angels. Lia wakes up in her dark house to the sound of someone sleeping.

• • •

Lia doesn't move in her bed. The ghouls are quiet, resting; someone else is home. She remembers Shrike's paternal care. He would send her off to bed with a threat.

"Boogie will get you if you don't hurry, little one."

She would run into the dark end of the house where her bed was as fast as her little feet would go, jumping under the covers, breathless, accompanied by her favorite spook. It would be ages of fear before she had her breathing under control, and the spook checked all the corners for goblins and Boogie.

• • •

She knows the Boogie Man now, better than anyone alive. Fear no longer plagues her. She is part of the darkness, a knowing servant. She is a child of the darkness, after all. Boogie protects her. They are lovers.

• • •

Lia wakes up with the light, deep red on a horizon of clouds: *red in the morning, sailors take warning.* Sometimes a sailor can even read mountain weather. She is the only one upstairs now, but she smells bacon frying, hears the spatter of grease between the meat and the metal.

She stands in front of the vanity and looks at her body, free of wrinkles, smooth defined muscles, pure, unblemished, white skin, the Devil's touch. She pulls a long, dark dress over her young body and looks into the tall mirror over her wash basin. Her gray hair is still held neatly by the braid she put in the night before. The age in her face, not disputed by the youth of her body now covered by the long dress, shows her to be 100 years old on this day, her birthday.

She has never once left this house since the day she was born. She tried once, to assert free-will. It was just before Boogie's first visit. As she stepped off the last step from the house, the landscape changed from the luscious green of the Appalachian summer into a hellfire and white noise. Her entire body was wracked with pain only relieved when Shrike grabbed her dress and pulled her back up the stairs. A cool evening breeze soothed her flush cheeks and she never set foot on the steps again. Shrike hadn't said a word. And from that day on, Lia knew the limits of her existence. And like a house-cat, she made the best of it.

Lia's distinguished elderly face now shows neat laugh lines, elegant crows feet, and sparkling blue eyes, very bright. Her gray hair is a multitude of shades. She splashes water from the basin across her aged face and grins to herself, not at all dismayed by the yellow of her old teeth flashing back at her.

It is Shrike at the stove. He hasn't visited her since Boogie took her. Lia swishes into the kitchen and sits in her chair. Shrike doesn't look up, continues poking at the bacon. "Mornin' Lia," he says like he'd seen her yesterday and the day before that.

"Why, Shrike, what a pleasure," Lia speaks softly, smiling a little crookedly. "Did Boogie send you to fix me breakfast?"

"No."

"Alright then, why?" She asks.

Shrike flips the bacon onto a towel and pulls plates from the cupboard. He serves two portions and puts a plate in front of Lia.

"Boogie didn't send me." He touches her shoulder with his claw like hands. The touch of his sharp fingers stings Lia's shoulder and she feels a burning sensation rise up her middle, fear and arousal. The sensation stops in her throat and the smell of the bacon almost repulses her as she feels his interest.

Shrike drops his hand away and sits down next to Lia at the table. He doesn't use his fork, just picks the bacon with his fingers. She hears the meat crunch between his teeth, sees his sharp tongue dart to get the crumbs, to lick the excess fat shining. She desires his slick mouth. She leans forward and Shrike spears a piece of bacon from her plate. He places it on her parted lips. She chews the bacon then asks Shrike.

"Where's Boogie?"

"Don't know. Who cares?" Shrike feeds her another piece of bacon; she is hungry for his claws.

She swallows the bacon almost without chewing this time. She feels it slide roughly down her throat. Shrike laughs at the discomfort on her face. "Ah, my brother's lover, what beauty." He strokes her right breast through the dark fabric of her dress and her nipple rises. She remembers her dream.

"Will I end up like my mother?"

Shrike laughs, and Lia knows. She really wants to ask "when?"

He looks out the window and stops touching Lia. She is relieved to have her body back for a moment. True fear begins to seep into Lia's flesh, an old, unused sensation.

"Boogie needs me. Now." Shrike says and looks at her, touches her face, Lia feels the wrinkles disappear, feels supple flesh on her face for a moment, Shrike's touch doesn't last, not like Boogie's. His hand trails away again and her flesh begins to sag almost immediately. Boogie hasn't touched her face in years.

She feels new desire. She desires Shrike's body inside hers. She wants to take his sharp body inside her womb — to feel pain there would be better than to feel empty. She wants him inside her insides. Shrike in her intestines, nestled in her colon, up against her appendix. She leans forward and this time he doesn't dodge her, can't. He takes her mouth up against his, darts his thin tongue across her teeth. Her old face is rejuvenated while flesh touches flesh.

"So what did you see last night?" Shrike speaks into her ear with a breathy low voice. "What did you hear?" He asks the same questions that Boogie usually asks.

"Shhh." She whispers in his ear and he stops talking. But she continues. "It's quiet in town since I started hearing the dying babies."

Shrike pulls away. "Babies?" He looks pleased.

"In my dreams." Lia squints at him, not understanding. "I had forgotten fear."

"I'm right on time," Shrike says and grabs Lia by the throat and drags her to standing. She coughs into his face and laughs. Physical pain doesn't often faze her. Boogie is never gentle. And Shrike never was, either; he trained her well.

"When was Boogie here last?" Shrike demands of Lia and tightens his grip on her throat. "Did you tell him you were dreaming?"

• • •

Shrike had always beat Lia for anything she did wrong as a child. Countless times he strapped his leather belt across her back, raising welts and beating the fear out of her. He would then lick the blood from the edges of the wounds. She didn't yell when he struck, she didn't cry, ever, even when his saliva stung in the sores.

But, Boogie removed the salty lake of uncried tears from her soul the very first time he entered Lia. It had been an enormous relief and at that moment Lia let hate and Boogie eat her soul.

• • •

Lia comes around from her reverie to find herself being led upstairs by Shrike. He is muttering something about babies and about his half-brother, the Devil, the infertile ass, how he has to do all the dirty work. Lia feels young inside out.

Boogie had come to her on her nineteenth birthday. Boogie knocked on Lia's window just after sunset. Lia had been in bed reading. She jumped at the noise and turned to look at the window. A handsome face was peering in, framed by the reddening evening sky and early spooks; and Lia felt shy. She opened the window anyway and the boy leaned in and kissed her hand. She let him climb into the room and turn out the light. The handsome boy touched Lia gently, her scars, her nipples. Lia felt drugged and a rare smile played at her lips. The boy stripped her and caressed her new curves. He kissed her navel and kneeled at her feet as if he were worshipping her. She let him lead her to her own bed and lay her down. He undressed in almost a single motion, his clothes seemed to fall away. He lay on top of her, and she felt a moment of agony as he entered her, and then she smiled in bliss into his fiery green eyes as he moved over her. That was the only time Boogie had ever been gentle in eighty-one years. Shrike had never tried to enter her.

• • •

Now, Shrike leads her to her own bed and tenderly takes her nightgown off.

"My half-brother did not tell me you were dreaming."

"I haven't seen him since it started." Lia whispers.

He kneels at her feet and delicately circles her navel with his pointy tongue. Lia wonders at Shrike's attention. She has only known Shrike and Boogie; Boogie was her only lover. The pleasure of Shrike's new caresses spin Lia past thinking. He buries his face in the hair between her legs taking in strong breaths, smelling her. His hands trace the lines of her legs, reach up around her, across her backside. He pulls her into his face. He explores her with his tongue. The pleasure is unbearable and Lia's knees give out. She lets herself collapse and Shrike catches her, directing her falling weight towards the bed.

"Mother of God," Shrike whispers.

Lia is taken by the softness of Shrike's touch. He knows the way in. He knows he will father the next heiress, and the one after that.

He wonders at his half-brother's absence for a moment. Did he want to break the chain? Why hadn't he been checking on Lia?

Shrike leaves Lia on the bed dripping their fluids.

Lia waits for Boogie's arrival, let him sentence her. Now that the act is complete, it is too late. She sold herself to Boogie on the night of her nineteenth birthday. She's pretty sure she knows what comes next.

It is the morning of her century and she feels a new powerlessness, worse than the day she tried to leave the house, a renewed fear. Boogie sees everything. Is this a test? She hears a door slam downstairs and her heart races up into her throat, the blood pounds in her ears and she cannot quiet her body enough to hear where the steps are going. The doorway is full and Boogie stands looking at her prone body. Lia stays still, expectant, waiting for punishment.

Boogie smiles at Lia and leans over her on the bed. He reaches between her legs and takes a fingerful of what's there. He smears it across her cheek and then rubs it in with his thumb. Her wrinkles smooth away. She doesn't dare move, yet, almost doesn't breathe. Her pulse is light and fast. Boogie pushes her gently towards the middle of the bed and slides down next to her. She remains limp, uncomfortable with this ancient feeling of fear of the unknown. She wants the security of a leather strap across her conscience; but, Boogie just touches her gently again, like the first time.

"My half-brother is good for something." Boogie sighs and strokes Lia's tense, aching belly. "He knows how to wait his turn." Boogie takes her in his arms. Lia knows her time is now; there will be another baby girl, and Boogie wanted it this way. **T:S**

God Words

Paul Woodlin

I like being out in the words, among the giant, usually solid nouns. I'll climb into their canopy of implications, where their myriad meanings branch off, intertwining with limbs from other words. You can peel away their layered adjectives, a rough bark that protects us from controlling them too much. A few times I pulled off so many, really dug deep into their reality, that there was nothing left. They were all bark.

Verb watching is my favorite sport, seeing what they are by what they do. How fast or slow, how carefully. A verb is a repetitive idea. Good thing there are so many kinds or I would get bored. Eventually.

Sometimes a verb meets an adverb and an intricate dance begins. Adverbs are meaningless without verbs, or nearly so, but so many verbs already have the meaning of adverbs within them. This leaves no room in the verb's mating pouches, and instead of a conjoining and the creating of new meaning, the adverb just clings to the verb's back, weighing it down.

I grew up in the forest I will forever feel is the most natural, so as I describe my travels to other words you should remember everything I say is relative to what I've known before. One forest is filled with words that have prickly "leaves" defending them admirably; I've never been able to climb them without getting wounded. Other forests are old, with roots that dig down deep into the soil of our imagination. Some are so easy to climb that they practically beg to be learned.

Sometimes the winds have blown seeds every which way, and I'll find myself in strange places, with words that don't sound like they belong together as the breeze shifts their branches into each other. It can be hard to write formal poetry with such words, since the sounds themselves take so much untangling and dragging along the forest floor. Pretty soon every sonnet about life includes unfortunate associations like wife and strife.

A Church Father wondered, if God created the world with words, what did they sound like? There was no air. God doesn't have a mouth. There was no one to hear, except angels equally spiritual in material if not in infinity. He wondered if the Word was instantaneous, or if it echoes in continuous creation until the end of the Word.

I used to search for those words. God words, so to speak. I searched forests for ultimate meaning, I climbed words, I dug at their roots, I mined for fossils. Then I tried to tear away the bark of a word for God whenever I found one, and stripped them to nothing. The trees fall down, and I don't read the Church Father anymore.

I eventually decided if any such Word exists, it isn't a word as we use it. We represent things with words, but God Words create things. If there are gods, I wish they were more careful, or happier. Never mind the sticks and stones, their Words could hurt you. **T:S**

The White Swan
Sonya Taaffe

The pale splinters of bone, black broken as teeth; piano shards. Blood misted like rust, oil-slick, smeared on the skin where sweat diluted. A wreckage of lamplight. He brought his hand down on the shattered keys two, three more times: strengthless, no damage left to do, a gesture of completion rather than the compulsion of rage. Half the strings had broken already, or slackened when their frame gave way, a jangle of steel tendons curling and twanging senselessly; everything snapped, dented, battered, rent; made dumb. The sounds were heartbeat and hard breath, torn wood and the silent slam of blood. Pain white as a halo around every movement of hand, elbow, shoulder, even the fingers unstiffening from their crushed clench flared like candle flames: a hanged man's hand of glory. He thought, absurdly, *What's black and white and red all over?* and his breath tore, too spent for a laugh. When he took a step backward, a pair of white keys, uprooted, skeletal blanks, cracked underfoot. Fingerbones. Her fingers, ground and twisted beneath the single, lethal step he had never taken; swift and tensile, strong over the black and white puzzle of notes, delicate and dangerous as the undertow in the music she played. Sweat burned his sight, salt for a wound. He could not remember which of them he had meant to punish.

Split fingernails, flesh beaten back to the bone, crazes and cracks and at least two fingers in need of splinting: a mess of blood and bruised, swollen barriers against any playing in the close future, an impossible distance. Perhaps it no longer mattered. On the couch unraveling mossily among shelves and milk crates of scores and sheet music and discrepant novels, he hunched sideways over the black, grinding ache and felt tears strand themselves in his throat; his eyes left high and dry. Blood stuck his hair to his temples, a shade he had never tried. The fine, flyaway corona that her fingers combed through, laughing over its unseasonal changes, leaf-bronze, fallen maple, pale as cornsilk or husked grain, dark as stained wood the week before and who cared? *I love your music.* No one came to concerts for the color of his hair. Across the room, most of the piano stood out starkly: upright or scattered where his fists had hammered and the little owl-faced thing made of engine parts — still smelling of oil, half-found art; she kept it atop loose pages — had gouged, driving out something from inside him, coiled tighter than steel wire, stretched tauter. Some notes might still sound, their tuning deranged. Not all the keys lay on the floorboards, the vine-patterned rug. A ruinous piece of performance art. Dismembered, eviscerated; or only damaged irreparably. Fear tasted very cold; he swallowed the tears that were not in his eyes, slowly moved wrists, fingers, bit down on the pain that streaked bone-deep. If she came home now, he wondered what he would say. This bloodied, sweat-stuck, tear-starkened shambles of someone she loved, exhausted fury as tangible an aftershock in the room as sex, and would she ask him how the rehearsal had gone? Would he ask her? His mind stopped, as against a wall: he could not picture her face, his words, anything.

Her hands, he knew. The discipline; the deft, driving need that spun in her veins where he felt his blood shivering now. The chance fall of notes like cards or stars that had brought them together, a drift of Rossini accompaniment picked apart into twelve tones, improvisation half-heard through a practice room door and he felt something in his chest shift, tighten, come apart, before he put one hand up against the door and pushed it open to find her, face framed in the memory of that surreal, singular phrase. She ate lemons, kissed acid into his throat. At night, the first time, he did not know which one of them had been more afraid, hungrier, more gentle. Her smile was something practiced that fractured true when she laughed. But she wound her music between their hands, their mouths, hair-slender and piercing, stitching skin to skin, until even simple exercises felt like her name spelled out in half-tones; until sitting in the audience dark, an afternoon spent listening through kitchen walls and bedroom doors, was a hand on her chopped, pitch-colored hair; was touching the rise of her hip. Her bones, her heartstrings. When he played, he never looked for her face out beyond the lights; wherever she sat, her breath was at his back.

Under his hands, the folk tune he had been exploring — not a Britten piece, something off the radio that had caught in his head as she quietly watched him drive; a cold sea-brim, a bone-white swan, he had not gotten all the words before he dropped her off for rehearsal and went home, something of the song's bitter salt chill gathering where he breathed — had broken apart, a frozen nova. She would have made it something rare and strange, metamorphic, as he always wanted to hear. Perhaps there had been variations weaving in her head even then, nothing conscious, music in her marrow and a word of loss or love under the surface of her gaze that he avoided. *I love your music.* Words passed back and forth like kisses from their first, maybe second date, something true to keep from saying another, more perilous truth; an old joke, sometimes still murmured late at night or before a concert, whoever bowed and took their place that night. No less true now; and even as he extemporized, expanded, closed back to the simple, recursive melody, he wondered what the words might have moved in her. *But aye you give me your own true love...* The thought burned, acid and gall. The simple, intractable ease of her playing: the one thing he had ever loved that was hers and hers alone. *How the white swans swim.* He thought, *She would have played it better,* and he heard the dissonant smash of notes, felt the impact in the heel of his hand, before he recognized the movement.

The blood was clotting between his fingers when he pulled a chair over, gingerly shoved two concertos and a fantasia onto the floor; a flinch of fire when he touched the gapped keys and he repeated the gesture, no artistry in it but pain. For a metronome, his heart and the sounds of stopped tears. Carefully, he pressed one surviving key, again and again, until the note receded into noise. A sound, no more; he could not identify its metallic burr, resonant as an old clock striking, plangent and out of tune, could not locate it anywhere on the broken rack of what had been an instrument. Another senseless noise, another tremor of pain, and another, another, another. This bone-picked, hurting song of envy, love, murder: what else was left to play? Under his finger, a black key clattered to the floor; he bent to lift it and lights wheeled in his skull, a tympani roll of blood. Nothing he could ever have stayed away from, as imperative as the first furious blow, as infallible as her face raising to him under fluorescent light, tone-rows and Rossini still dissipating in the doorway. The storm door dropping shut, caught against a shoulder while hands shifted for house keys, a sliding click of tumblers and her quick, loping step, he heard: his face tightened and he did not know the expression. This piece, this melody stripped from the skeleton of whatever they had had between them, was his. This damage, this transformation. His hands.

I love your music. The bones played of themselves. **T:s**

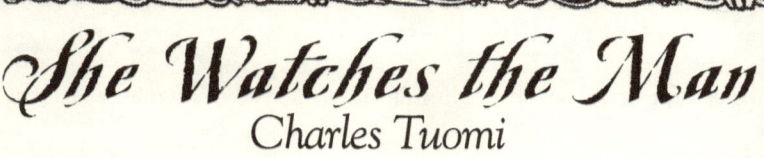

She Watches the Man
Charles Tuomi

*S*he watches the man.

And oh yeah, sugah, she talkin' 'bout
the MAN:

Walkin' (check that) *saunterin'*, as in:
The MAN:

Positively *saunterin'* down that mo-fuckin' hill, gold patches of late summer afternoon sunlight streamin' through bright green tree leaves, lightin' him up likes a fireworks display. *Saunterin'* with what could be perceived as a distinct air of *joviality* down that steep, cracked sidewalk on the other side of the street, got himself some eyesglasses and a tweed jacket and a baseball cap with white letters on black fabric that'd be too far away to read jes yet, sugah, if'n she could read at all.

Shee-it, she whispers, one and a half syllables through a mouth with jes them four nasty brown peanuts for teeth.

Shee-it, it's the MAN:

Half-grinnin', half-cocked, half-fallin' over, looks half out of his mind, but oh lawd ain't he all the way into hers.

Shee-it, she whispers. *Shee-it*, sugah, ain't it jes like
the man:

Saunterin' down Crew Hill, jes 'bout past that big ol' lilac in front of the clinic now, and she sees it: shee-it. He tilts his head a little bit, toward the pink purple blossoms.
The man:

Got himself some big mo-fuckin' nostrils, yo. They open up wide and
the man:
inhales, deep and slow. That half-smile turns into two thirds maybe of a grin.
He don' slow down, he gots business, yo, he don' stop, but
the man:
oh yeah, the man:
He smells the flowers.

• • •

She watches the flower shop.
Two doors in from the corner of the bottom of Crew Hill and Cooper, got a window
full of bright colors and vases done give her a headache to look at some days and a nice
old guy with big glasses that runs it. Sees him smilin' outside some days, sweepin' the
shee-itty-ass pavement and whistlin' show tunes and wavin' at cars. Some days she sees
him but not today, because today it's
the man:
Strollin' through the doors of
the shop:
jes 'bout four minutes 'fore the ambulance and the po-lice. And then it's
the man:
Leavin' jes when they get there, holdin' the door for the paramedics, tippin' that
cap like he was a
genteel-man in one of those ol' movies as they goes rushin' inside.
Got himself a bouquet of roses under one arm.
the man:
Still grinnin', heading right back towards her.

• • •

the lady:
who's yo, what a mess.
Crumpled up in dirty pain like her bags of trash on a wet park bench, stinkin' like
her cancers, sweet and sour, make your eyes water, yo, don' get too close.
Got bumps all over, got 'em inside and out, and hands like rubber gloves blown up
like balloons: swollen bad, with puffy thick little fingers done shrunk, and don't they
hurt like the hell where she's headed, which might be better, sugah, than the hell where
she is.

• • •

The park:
Is what they call the place, patch of dirt and a strip of see-ment on the side of Crew
Hill, got nineteen blades of grass and three posts (used to be a fence) and a broken kids'
swing and jes the one bench that ain't been smashed.
The park:
is where

the lady:
gonna die.

• • •

Because today it's
the man:
glidin' now, as in
the MAN:
effortlessly *gliidin'* up that hill, other side of the street now, yo, *her* side, maybe *her* turn, sugah. *Gliiidin'* and grinnin' and stickin' his big white nose in all them flowers he got and sniffin'.
the lady:
wipin' a tear from a red-yellow eye and watchin'
the man:
getting' closer, and
the shop:
where the old guy's done already gone. Got some woman cryin' outside on the sidewalk and the po-lice car's lights flashin' and the paramedics shakin' their heads and shruggin' like there was nothin' they could do.

• • •

the man:
stoppin' in front of
the bench:
where
the lady:
tries to sit up for
the man:
bends down, puts his mouth near her ear, smellin' like roses, less maybe it's the roses he's holdin'. Says one word to
the lady:
then
the man:
takes her hands in his hands and hands her the flowers and winks and glides away and
the lady:
thinks, check it out sugah I got roses and hands that don't hurt no more and a word from
the man:
who said *Soon.* т:ѕ

Revenge in the Funhouse
Ruth Nestvold

mbrosia is well aware that John-Boy is staring at her boobs whenever he thinks no one is looking. The little dweeb is just reaching *the awkward age* when a guy starts developing that life-long fixation on the movement in his pants and finally becomes a man. His Uncle Bill is staring at her too, in between attempts at getting a better look down Magda's blouse. Magda is John's mother. Her husband Lionel doesn't seem to have a clue about all the sexual tension in the autogiro. He just guides the flyer unerringly in the direction of Ocean City, intent on their weekend *odyssey* to the brand new funhouse, *Neuromancer,* a tall white marvel full of the latest in illusion, a maze of mirrors and machines and virtual reality.

Ambrosia *is,* not Ambrosia *was.* At the turn of the new millennium, the use of the present tense is a very common device to indicate that the author has literary aspirations for her work, a kind of in-your-face sign that you'd better take *this* author seriously, and an accepted literary convention. I need all the help I can get, even if it's from convention. In the hands of a skilled author (can I be? will I be?) literary conventions signal very quickly what kind of fiction a reader can expect, or provide a shortcut to establishing character, e.g. the pre-nubile blonde with the pouty lips.

Ambrosia bites her full lower lip and looks out the window of the autogiro, ignoring John-Boy's hand on the seat next to her bare thigh. He is so transparent, just like language is supposed to be according to the philosophy of realistic fiction. The reader should never be aware that he is reading, he should be swallowed whole by the fictional dream. The way Uncle Bill would like to be swallowed by Ambrosia's oh-so pouty lips.

But at least old William is a bit more subtle about his train of thought than fourteen-year-old John-Boy. Ambrosia has learned all about that train of thought in the last year. She has just reached the ripe age of fifteen and is very well developed for her age; she left *the age of innocence* behind her with her training bra. She knows what moves men, and she has precociously decided to use that knowledge. Her old lady didn't figure out the secret until she was over forty, and now she is too old to take advantage of it. Old and bitter.

That isn't going to happen to Ambrosia. She figures a woman is a fool not to use her real power, the curly matter between her legs and not the gray matter between her ears. Her mother always put her faith in gray matter. Now John's mom, Magda, there is a woman who knows where real power lies.

Magda is still a beautiful woman, although she too is old to Ambrosia's way of thinking. But unfortunately, "beautiful" is not a very effective adjective. When it comes right down to it, there isn't enough description in the foregoing paragraphs, period. The introduction of the main characters is progressing well enough, but the reader still has too few sensory details to anchor her in the story. Bleached blond hair, while a telling trait, (much better than dyed red), is hardly enough. Metaphors and similes are missing entirely. The other autogiros they pass gleam in the sun like. Magda's dark hair curls against the back of her neck like. And none of the senses has been invoked other than sight. Surely something smells.

Despite the open windows, the air in the autogiro is redolent with sweat, the sun warm on the skin of Ambrosia's bare arm where it is propped against the glass of the little flyer. She imagines she can distinguish the smell of the different occupants; Lionel's laced with some male cologne or aftershave, Uncle Bill's sharp and pungent, Magda's tangy, John-Boy's acrid with his nervousness and anticipation. It's obvious enough what he wants from this outing; he wants a repeat of that painful incident after one of their *nights at the circus* when she was drunk and he said he'd take care of her. Bent over the seat of the toilet, her bare knees cold on the floor tiles. He thinks the funhouse will give him the *chance* he needs, a dark corner, a *bleak house*, a girl who needs help, a fantasy fulfilled. He thinks she likes it, that she asked for it, but all she likes is his family's money and their autogiro and the way Magda has Lionel and Bill eating out of her hand.

She has very different plans for the funhouse than John-Boy, and we finally have our conflict. It is, however, rather late in the narrative to first introduce the conflict, which should be clear as early as possible to ensure that the reader will stay with the author until the end. We haven't even gotten to the funhouse yet! But in my own defense, I am doing my best to make it clear the reader can't expect a conventional story here — using the device of present tense, strewing the narrative with titles of great literary works, and interrupting the narrative flow with a steady stream of authorial comments. Still, by now most readers have probably thrown this thing across the room, totally fed up with a story which doesn't live up to the implied expectations of a work with the word "revenge" in the title. The story is breaking the implicit contract between author and reader, trying to drag her into things she has no interest in being dragged into. A little like Ambrosia after the circus.

But soon it will be her turn. John-Boy is all but panting, the little finger of his right hand sneaking across the back seat of the autogiro, trying to slip unnoticed beneath her thigh.

And I still haven't gotten them into the *Neuromancer*.

Ambrosia will solve that problem.

She has heard the new funhouse is white, but it is actually more of a cream color. Ivory. It doesn't look much like a funhouse either. It is an oblong tower with crazy windows at odd angles and stairs on the outside leading nowhere, or leading into painted stairs which go in another direction in an impossible way, phallic homage to M.C. Escher and the mind-bending properties of surrealism, *uncharted territory*. Of course, it is unlikely a fifteen-year-old blond bombshell would describe the funhouse in quite this way: this is obviously another case of authorial intrusion. Mid-twentieth century fiction rediscovered the technique of the selfconscious narrative, which draws attention to its own fictional nature. The eighteenth century novelists Henry Fielding and Laurence Stern were masters of this, but the fad went out when realism came in. *Tom Jones* is now an aging pop singer. (I will not, however, go into the realism of this particular phenomenon.)

The funhouse is not realistic. It apes reality and distorts it, picking it up and spitting it out in a totally different shape than it was before. The people leaving the tower look slightly *dazed and confused*.

"Wow," says Uncle Bill, but his voice lacks conviction.

Lionel takes off his glasses and rubs them on his Matchbox 20 T-shirt, no longer trusting the corrective powers of concave lenses.

"I think I would rather go *to the lighthouse*," Magda says. She is staring at the ivory tower of the funhouse, the flirtatious laughter gone from her eyes.

Uncle Bill nudges her playfully with his elbow. "And I'd rather go *under the boardwalk*." Nudge, nudge, wink, wink.

Okay, so maybe older men aren't always more subtle.

And Lionel is still cleaning his glasses.

Ambrosia turns to John-Boy and giggles self-consciously. "It looks like we're on our own."

Little Johnnie swallows. Gone is the bad guy of her dreams, and in his place stands a nervous adolescent, his face turning red and sweat beading his forehead.

But that is part of his power, part of the reason she has to have revenge. He controls the images, and his interpretations hold sway. Right now, he is imagining getting her exactly where he wants her, on her knees in a dark corner. Himself he sees as a young version of his uncle, dark-haired and dark-eyed, a future lady's man. But he's also the kid who buys her sodas in the afternoon and somehow manages to get her beers in the evening and makes her feel too sorry for him with his red face and sweaty hands to be able to tell on him.

Still, she's sick of the way *she* is always the one who has to nod and smile and pretend, despite her new-found power.

No more.

She takes his hand and laughs gaily, pulling him across the sand to the surrealist monstrosity of the funhouse.

You see, we are finally getting them into the funhouse, and the momentum has been enough to keep the narrative going for an unconscionably long time. I am close to violating my contract with the rest of my readers, the ones who *don't* want a plot. Although I have it on very good authority (a multiple Hugo and Nebula winner, no less) that there is no such thing as a plotless story. Plotless is synonymous with "sucky" and "unsold." (Ibid.) Unfortunately, I have it on yet another authority that plot is dead, or if not dead, at least unforgivably naïve.

Can you blame me for being a bit schizophrenic?

By this time, Ambrosia has managed to lose her nemesis long enough at the virtual reality terminals to steal a kiss and a key from the janitor. She finds John-Boy glassy-eyed with illusion and is only able to drag him away with the promise of the tumbling-barrel, upstairs with the other old-fashioned attractions that don't rely on advanced technology for disorientation and confusion.

She allows her skirt to fall up around her waist often enough to leave him glassy-eyed in a different way, so that she can easily lead him up yet another flight of stairs into the hall of mirrors.

The hall of mirrors takes up a whole floor of the funhouse, and, according to the *Guinness Book of World Records*, is the single largest collection of mirrors in the world. Mirrors to make you fat, mirrors to make you thin, mirrors to make you tall, mirrors to make you short, mirrors to make you old, young, ugly, beautiful. Ambrosia isn't too sure about the lack of technology.

"Wow, Ambi, look at this!" John cries, standing in front of a mirror that makes him into a God.

"Yeah, John, that's really cool." Little Lord John-Boy, frolicking among the mirrors. This would be easier than she expected.

Now, seeing as Ambrosia is not an Author, but only a *Lolita*, a little blond bimbo, she cannot play God. Playing God is reserved for omniscient, authorial narrators, not limited thirds. I, however, *can* play God. I am authorial, I am omniscient, I am Woman, I am roaring, and I am screwing up the point-of-view royally. Maybe it's time I got back to limited.

When Ambrosia stands in front of the mirror, it only reflects back a *baywatch* babe. BUT — she has the key. And she has her nemesis where she wants him.

She slips between reflecting plates of glass while Johnnie cavorts in front of the mirrors, wallowing in the joys of distorted solipsism, making noises at his many reflections similar to those he once made over her heaving back.

It is more difficult than she expects to find the door again, but finally she's out of the hall of mirrors. She leans against the wall of the stairwell and heaves a sigh of relief.

Now she can lock the little bastard in, give him a scare. That will teach him. She digs in the pocket of her skirt.

The key is gone.

Behind her, she hears the click of a door locking.

Ambrosia blinks. It can only be Johnnie himself. She didn't see anyone else in the hall of mirrors just now. She wanted to lock him in with them, teach him a lesson, but he thinks they're cool, he *wants* to be alone with them.

He wants to be alone with them more than he wants to be alone with her.

She shakes her head, still not quite sure what happened there. She must have lost the key in the tumbling-barrel while she was showing off her tanga. Too bad. Obviously, the revenge she plotted wasn't any good anyway. Must be because she isn't an Author, just a *Lolita*.

Ambrosia doesn't feel like going through the different levels of illusion in the funhouse anymore, so she heads for the elevator, which takes her past the tumbling-barrel and the virtual reality terminals and the singing fat lady and the maze and the *mission to Mars* and the journey *across realtime* and *the jungle*. She leaves John to his mirrors, a boy who will never grow up because the adolescent initiation story died in the funhouse over half-a-century ago.

The sunlight reflecting on the sandy beach of Ocean City hurts her eyes after the dark and the artificial light in the funhouse. She strolls down the boardwalk leading away from the building. *All's well that ends well.* The view is a hell of a lot better out here where there are no mirrors to distract you, like at the top of that silly ivory tower. Not that Ambrosia has anything against mirrors, no, not at all. But the guys on the beach in their skin-tight Speedos are kind of cute too. John-Boy wears boxer shorts.

Ha! I'm achieving resolution! And not only that, I have made John looked ridiculous, carried out my *revenge in the funhouse*, gotten over my *anxiety of influence*, locked postmodernism away with its mirrors, and freed myself from plotless maniacs. The *metamorphosis* complete, I can now celebrate *the awakening* and allow my point-of-view character a little fun — including a couple of *baywatch* studs.

Ambrosia straightens her shoulders, pulls the rubber band out of her bleached-blond hair, and places the ball of one perfect foot in the hot sand. **TIS**

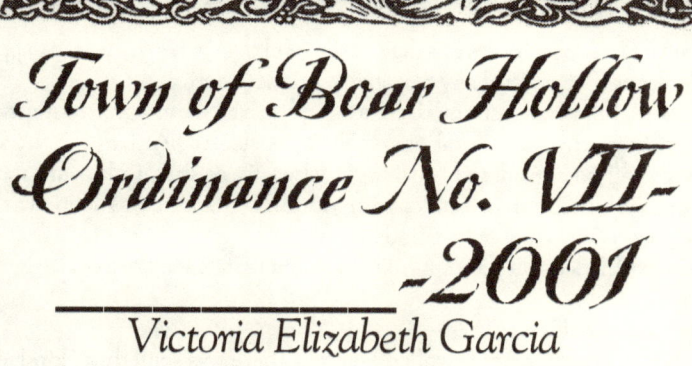

Town of Boar Hollow Ordinance No. VII- -2001

Victoria Elizabeth Garcia

TOWN OF BOAR HOLLOW
ORDINANCE NO. VII-_____-2001

AN ORDINANCE TO ABATE THE DISTURBANCES CAUSED BY
DOGS RUNNING AT LARGE

BE IT ORDAINED BY THE TRUSTEES OF THE TOWNSHIP OF BOAR
HOLLOW:

Section 1: Authorization
This law is enacted pursuant to OAS 3-19-23.1(d), which authorizes Municipalities
of this State to enact Ordinances for the preservation of the health and wellbeing of
the citizenry.

Section 2: Purpose
Whereas the citizens of the Township of Boar Hollow have weathered disturbances of
both mind and health caused by the presence of unmanaged dogs within the Township
limits, the Township hereby enacts this Ordinance to provide for the protection and
wellbeing of its citizens.

Section 3: Dogs Running At Large
(A) It shall be illegal for any animal which may reasonably be construed as a dog, to

run at large. A dog shall be considered to be "At Large" when his actions, appearance, or demeanor are beyond any reasonable human control.

(B) Any dog who, when restrained, creates a disturbance through barking, menacing behavior, or other manifestations, shall be considered "At Large."

(C) A dog shall be considered "At Large" when he or she displays an uncommon fascination with human death or with Mortal Human Vice, as defined in Title VI, Section 7-9-36(A)(2) of this Code.

(D) No dog which does not possess a Culpable Mental State shall be found to be At Large.

Section 4: Erica Miller

(A) She had a large nose and swollen feet, but there was something kind about her eyes.
    (1) If you stared at her long enough, you'd find that the kindness leached from her eyes into the rest of her face, making the crags and bumps in it beautiful.
    (2) But if you looked away even just for a second, she'd turn ugly again.

(B) She gave a dog a reason to howl.

Section 5: Miscellaneous Prohibited Dogs

The following Dogs shall henceforth be illegal:

(A) The Gray Dog with the white eyes who sits on the roof of the School.

(B) The Dachshunds from the Cemetery.

(C) The Litter of Wire-Haired Pups with the Extra Legs.

(D) The ones with Wings. The ones with Metal Teeth. The ones that eat marrow with fire and dirt.

(E) Any Dog whose existence was not known, and whose Like has not been seen, before the death of Erica Miller on the Fourth of July, 1999.

(F) The Red One.

Section 6: Warnings Given

(A) Each Dog whose conduct renders him At Large, or whose existence is otherwise Illegal shall be notified of his Illegal status and required to report for trial. Trial shall be held within thirty days.

(B) Notice of each Illegal Dog's status shall be posted in three public places throughout the Township.

Section 7: The Only One

(A) Some dogs wait for decades to find the Right One.

(B) She laughed when he rubbed his muzzle against her neck.

(C) The Red One's ears were torn. His coat was full of maggots that burrowed into him, whispering.

(D) He'd been known to lick the salt and blood from women's fingers before.

(E) When he licked her hands, he could taste the thoughts in her head. He could taste the breath in her lungs. He could smell her heart as it thrashed inside her.

Section 8: Things that Die
(A) Legality and Death:
    (1) A Legal Dog may carry a leg in its mouth.
    (2) A Legal Dog may drag a carcass through a window.
    (3) A Legal Dog may wag its tail and hope for a piece of hide from a slaughtered calf.
(B) Illegality and Death
    (1) He covered the gashes with his paws. He tried to pack the wounds with earth. She wouldn't stop screaming.
    (2) When he knew that it wouldn't work, he lay down with his head on her chest and licked the sweat from her lips and chin.
        (a) A Legal dog would never do that. A Legal dog wouldn't spit up when the blood died.

Section 9: Procedure
(A) All Illegal Dogs will be brought before the Court and required to provide an explanation.
(B) All Illegal Dogs have the right to an attorney.
(C) After providing an explanation, all Illegal Dogs will be promptly sentenced.
(D) The Red One is not entitled to an attorney.

Section 10: Protections
(A) They swarm through the Township because they want pieces of her. They want bites of flesh, swallows of marrow, chunks of bone. They want streamers of gut to run through the streets with.
(B) The Red One lies guarding the front porch of her house. He growls at the shadow dogs, the dogs that swim in the air, the dogs that flash and prance and snap. He hasn't eaten for days. The only thing that nourishes him is the film of fat on his muzzle.
    (1) He deserves to starve.

Section 11: Penalties
(A) All Illegal Dogs shall be burned, skewered, drawn, quartered, boiled, pressed, and skinned.
(B) All Illegal Dogs shall be shot, hung, shredded, dismembered, and drowned.
(C) All Illegal Dogs shall have iron bars shoved through their heads.

Section 12: Emergency Preparedness
The Trustees must be prepared to defend the Corpse of Erica Miller against the predations of the Illegal Dogs. The Trustees must be prepared to take up arms. They must be

prepared to send their sons, daughters, wives, and husbands to their death in order to defend the Corpse of Erica Miller. The Trustees must be prepared to incinerate everything, except for the home of Erica Miller, which must stand, untouched, throughout eternity. The Trustees shall be, and are, glad to die in its defense. The Town Clerk and the Mayor are glad to die. The Red One is glad to die. The only thing in the Township that is worthy of life is the Corpse of Erica Miller.

Section 14: Repealer and Savings Clause

(A) Any provision of any section of any previously-enacted portion of the Boar Hollow Township Municipal Code, or of any previously enacted Ordinance, which is found to be in conflict with this Ordinance is hereby repealed.

(B) No law of the State of Oregon, the United States, or any other tangible or incohate sovereign shall be found to conflict with the provisions of this ordinance.

(C) The provisions of this Ordinance are fully severable.

(D) Her life is gone. He'll save her death. He'll trot along with her death in his mouth and maybe she'll stroke his head.

INTRODUCED, read and ordered published this ___ day of _____, 20__, and a public hearing fixed thereon for _____, 20__.

PASSED, adopted, signed and approved after public hearing this _____ day of _____, 20____.

TOWNSHIP OF BOAR HOLLOW

BY:_____
Mayor

ATTEST:

_____
Town Clerk

ATTEST:

_____
Forever

ATTEST:

_____
And never again. ᴛɪs

Lost

Jeff VanderMeer

"*A*re you lost?" it says to me in its salt-and-pepper gravelly moan of a voice and for a long moment I can't answer. I'm thinking of how I got here and what it might mean and how to frame an answer and wondering why the answer that came to mind immediately seems caught in my throat like a physical kind of fear, and that line of thought leads to this: remembering the line of color that brought me here: the spray of emerald-velvet-burgundy-chocolate mushrooms suddenly appearing on the old stone wall where yesterday there had been nothing, and me on my way to the university to teach yet another dead-end night class, dusk coming on, but somehow the spray, splay of mushrooms spared that lack of light; something about the way the runnels and patches of exposed understone contrasted with the otherwise gray solidity that brought me out of my thoughts of debt and a problem student named Jenna, who had become my problem, really, and I just

stopped.

right there.

and stared at the tracery of mushrooms, the way they formed such a uniform swoop across that pitted stone, and something about them, something about that glimmer, reminded me of my dead wife and of Jenna — the green was the same as my wife's eyes and that of Jenna's earrings, and I remembered the first time I noticed Jenna's earrings, and how it brought a deep, soundless sob rising out of my chest, my lungs, and I stood there, in front of the whole class, bent over, as if struck by something large and invisible, and how ever since I cannot tell if my fascination with her has to do with that color and my need for companionship or some essential trait in her, and how ironic, how sad, that she misunderstood my reaction and began wearing the earrings every day, until that physical pain inhabiting my body became a dullness, like the ache in an overused muscle, which I hated even as I found myself falling for Jenna…

and all of the time.

the whole time.

The light was fading except across the wall, and people in overcoats were walking past in the clear chill, under the embering streetlamps, and I could smell something other than the dankness of the wall as I traced its roughness with my fingers. It must have been a woman's passing perfume, but for a moment I smelled my wife and the emerald color of the mushrooms, the memory of her beneath me, the smell and feel of her—all of this was the same thing, and when I started walking again, I didn't go straight. I didn't head for the ivy-strewn facades of the campus buildings. Instead, I turned

I turned and turned and turned.

turned as if turning meant wrenching my life from a stable orbit.

To the right I turned to follow the scatterings of mushrooms, and I don't know why, if I was just curious or if I'd already been captured in some way, because it wasn't like me. My dad had always said, before he passed from cancer in a very orderly way, that "you have to make a plan and keep to it." He said it to me, my mother, and my estranged sister, and he meant it. Routine was a religion for him, and we made it ours. Set meals. Set appointments. Set activities. I remember, when I turned eighteen, planning my rebellion, figuring out what I was going to do first and second and last, so I could savor my rebellion even as I… planned it. Less satisfying in the execution, the sex quick and lonely and not with someone I loved, the beer and pot putting me to sleep too quickly, waking to a cat licking my face, out cold on someone's sour-smelling lawn.

But I turned the corner, followed the mushroom trail, which moved up and down the wall like a wave, now mirrored on the wall that had sprung up opposite it — and ahead the ache of a dull red sunset, which bathed the mushrooms in a crimson glow, and,

suddenly, it wasn't that night

that place,

but a two-lane road the year before, the lights of our car projecting through the murk as we drove down a corridor of night. She was driving, and had the pursed lip look of concentration that I loved about her, and which I never told her I loved because I was afraid that if I told her, the expression would become different in some essential way, and I never wanted that to happen — never wanted her to be a different person, either, when we made love, staring at her face and seeing that same look of concentration, of being fully engaged.

wanted no self-consciousness from her.

wanted her lilting laugh to remain spontaneous.

wanted her.

I wanted her to always preface her questions to me with "Let me ask you a question."

But a look of concentration doesn't mean concentration, and when I said later, in response to the ever-present question, until I had exhausted the gauntlet of friends, family, strangers who didn't know, the ordinary words "car crash," I couldn't help but associate that look with her death, and thus her death with our sex and our conversations and our holidays, and all I really wanted was a way to break that linkage, in almost the same way I wanted the trail of mushrooms to come to an end, because, honestly, where could they possibly lead that would be good for me? Ordinary thoughts, the thoughts we all have: that I was already late for work; that Jenna would miss me or she wouldn't; that this would be my fifth absence this semester and how many did there have to be before they let me go.

My legs didn't seem to have questions, though — they carried me forward. I followed the mushrooms because of the sparkle in Jenna's earrings, the gorgeous color of my wife's eyes. I followed the mushrooms because I can't say my wife's name. If I say her name, if I write her name, I will lose it — the name and my self-control. When I hear her name said, that is enough to conjure up the trail of evidence, the linkage. Unbearable.

The red of the sunset had become as green as…

A few people dressed in the outlandish garb I'd become accustomed to on campus pushed past me, and ahead, partially obscured by the lack of light, the spires of an old church or series of churches. Crennelations. A darkness that came from age, inhabiting the corners of the spires. A few circling birds or bats. It reminded me of the vacation my wife and I took to Eastern Europe one year, which made all that was ancient about my university employers look petty and cheap and just-yesterday. She fell asleep in the train from Berlin to Prague. I saw her face, framed by the reflection of the landscape rushing past the window, without lines or care, saw how her arms lay at her sides. She felt secure. She felt safe, I could tell.

Spires, though. I couldn't remember spires anywhere off-campus. I couldn't remember churches. Had I somehow ended up back on campus? It's true I had certain routines that meant I hadn't explored the city as I might have, and my wife to distract me, and then my grief.

Two youths ran by holding flags with symbols on them that I'd never seen before. I saw a man wearing a goat costume. I saw a woman with no legs "walking" on stilts. Fraternities and fraternity jokes came to mind, although there was something too solemn and formal about them. I had lost the thread

of the mushrooms.

no longer followed them.

just walked forward.

randomly.

Bathed in the green light of my wife's death. I turned as if to head back, except where I had come from no longer existed. It was as gone as the swathes of darkness my wife and I left behind us in our little car, headed home from a colleague's party, on the two-lane road at three in the morning.

More people crowded out onto the streets and I came under the weird light of gargoyled lampposts and buildings crowded and hunched in shadow to all sides, cut through by the narrowest of alleys. A festival of some kind, and I was in it or out of it or outside of it but caught up in it and the people kept pouring out of nowhere in their strange clothes and their strange accents and the strange look in their eyes and so I laughed with them and clapped my hands when they clapped their hands, and when the parade came by with animals foreign and fey, when the jugglers and the fire-eaters and the retired soldiers from distant wars, wearing uniforms I'd never seen before, when all of this converged, I tried not to think about it, tried not even to smell the stench of beer in the drains, the stench of vomit, of piss, tried to misread the mischief and malice in the eyes of those whose gaze I met. I realized this might be

a break in the linkage.

a severing of routine.

a way out.

Had I missed how random my world had become since my wife had died? Had my grief obliterated the real world for me?

● ● ●

And so all of these thoughts overwhelmed me when I woke from my hiding place in an alley the next morning, having slept on garbage and filth, to find it — wearing a large gray felt hat, small as a child but with the wizened features of something already dead — staring down at me. It had long claws that dragged down below the sleeves of its robes. I could not look it in the face. It swayed back and forth as if in trance, and it said to me, as I looked up at it with a disbelieving smile on my face, "Are you lost?"

And.

I thought about how I had gotten to this point.

I thought about Jenna and I thought about my wife and I realized I didn't love Jenna, that I didn't even really like Jenna, and with that thought came a kind of release and I was back on the two-lane road in the darkness and this time I welcomed it, brought it to me, soaked up those last few miles before she lost control of the car and swerved into the path of oncoming headlights connected to god-knows-what kind of vehicle, the same look of concentration on her face mixed with anger, because I was looking at her not at the road, arguing with her about some stupid point of routine that didn't make any sense to anyone but my father, and I wonder if she saw, in those last moments, some kind of entry to this place, and if she saw something that made her swerve, and it wasn't my fault at all, I wasn't the distraction that killed her.

"Are you lost?" it says to me and I'm more frightened than I've ever been before, even when my wife died in front of me, and I say, "No. I'm not lost. I belong here."

And I do. **T:S**

Fancy Bread

Gregory Feeley

*T*he ogre lifts his rockslide face and sniffs, cavernous nostrils distending. With a howl of rage — Jack can whiff his breath from where he hides — he stamps the tree-wide floorboards and cries out in a bowel-solving roar:

> Fee, fye, fo, fum!
> I smell the Blod of an Englysshman!
> Be he quicke or be he dede,
> I'll grinde his Bones to make my Brede!

Behind the oven grate, Jack feels his shanks quiver as though struck free from his spine. Wolves came down once from the hills and snatched a village child, and crows pluck corpses on the gibbet; but never did Jack imagine that his end might be another's maw. It is a terror beyond reckoning: his sweet flesh guttled like dough.

The ogre's goodwife assures him that what he smells is simply the remains of the boy he ate yesterday. Jack squitters in terror but the ogre seems mollified, for he sits down to be served a tremendous meal. The broth he slurps reeks of a mutton unknown to Jack's nose, and his stomach clenks at his mouth's watering. The ogre calls for a loaf, and when he sops then cracks loudly, Jack knows what he is crunching.

The din allows Jack to shift his cramped feet, stirring wisps of ankle-high ash which conceals hard lumps that bump his toes like riverstones. At last he sinks aching to his hams, and in the humdrum of the ogre's guzzling — even terror sates with surfeit — he nudges one of the lumps and discovers it an unrelieved crust. Jack brushes away bits of ash with wonder: the ogre, strong enough to disjoint him like a hen, owns no leaven.

Barrels of ale sluice the ogre's gullet as Jack squats in a plague pit of bones and ash. He cradles a rock of grain, pitiful weapon, and wonders at its coarseness. A memory stirs from childhood, the voice of traveling player declaiming on market day:

> *Tell me, where is fancy bread,*
> *Or in the heart, or in the head?*

Hungry with no market-day bun, Jack had yearned for fancy bread, sticky with sugar and finer than cake, something he had tasted one on Whitsunday. Later he wondered whether the player's question meant that fancy bread might exist only in the head, never to be tasted in the stomach. Bread with dough smooth as milk, bread so soft the toothless could eat it without sopping first. Had such yearnings led him in time to the hedge of the ogre's castle?

Replete and belching, the ogre nods at table like a swaying oak, knocks his spoon to the floor, and soon is snoring deeply. Fearful beyond measure — the goodwife does not come to aid him — Jack slowly pushes open the grate and creeps from the oven's belly, leaving ashy footprints even an ogre could follow.

It seems greatly daring that in his flight Jack could pause to pick up the spoon, but even in his terror he realizes that no man can be eaten twice. It is as long as his arm and heavier than any Jack has held, so he clutches it the harder and sneaks past, breaking into a run at the door.

Later he would try to recall whether he had heard a roar as he burst into sunlight. He had not looked back, and ran half a mile before slowing. The spoon is crusted with porridge, and when Jack finishes gasping he sniffs, then tastes it. The oats are merely greasy, but the tip of his tongue thrills at the metal's touch. It is silver, and he later sells it for six shillings. A shard of crust lodged in his pocket he discards with a shudder.

He never again tried to rob an ogre's fastness, a lesson learned if not remembered. (Once he saw a widow lay her dough on a bed of coals then sprinkle it with hot ashes, and shivered with sourceless dread.) Curled under a pew that night, cold and still hungry, Jack worries the experience for what else he can take. The day is already falling from memory like a cinder from burnt fingers, but as Jack nestles into the rug of sleep a shard presses hard against him, sharp so he feels every word: Bread made with men's bones never rise.

•••

Starvelings bedded under hedges never rise, either, but rather turn coldly stiff, in glorious reversal of the Devil's fell offer to change stones into loaves. Jack feels hardened to petrifaction, but his limbs yield, if complainingly, as he crawls forth, brushing crumbs of dirt from his coat, to blink at the morning's pale glare. Gazing across the fields in the breath-steaming chill, he recognizes barley and, farther on, what looks to be rye, but nothing that nods like wheat-stalks. Nor pasturage for miles now: it's crusts and tubers Jack has to look forward to, assuming he is not offered a hail of rocks.

The rutted path is muddy, but Jack is glad enough to see no lace of frost upon the standing water. Frozen roads traverse better and stink less, but it's a thin coat Jack wears this early March day, a hungry season with the winter stores dwindling and naught but peason planted. The wheel ruts are not deep, so the land is not yet too soft for fellers' carts; but Jack can see that felling time is over early here. The woods, like a sexton's hair, have receded steadily over the years, and the open fields show few stands of any size.

The sparsely hedged fields also offer few means of concealment, and Jack walks bent and brisk when a rise threatens to bring him within sight of harrowers, who will soon be out. He knows enough not to fear pursuit — no rustic will leave his work to accost a sturdy wayfarer a field away — but word travels fast even in villages, and he does not want suspicion running before him.

But no one is abroad at this least pleasant hour, too early for laborers and too late for the rogues who walk the roads at night. Other travelers — the tag-and-rag army of vagabonds and abandoned women who fill the highways — will be out soon, and Jack does not care to be numbered among them. If he has not a horse and a fine plumed hat, he must distinguish himself otherwise.

The first cottage he sees is not promising; but the men are out by now, so disappointment is not likely to prove calamitous. Jack cannot suppress a quaver of fear at approaching a strange door, but is reassured by the knowledge that most peasants (with dangerous exceptions) are stupid as dirt. Ignorant of the ways of cozenage, they substitute a brute suspicion of all strangers: which, being surmounted, could leave them defenseless as hatchlings.

Jack sees no chickens in the yard, but no dogs neither. He fingers his beard for crumbs, then spits three times on his right hand. The effort produces a loud rumble in his stomach. Emboldened by such perceptible evidence of want, he knocks upon the door — not confidently, as serves some circumstances, but weakly as he thinks will be heard.

He is bent to one side as the door is opened and a servant girl looks out. "Ah, mistress, a cup of water in Christ's name. I am set upon and robbed of my wares, and beaten half to death besides."

He steps back at this point, rather than forward as the servant fears, and staggers with a soft groan. The servant gasps — he is listening even as he grimaces — and before she can speak he brings up his hand and feels tenderly the back of his head. The pig's blood (from yesterday's unsuccessful venture) has dried in his hair, but enough comes away to redden his wet fingers and gives a half-clotted appearance.

"Jesu!" the girl exclaims. "Does it hurt?"

"More now than last night, though it scarce seems possible." Jack looks at her ruefully. "I hid my face in my hands, but they kicked my ribs till I feared they be stove in. And my wares—" Here he sighs as if at the cruellest stroke of all. "My lace and pins and buttons, which I have three times sold thy lady in the spring, are stolen me."

"The goodwife is not in," says the witless creature. At this Jack lowers himself to the ground, as though his legs were failing him, and cries out briefly as one ham touches the packed earth.

"My teeth are not broke," he says, touching them, "but I am sore dry. Is there water here cleaner than the ditch's where I lay?"

The bird rushes for a ladle, and Jack looks up to peer through the door. It is a meaner cottage than will yield much. Servants in London eat better than freeholders here, who have a servant only because the tide of workless women and men spill into any house open to them. Jack guesses that the goodwife has lain in yearly, and is worn enough to need a drudge with the surviving brats, one who can moreover bend her back at harvest and spend winter weaving hemp or flax. A wolf gauging the gauntness of the deer, Jack judges this freeholder not far from becoming a landless laborer himself.

As if in confirmation, he hears a babe's squall. Any mother still alive to give suck will be nearby, and Jack decides to work fast. He is rising as though painfully when the girl returns, dipper in one hand, a crust in the other. "Will you report this to the Justice?" she asks him.

"Lord, no, girl!" he cries in feigned alarm. "The village justice likes not wanderers, and is like to demand I prove no rogue myself. And how could I do that, with my wares gone?"

The girl crinkles her face in confusion, and Jack knows he is home. He drinks avidly (good water is scarce on the highways, and this is at least unclouded) and quickly examines the bread, as a merchant might eye a bolt of cloth. It is brown as her muddied hem, and smells to be rude maslin indeed, containing scant wheat and even some barley with the rye. Jack's stomach clamors loudly and he eats, tasting barley in the hard and ill-risen bread, which will rest heavy in the stomach without filling it.

He thanks the girl and returns the dipper (it is of no value anyway) before commencing his cast. "Good woman, where shall I go now?" he asks earnestly. "I have no goods, nor means to return to London Town" — the name never fails in its effect — "so must offer my hands and strong back to earn my bread. Tell me where an honest man should go to find work."

The cony looks ready to cry. "There is no place, alas," she says. "Come you from a parish where work awaits every man willing? What a wonder if so!"

Looking suitably stricken, Jack protests his readiness to work and offers to perform any chore, however onerous, this freehold wants done. He straightens his back with scarce a wince to demonstrate resolve, and senses he is on the verge of being asked within — it is all he needs — when the sound of voices in back snaps the girl's head around as if on a string. Jack's labours are undone in an instant, a card-castle struck by wind, for the mistress of the house comes around, swollen-bellied, suspicious, and blanched of charity, and Jack is dealt with briskly. She does not recall past dealings with the pedlar, has no work to give him, and directs the injured man to take his knocks to his own parish, whither the Justice will speed him if he thinks to dally. And so Jack is sent back along the road, with no solace but the crust and his memory of the girl's hurt eyes, bereft as though bidding him to return and devour her.

•••

No beer, scant bread, and uncertain fortunes ahead. Jack does not know the name of the township he is near, and would not betray ignorance by asking. It is not however a fortunate one, for the next bread he eats (a day later) tastes of vetches, what market-town folk call "horse-bread" who never have to eat it themselves. Cottagers are running low on corn, which a cold winter burns like wood: it will be gaunt weeks before the spring barley is up. Jack keeps an eye out for a servant-girl from a richer household than the cottagers', but doors remain closed to him.

A village where you are not known is like a cow that has not yet been milked. Jack moves carefully through the parish, alert both to danger and opportunity. One morning he steals a chicken, which he plucks, roasts, and eats entire before he hears the halloo. On another he helps a goodwife whose husband has broken his leg: he hauls sacks of grain by cart to the miller, but gets nothing for it but dinner, for the woman watches closely all the while.

He stands agape at the mill, which growls and creaks like a giant's wagon, and returns the suspicious looks of the miller and his son, who know everyone living in the village. The goodwife's grain — it is barley, with not a peck of wheat — disappears into the grinding maw, and Jack feels a nameless dread that moves him to stand in the doorway. The goody attempts to oversee all stages of the operation, and quarrels fiercely over the division afterwards.

"He hath a magic thumb," she complains to Jack as he pulls the cart — now, from the millstream, mostly uphill — back to her farm. And Jack thrills to think of the ways a miller might divert more than his rightful sixth part of the grain. He wishes to know more, but is fed and dismissed directly they return.

The spring brings rains, and too little sun otherwise. Apprehensions of a poor harvest settle like an ache into the bones, and fear of the dearth grips all. Jack catches an ague and coughs for weeks, but the lengthening days save him. With the haymaking there is work for all, and Jack labours like any vagabond for his bread and ale. One tumble behind a hedge with a doxy whose man had been arrested, one sheaf of ballads taken from a vagrant who lay sleeping, and it is hard sweat for the rest of his gettings. Jack enjoys selling ballads, which are light for their value and allow him to deal with better customers than farm wives; but they are hard to procure save in London, where he cannot now go.

To avoid charges of vagrancy, he long claimed to be carrying a letter to a nobleman in another county, but a Justice of the Peace once read it, found its date long past, and destroyed it. Lately he has employed, with more success (though he hates using it), a letter attesting that he had been whipped as a vagrant and was being sent back to his parish. But now he swims safely in the great school of available laborers, their numbers swelled (he learns by always listening) not only by vagrants but also former husbandmen, forced off their land by falling prices and poor harvests. The engrossment of holdings is under way in the lands of corn, as it hitherto had been in the lands of sheep.

Jack hawks the ballads between the mill and the inn, speaking smoothly and pretending at times to sing from one. He catches the interest of a yeoman's wife, who fixes him with a saucy eye (or so he takes it) and asks him what the songs concern.

"Marry, here is a song of a new way to make bread," he says smiling.

"A new way? And what might that be?"

"Why Madame, they employ *up and down husbandry*," he replies with a leer.

The woman barks a laugh and pays tuppence for two. Boldly he asks how bread is made in her master's household, and she directs him to follow her servant. He gets a half-loaf of cheat bread — his first taste of wheat this year — handed him from the back door.

Standing in the chill air, with the hens keeping their distance and ducks jeering from the safety of their pond, the bread's soft texture and sweet taste awakens in him a rage never again to eat worse. No longer should Jack bend his back for brown bread, heavy with ill-ground pease and beans. If cozenage proves no perch, he shall not slip down but claw up.

Next morning he assaults a yeoman leaving the inn, gets three shillings but must hide in the woods for days, where rains fall incessantly and the boughs wave overhead as though bearing his swinging form. He crosses water, is attacked by dogs, travels roads by night and is set upon and beaten unconscious. Discovered by a constable searching for the robbers of a merchant party, he finds himself giving evidence with them before a Justice. Imitating the merchants' accents and manner, he portrays himself as a journeyman bearing papers for his master, all now lost save for a scrap of ballad he had bought at a crossroad. He produces the scrap and is luckily not asked to read it.

Outside he is invited to accompany the travelers, who are going to Portsmouth. They are undeceived by his claim to be of their trade, but seem amused by his brass. Their party is bound for France, a land rich in opportunity, where gold flows only upward but one may catch some drops, like water from a fountain, as they flee the stony earth.

Jack accompanies them through counties he has never seen, past lands given over entirely to sheep, enormous manors glimpsed at a distance, and the occasional rubble of an abandoned monastery. These sights trouble him, stirring dim memories at the edge of sleep. Jack knows never to speak of the misted events of his sloughed-away past, and as they continue south (it is days before he wonders why merchants don't ride) the recollection of monks driven forth, horsemen wheeling angrily, and ragged crowds waving sticks fill his dreams, spurring his impulse to keep moving, put distance between himself and the tall stone structures that loom in his memory's mist.

They spend only a day at port and leave by night, which tells Jack all he needs to know about the nature of this venture. Upon crossing a stomach-tossing sea, they alight on a darkened coast, unload sacks on the beach, and take on bales after murmured converse with shadowy figures. The ship docks next day at Le Havre, but Jack never learns what becomes of its cargo, for he is taken by two of his partners to a tavern and bid watch the door as they meet with others within.

Until he learns the language, Jack is like a toiling ass, that obeys its master without comprehending his speech with others. No questions are asked him, and his only requital is the ass's: that he is fed.

• • •

The foreigners' tongue yields its meaning only word by slow word, but Jack survives by reading faces, intonations, and the logic of the moment. It is a land of nothing familiar, where friars walk the streets like plump capons, villages are the size of market towns, and authority is everywhere. Ecclesiastical or seigniorial, its charge is ubiquitous, as though gold held the power of lodestones. The land is tax-ridden but people still need salt, needles, sometimes lace and ribbons. Jack carries loads and stands by during transactions, is taught little but learns withal. Conning is slow while cunning must be quick.

Jack dislikes voyages by water, during which he can see his death, so remains in the towns, with their crowded anonymity and city pleasures. It is a world at times comprehensible (men's appetites and frailties do not change with their tongues) and at times cast upside-down: the flurry of laws and regulations, which bind the poor man, the farmer, and even the prosperous bourgeois, have left the modest fraternity of corn untouched, and their cost may rise unchecked as any bishop. Bakers labor under strict laws and may not raise their prices, but the loaves themselves can shrink as grain grows scarce, shriveling and hardening as they approach the condition of stones.

English prices soar in time of dearth, but there is something different here, though Jack cannot figure out how. He labors for his merchant masters, inherits their cast-off clothes, and after an eventual falling out continues on his own. He has learned to deal in cash, which fascinates him. Gold and silver have flooded into Christendom, from the cities and mines of distant lands. They pay for everything, including blackamoor slaves taken to other lands, from which sugar, tobacco and maize appear. Sugar and maize you can put in your stomach or sell for cash, which pays for everything. Listening to merchants discourse in taverns, Jack hears this and marvels, even as brown bread softer than he once imagined white could be rests on a plate before him, sliced rather than torn, and oft smeared with gold-colored butter.

A cold winter hones the edge of hunger, but it is the wet spring that fans the fear. Prices for grain — here called *bled* — begin to rise even before it is clear that the rains have sufficed to stunt or mildew it, and when the summer barley comes off the field it is not sent to market: noblemen, chapter-houses, millers, and the larger farmers hold onto their stores, waiting for the price to rise further.

This scarcity drives prices aloft like startled birds, and the market loaves cringe in response. Hungry peasants begin streaming into town, and are driven back through the gates. Jack, seeing his expenditures rise, knows he must venture out into the countryside, whence comes the produce that feeds and clothes the towns.

The *chasse-coquins* stare suspiciously as Jack strolls through, but their charge is to keep the poor out, not foreigners in. Solitary travelers look vulnerable, but Jack keeps to well-trafficked roads, conducts his business in busy market squares or the front rooms of inns, and is out of sight by nightfall. Other merchants have heavier pockets, but Jack moves faster, making small transactions quickly with coin kept on his person. Like a grain smaller than the gap between millstones, he moves through the workings unmarked.

Jack is used to avoiding the hand of authority, but discovers that its absence also grasps. Forestalling — the buying up of grain before the markets open — is not forbidden here, and it sweeps through villages like an invisible hand, gathering up what is suddenly precious. Jack had always assumed that grain was bound to the earth, to be consumed near the land that yielded it up. Here *bled* is like water, that can flow freely to reach its natural level: that being where the most gold lies. Such dissolution, as though by channels invisibly scored, draws the very substance of bread irresistibly through the peasants' desperate fingers.

And as the bread flees the land, the countryside rebels. Throughout the summer it is war, as merchants seek to move their grain to higher-paying markets and the *paysans*, like headless armies, mobilize to prevent its leaving their county. Jack is traveling these weeks, and discovers that regrating is not only permitted, but is enforced by the Crown when the merchants are able to appeal for armed escorts. Disbelievingly Jack watches the *marechaussée* charging bands of thirty or more peasants armed with staves and pitchforks as merchants quickly load their sacks onto boats and push off downriver.

"Fewer customers?" he asks the innkeeper that night, for his tables are nearly empty. The man regards Jack without warmth, as though the ambivalence of his position were mirrored in the less than reputable-looking foreigner. The cost of bread has doubled for him as for everyone else, but the troubles have brought traders to his place, and he feels little affinity with the violent peasants in the fields.

"They will return for the harvest," he says shortly.

When harvest comes, the large farmers hire fewer hands. There has been little work all summer, for the towns that purchase the countryside's labor must now pay more for *le pain*, so can afford less of all else. The superfluity of workers drives down the wages of those who are hired.

These processes, running in train like an irresistible mechanism, first catch up the poorest, then the rest. By fall the peasants are seeking anything to put in their grain: chestnuts, millet, cabbage stumps and discarded husks, acorns not yet found by pigs, half-germinated seeds from their own small plots. Peasants mix darnel and hemp with their dwindling corn, and produce bread that makes them stagger and reel. As hunger turns to starvation, their skin begins to bruise black.

Jack would not scruple to haul bushels from the parish, but his practice lies elsewhere. A moonless night finds him at a crossroads watching as sacks are unloaded from a wagon and packed onto quiet horses. The sacks contain grain, their contents inspected by the buyer in a barn where Jack led him ten hours before; Jack has kept watch over them since. He is paid not on the spot but upon presentation of a receipt hours later and miles away.

"Gold for paper," remarks the trader, folding the scrap Jack gave him and tucking it away. His table is covered with papers, which he must hold close to his face to read in the early dawn.

"Paper is not gold," Jack replies shortly. He only agreed to defer immediate payment because he knows the trader plans more purchases and shall need his assistance.

"You think not?" asks the trader. "Here is a kind of cash," he says, picking up a sheet. "It is the receipt given a landowner when his grain goes to the warehouse." There is an amount specified; Jack can see the number. It is not the price the landowner was paid, but rather what he wants for the grain, for which it shall eventually be sold. The paper is itself of value: the landowner has sold it, like gold.

Jack smells a gull: the man who accepts bills for cash will soon find himself holding trash, his labors and payment fled. He suggests to the trader what a man left clutching such paper might do with it.

"You are wrong there, my friend," says the trader with a smile, as though to suggest that he who lives as a rat in the granary should not expect to understand the owner's dealings. He explains that credit may connect seller to buyer when their lines are too short to meet. With credit — the assurance of gold, though it not be present — enterprises might expand, ventures find footing. Wealth that resides only in land cannot move, but credit can spread like knowledge, allowing at last money to grow.

"Then you are a Jew," exclaims Jack, at last understanding.

The trader bursts into laughter. "What century do you live in?" he asks.

Jack does not trouble to answer that, for his country and time are unchanging. He lives in the land of *le pain*, without frontiers or landmarks save for the mill, the market, and the city gates.

In time Jack comes to buy and sell, though only in small, swift transactions. Sellers and merchants are not anxious to travel to meet, and Jack moves between them, first as courier then as agent.

Sometimes they write letters, which Jack conveys. He cannot read them, but the faces of the recipients as they scan them tell him enough. He is never cheated, and the grain spills quietly, some lodging in his pocket.

One afternoon he hears a mother sing to quiet her fretful babe:

"Our land is called poverty,
Where one does the dance of hunger.
You have milk now, but where shall come your bread?
Taller you may grow, thinner surely."

A winter blaze crackles in the fireplace. Sitting before it as snowflakes fall through the night sky, Jack thinks briefly of children and mothers. It is difficult to remember that he once stole crusts and hid quaking.

"It is an old system," the trader tells him, the last time Jack sees him. "The tenant's share of his crop is too small for him to afford improvements, so the landlord's share also remains scant. But it comes to him without labor; and it is moreover a difficult thing to combine fields and enjoy the resultant economies. Driving tenants off land brings difficulties: and not just angry peasants. Like the Earl of Leicester, remember? Who enclosed his fields, and later said in remorse: 'I am like the ogre in the old tale, and have eaten up my neighbors.'"

Jack starts at this, but only for a moment, as the tale has none to do with him. You don't eat up the one who escaped.

• • •

Jack rarely eats fancy bread: it pleases him more to get good brown bread, not the kind here called *cannine* but the better quality, and eat it sliced thick with drippings. The innkeeper tells him that such barley bread is so called because many years ago it was judged good enough only for sheepdogs. They laugh at this together.

These days Jack rides, as beggars do not. Vagrants cannot accost a mounted man, although he once has to lash at the face of one who tries to seize his reins. What he sees mostly on the road are children: beggars sent wandering by parents with families too large to feed, and all less fortunate still. They look up beseechingly but offer no threat. Did Jack's taste run to boys, he might have his fill.

One he sees as he stops to drink at a stream. Jack has pulled off his boots to cool his feet, and is sitting at his ease, eyes half-closed, before he sees the boy standing in the bush. At first he supposes an attempted ambush, but then realizes that the whelp is simply too slight — too *faible*, as they say — to notice immediately.

"*Abandonné par tes parents?*" he asks lazily, pulling his boots closer.

The boy simply watches him. The fact that he does not shift his gaze past Jack tells him that he has no confederates nearby.

"They are good boots," he tells the boy. "You are right to covet them." He wishes to draw attention from his saddlebag, where the gold is. It occurs to Jack that the gold he is carrying constitutes, in a sense, the corn that this boy has not eaten, whose lack broke his family apart.

The boy's attention, however, is fixed upon Jack's wallet. "Do you have any bread?" he asks at last.

Of course Jack has bread in his wallet, and meat besides. "There was bread in my stomach this morning," he answers. "But where is it now?"

"Shit along the road," the boy replies.

Jack realizes the boy is older than he looks, meaning small for his age. "Older brothers, eh?" he asks. "Too many competing mouths."

It is his third question, but the boy has answered only the second. He does not look as though he could last long on his own, so must have been cast off recently. There is no sign of emotion on his face, only a certain cunning, which did not this time avail him.

"The boots would have bought you food, had you got them," Jack says. "You have to snatch fast, if you would rob an ogre." As he returns to the road, he sees a stretch of stone wall beyond the trees farther downstream. An old mill, where stone teeth grind the farmer's grain (and swallow much of it), or a monastery, where the flour rests comfortably? Neither holds terrors for Jack.

A cold wind rises, but Jack's coat is leather. You need not answer riddles to survive, for riddles only answer what others think to pose, and it is what they don't think that you must know.

Jack once heard a riddle, and now knows the answer. Though the heart is closer to the stomach, it is the head that feeds it. All else is fairy gold and melts into air: the realm of mere wind and words, the province of the *faible*. **T:S**

Forrest Aguirre Forrest is a recipient of the World Fantasy Award for his editorial work on the anthology *Leviathan 3*. He also edited the *Leviathan 4: Cities* anthology and is currently editing *Muses* (Wheatland Press) and *Text: Ur — The New Book of Masks* (Raw Dog Screaming Press). His short fiction has appeared in a wide range of publications including *Flesh & Blood*, *The Journal of Experimental Fiction*, *Exquisite Corpse*, *3rd Bed*, *Notre Dame Review*, *Prague Literary Review*, *Redsine*, *Polyphony*, and many others. He has work is forthcoming in *The MacGuffin*, *Polyphony*, and *Surreal Magazine*. Forrest's first book length collection of stories, *Fugue XXIX* is forthcoming from Raw Dog Screaming Press. He has recently finished his first novel, *Swans Over the Moon* and is working on his second novel, tentatively titled *Archangel Morpheus*. Forrest lives in Madison, Wisconsin, with his wife and four children, who tend not to read his writing.

Greg Beatty has a Ph.D. in English from the University of Iowa, where he wrote a dissertation on serial killer novels. He attended Clarion West 2000, and any rumors you've heard about his time there are, unfortunately, probably true. His main project for 2005 is to publish a children's picture book titled *The Man Who Gave Orders to Cats*.

Leah Bobet lives in Toronto, where she studies Linguistics and works in Canada's oldest science fiction bookstore. Her work has appeared recently in *Strange Horizons* and *Realms of Fantasy*, and is upcoming in *The Year's Best Science Fiction and Fantasy for Teens*. She is currently working on the second novel in a series about hockey, magic, and urban planning.

Steve Carper has been worddrunk since his mother told him bedtime stories about the Three Rocketship Bears. He lives in a house containing approximately one billion words by other writers lightly spiced with a million of his own.

Brendan Connell was born in Santa Fe, New Mexico, in 1970 and currently lives in Ticino, Switzerland, where he teaches English and writes. He has had fiction published in numerous magazines, literary journals and anthologies, including *The Journal of Experimental Fiction*, *Fantastic Metropolis*, *Flesh & Blood*, *Leviathan 3* (The Ministry of Whimsy 2002), *Album Zutique* (The Ministry of Whimsy 2003) and *Strange Tales* (Tartarus Press 2003). His first novel, *The Translation of Father Torturo*, has recently been published by Prime.

Ian Creasey lives in Yorkshire, England. He has published a couple of dozen stories in various magazines and anthologies.

Jetse de Vries is a technical specialist for a propulsion company, and used to travel the world for this. Of late, due to the increased time both his story writing and co-editing *Interzone* with Andy Cox, Peter Tennant and David Mathew is taking up, he's trying to settle into a desk job. Further examples of his writing can be found in *Nemonymous 4*;

the Journal of Pulse-Pounding Narratives, vol 2; and the *Amityville House of Pancakes*, vol. 1. Which makes him a sort of late-labelled, experimental pulpster with a modern sensibility, and a wicked sense of humour, all drenched in stylistic excess. And all he really wants to do is write SF…

Gregory Feeley published his first story in 1977, and was nominated for the Philip K. Dick Award for his 1990 novel *The Oxygen Barons*, but is best known for the novellas he has produced over the past dozen years, many of them dramatizing episodes in the period between the Renaissance and the Enlightenment, when the modern world was taking form. This year he has has published *Arabian Wine*, a novel about coffee, trade, and the emergence of capitalism in Europe. Some of these themes recur in "Fancy Bread," a story that reminds us, as Piero Camporesi showed in his *Bread of Dreams: Food and Fantasy in Early Modern Europe*, that in the centuries before industrialization, the bread that formed the main staple for Europe's peasantry was life itself.

Automated interactive bio simulation for **Toiya Kristen Finley:***
1. Toiya is a) not a robot, b) a twenty-something-or-other, c) a reject afrocentric name from the 1970s that does not have a prefix of "La-," "Sha-," or "Qua-," d) all of the above.
2. Toiya lives in a) a blue state, b) a red state, c) a mauve state, d) an emotional state.
3. Works by Toiya can be found in a) *Los Archivos Babel'nios*, b) *The Nerf Herder Private Collection*, c) *The Dr. C. Kinbote Memorial Library*, d) none of the above.
4. Toiya has edited a) *Alternate Realities Viewed Through Prescient Mirrors: A Literal History*, b) papers of online composition students, c) a university journal with a weird name, d) a couple of the above.
*Bio valid only if Toiya Kristen Finley is an actual being.

Timalyne Frazier graduated from Marlboro College with a BA in Literature and Creative Writing; thesis title: "Sex as a Literary Device." Her fiction has been published in *Tomorrow SF* and *Polyphony*. She won third place in a Playboy Fiction Contest and Runner-up in Asimov's Contest. She was also the 1995 West Coast recipient of the Susan C. Petrey Clarion Scholarship. Timalyne and her father, Robert Frazier, are possibly the first parent/child duo to have completed the Clarion Workshop, though many years apart — he attended Clarion East '80. Timalyne's poetry has appeared in *Nantucket Magazine* and *Clean Sheets*. She currently lives in Marlboro, Vermont with her husband, two daughters and three cats.

Victoria Elizabeth Garcia lives in Seattle with her husband, writer John Aegard. There, she listens to The Mountain Goats, cares for a surly but loveable little dog, and dreams of grad school. Her fiction has appeared in *Polyphony* and *Rabid Transit*, and will soon appear in *The Indiana Review*.

Greer Gilman's elusive novel, *Moonwise*, will reappear this summer in hardcovers, from Prime Books. It won the Crawford Award and was shortlisted for the Tiptree and Mythopoeic Fantasy Awards.

"Jack Daw's Pack," which is set in the mythscape of *Moonwise*, first appeared in *Century* (Winter 2000), and was a Nebula finalist for 2001. It was reprinted in the *Fourteenth Year's Best Fantasy and Horror*. It is the first story in the Ashes cycle, a triptych of variations on a winter myth. The second, "A Crowd of Bone," won the World Fantasy Award for Novella in 2004. She is working on the third.

Her poem, "She Undoes" has been reprinted several times, most recently in *Jabberwocky*.

Ms. Gilman was a John W. Campbell finalist for 1992. She has been interviewed by Michael Swanwick for Foundation, by Sherwood Smith for the SF Site, and by the Harvard University Gazette.

A Fellow of the Lithopoeic Society, and a sometime forensic librarian, she lives in Cambridge, Massachusetts, and travels in stone circles.

Jeremy Robert Johnson is the author of the 2005 cult hit *Angel Dust Apocalypse* as well as the acclaimed novel *Siren Promised* (with Alan M. Clark). His short fiction has been included in many anthologies and magazines and has twice been nominated for the Pushcart Prize. Jeremy is currently pretending to be hard at work on his next novel, *Extinction Journals*. For more information, ballads, dangerous break-dancing advice, and blog-type business, head to the cleverly named www.jeremyrobertjohnson.com.

Darja Malcolm-Clarke has masters degrees in Folklore and English and is working on a PhD in the latter at Indiana University, studying speculative literature and feminist critical theory. She attended Clarion West in 2004 and lives in numinous southern Indiana where cornfields watch and old buildings of limestone lie in wait. The walnut trees in her backyard relayed to her the sibyl's story.

Anil Menon worked for about nine years in the software industry, worrying about things like secure distributed databases. Then he shifted to a different kind of fiction. He is a 2004 Clarion West graduate and his stories have been accepted for publication in *Albedo One*, *Chiaroscuro*, *Fusing Horizons* and *Strange Horizons*. His edited volume, *Frontiers of Evolutionary Computation* (Kluwer Academic Publishers) was released in February 2004.

Th. Metzger is the author of three novels, *Big Gurl*, *Shock Totem*, and *Drowning in Fire*, a collection of short fiction, *This is Your Final Warning*, and two works of investigative history, *Blood and Volts: Edison, Tesla and the Electric Chair*, and *The Birth of Heroin*. He is also the author of *Select Strange and Sacred Sites: The Ziggurat Guide to Western New York*. A number of the feature articles he's written for *City Newspaper* can be found at: Rochester-Citynews.com.

A former assistant English professor in the picturesque town of Freiburg on the edge of the Black Forest, **Ruth Nestvold** has given up theory for imagination. The university career has been replaced by a small software localization business, and the Black Forest by the parrots of Bad Cannstatt. She lives with her fantasy and her family and her books in a house with a turret and has sold stories to numerous markets, including *Asimov's*, *Realms of Fantasy*, *Strange Horizons*, and the anthology *Realms of Wonder*. Her novella "Looking Through Lace" made the short list for the Tiptree award in 2003 and was nominated for the Sturgeon award.

Mike Philbin is the man behind the surrealist writing entity Hertzan Chimera R.I.P. who gave us *Szmonhfu* (novel), *United States* (novel), *Animal Instincts* (collection), *Spidered Web* (non-fiction horror-author interviews), *Chim+Her* (female collaborations), *Chim+Him* (male collaborations), the annual *Chimeraworld* anthology and website Apocalypse Fiction's *Fuck Star* series (co-written with MF Korn and Alex Severin). He is now relaunching his writing career with a fresh blend of sf-horror.

Mike's new novel *Yôroppa* is due from Hellbound Books in early 2006 and his (autobiographical) *The Life and Death of Hertzan Chimera* is due from Cyber Pulp in a few weeks time.

In the past few years **Tim Pratt** has lost a Nebula, a Campbell, and several Rhysling awards. His first novel, *The Strange Adventures of Rangergirl*, will appear in December 2005, and he has fiction upcoming in *The Best American Short Stories: 2005* and *Polyphony 5*.

The entelechy existing in contemporal memory as **Lawrence M. Schoen** bears both intrapsychic and ruminant epidermal markings of its culture's epistemological terminal experience and is entitled to an honorific which in past eras resulted in circumspect respect and facilitated preferential placement in consummatory emporia. Eschewing its scholastic obligation the entelechy has instead opted to serve as a conduit between the corporeal world and alternate possible realms of existence. Were that not sufficient evidence of interpersonal depravity, it further scribbles these data of a nonverifiable nature and conspires with cognitive hives of exsanguine editors and phlegmatic publishers to distribute its untenable speculations to the innocent masses, and not merely in its primary linguistic configuration, but throughout the planetary sphere, indulging in transfiguration into configurations favored by the Dutch, the Portuguese, the Greek, the Fins, and most sensibly the warriors of the Klingon Empire. Alas, your own insistent optically-aided instantiation reveals its infection has spread. Condolences.

Ken Scholes is a native of the Pacific Northwest, spending most of his early years in and around the Seattle area. After a first drink, Ken will tell you all about growing up redneck. After a second drink, he'll tell amusing anecdotes involving his childhood bicycle. After a third, he'll admit to having been a security officer, a soldier, a label-gun repairman, a receptionist and a Baptist minister before finally settling into nonprofit management where he's spent the last ten years. Four drinks, and he's impersonating the Queen, singing hymns extolling the many virtues of Tapioca pudding and effectively wowing people with his rapier wit and singular charm. No one's ever stayed for a fifth drink though theories abound.

Ken started writing stories in the first grade. He started submitting stories in the tenth grade and then, after a long break, started selling some of them. He has work appearing in *Talebones, Fortean Bureau, Twilight Showcase, Lone Star Stories* and the anthologies *Best of the Rest 3: Best Unknown Science Fiction and Fantasy of 2001* and *L. Ron Hubbard Presents The Writers of the Future, Volume XXI*. His speculative fiction has won honorable mention in several venues including *Year's Best Science Fiction* and he is a winner of the Writers of the Future contest for 2004.

Ken lives in Gresham, Oregon, with his amazing wonder-wife Jen, two cats, five guitars and more books than you'd ever want to help him move.

Dean Wesley Smith is the bestselling author of over seventy published novels and a hundred or so short stories. His next novel coming out in August is *All Eve's Hallows*, a contemporary fantasy novel. His most recent short story appeared in *Ellery Queen*.

Sonya Taaffe has a confirmed addiction to mythology, folklore, dead languages, and all the places these intersect. Her short fiction and poetry have appeared in various magazines, including *Not One of Us, Realms of Fantasy, Mythic Delirium, Flytrap*, and *Say...*, and her poem "Matlacihuatl's Gift" shared first place for the 2003 Rhysling Award. A respectable amount of her work has recently been collected in *Singing Innocence and Experience and Postcards from the Province of Hyphens* (Prime Books). She is currently pursuing a Ph.D. in Classics at Yale University.

Mikal Trimm is a short-story writer and Rhysling-nominated poet. And he's *still* not famous.

Jeff VanderMeer has novels forthcoming from Bantam Books, Tor, and Pan Macmillan. At a prep school event in 2004, a sixth grader came up to him with 200 pages of a handwritten novel and said, "Mr. VanderMeer. I hope you can help me. I'm working on a novel and it feels like it will never end," to which he replied, "Me, too, kid. Me, too."

Carrie Vaughn's novel *Kitty and the Midnight Hour* is due out November, 2005. She lives in Boulder, Colorado.

Paul Woodlin has been published in *The Leading Edge, Leafing Through*, and *Fantasy, Folklore, and Fairy Tales*. He graduated from Odyssey in 1999 and attended Dean Smith and Kris Rusch's classes in 2003.

The Beasts of Love:
Stories by Steven Utley
With an introduction by Lisa Tuttle. Utley's love stories spanning the past twenty years; a brilliant mixture of science fiction, fantasy and horror.

Weapons of Mass Seduction:
Film Reviews and Other Ravings by Lucius Shepard
A collection of Shepard's film reviews. Some have previously appeared in print in the *Magazine of Fantasy and Science Fiction*; most have only appeared online at *Electric Story*.

The Nine Muses
Edited by Forrest Aguirre and Deborah Layne
Original anthology featuring some of the top women writers in science fiction, fantasy and experimental fiction, including Kit Reed, Ursula Pflug, Jai Clare, Jessica Treat, and Ruth Nestvold. With an introductory essay by Elizabeth Hand.

Polyphony 5
Edited by Deborah Layne and Jay Lake
The fifth volume in the critically acclaimed slipstream/cross-genre series will feature stories from Jay Caselberg, Ray Vukcevich, Jeff VanderMeer, Theodora Goss, Leslie What and Nick Mamatas.

Polyphony 4
Edited by Deborah Layne and Jay Lake
Fourth volume in the critically acclaimed slipstream/cross-genre series with stories from Alex Irvine, Lucius Shepard, Michael Bishop, Forrest Aguirre, Theodora Goss, Stepan Chapman and others.

Polyphony 3
Edited by Deborah Layne and Jay Lake
Third volume in the critically acclaimed slipstream/cross-genre series with stories from Jeff Ford, Bruce Holland Rogers, Ray Vukcevich, Robert Freeman Wexler and others.

Polyphony 2
Edited by Deborah Layne and Jay Lake
Second volume in the critically acclaimed slipstream/cross-genre series with stories from Alex Irvine, Theodora Goss, Jack Dann, Michael Bishop and others.

Polyphony 1
Edited by Deborah Layne and Jay Lake
First volume in the critically acclaimed slipstream/cross-genre series with stories from Maureen McHugh, Andy Duncan, Carol Emshwiller, Lucius Shepard and others.

All-Star Zeppelin Adventure Stories
Edited by David Moles and Jay Lake
Original zeppelin stories by David Brin, Jim Van Pelt, Leslie What, and others; featuring a reprint of the zeppelin classic, "You Could Go Home Again" by Howard Waldrop.

American Sorrows:
Stories by Jay Lake
Four longer works by the 2004 John W. Campbell Award winner; includes his Hugo nominated novelette, "Into the Gardens of Sweet Night."

Greetings From Lake Wu
Jay Lake and Frank Wu
Collection of stories by Jay Lake with original illustrations by Frank Wu.

Paradise Passed:
A Novel by Jerry Oltion
The crew of a colony ship must choose between a ready-made paradise and one they create themselves.

Twenty Questions
Jerry Oltion
Twenty brilliant works by the Nebula Award-winning author of "Abandon in Place."

Dream Factories and Radio Pictures
Howard Waldrop
Waldrop's stories about early film and television reprinted in one volume.

Thirteen Ways to Water
Bruce Holland Rogers
This collection by the Nebula and World Fantasy Award winning author spans a period of ten years and brings together several award winning stories.

Colophon
Stephen R. Stanley

*W*hen Jay asked me to design this anthology I didn't hesitate to accept. Book design is a passion. As he described his vision, a style-rich collection of stories and a design to match, my creative mind raced through the possibilities. The opening page for each story could be ornamented like *The Book of Kells*. Or I could custom design each story — varying typefaces, sizes, layout styles to match each story's tone. A daunting solution, but one better reserved for a magazine. In a book such a design would remind readers of why the word "hodgepodge" was coined.

After similar brainstorming blew itself out, I reached predictable (for me) conclusions. Any experimentation that reduced either legibility or readability (first cousins, not twins) was against my design philosophy. Typography for fiction should be elegant, beautiful — brutal when appropriate — but always invisible while being read.

There are few places where a designer can strut and fret around in a book of fiction without getting in the way. Two such stages are page design and the treatment of chapter — or in this case, story — openings.

The tradition of book design extends beyond Gutenberg back to illuminated manuscripts such as *The Book of Kells*. Indeed, early mass-produced books emulated the look of hand-scribed tomes so as not to jar the world with a new technology (moveable type) and incur the wrath of the Church. The subterfuge didn't work. Gutenberg and other early publishers were persecuted as being in league with the devil. Eventually, typefaces evolved beyond script and book design was refined. Moveable-type tech promoted the explosion of mass-printed books and the access to information that contributed to the Renaissance.

Perhaps the first thing you noticed when you opened this book was its design: its asymmetrical layout. This is one of many classical book designs. (Hundreds of books about book design are available. I recommend Jan Tschichold's *The Form of the Book, Essays on the Morality of Book Design*.) Some designers believe this is the only true format for a book. "Pure" ratios of text block to page size (based on the Golden Mean or other mathematical formulas) leave even greater margins. Out of economic necessity most modern designers don't consider classical book design traditions for works of fiction. Publishers often can't afford the indulgence. The style is appropriate as a showcase for the richness of the stories in this anthology.

William Morris, when he founded the Kelmscott Press in 1891, championed the return to Medieval book design, but he couldn't help stamp his work with a Victorian sensibility. He revived the ornamental title page and border, reminiscent of hand-illuminated manuscripts. I've adapted one of Morris's border designs to use with the beginning of each story.

Other factors of style — choice of typefaces, sizes, placement of folios, etc. — were decided with careful regard to those two cousins Legibility and Readability. Once a reader gets into a story (beyond the ornamental first page) a designer must make sure that no typographic tricks get in the way of the images woven by the text. That is especially important to these stories, which are redolent with imagination.

Speaking of the stories. I hadn't realized the challenge Jay's selection would bring to the design of this book until I started prepping the manuscripts. Some of the authors have experimented with typography as part of their storytelling. This made the design of the collection as a whole a bit more difficult. I hope those tales work in a way close to how the authors conceived them, that my typographic interpretations mesh with their visions.

When all is said and done, even if design adds an extra level of style to a book, the magic of a story resides in the uninterrupted flow of words: in the simple experience of reading. Which explains my passion for book design. T:S

Colophon

TEL : Stories was produced on an Apple Macintosh PowerPC G5 using Quark XPress 6.0 software. The Goudy family of typefaces designed by Frederick W. Goudy (1865-1947) was used for body text: ten point type on two points of leading. Story titles and initial capitals were typeset in Ovidius-Demi. Printed in the USA by Lightning Source.

www.ingramcontent.com/pod-product-compliance
Lightning Source LLC
Chambersburg PA
CBHW031111260626
47172CB00001B/321